DATE			

1942

. . . Shh." Paul's warning came as a
soft hiss, barely reaching her ears. What
had he heard or imagined this time? Charlotte
held her breath and listened, so hard she could
hear her own heart beating and Robbie's
soft breathing next to her. Then she heard
it too, upstream. The scrape of wood
against rock. A splash and the
gentle thwack of a rope being
tossed to shore. . . .

HISTORY MYSTERIES FROM AMERICAN GIRL:

The Smuggler's Treasure, *by Sarah Masters Buckey*
Hoofbeats of Danger, *by Holly Hughes*
The Night Flyers, *by Elizabeth McDavid Jones*
Voices at Whisper Bend, *by Katherine Ayres*
Secrets on 26th Street, *by Elizabeth McDavid Jones*

Voices at
Whisper Bend

❧

by
Katherine Ayres

Published by Pleasant Company Publications
© Copyright 1999 by Pleasant Company
For information, address: Book Editor, Pleasant Company Publications,
8400 Fairway Place, P.O. Box 620998, Middleton, WI 53562.

Printed in the United States of America.
99 00 01 02 03 04 RRD 10 9 8 7 6 5 4 3 2 1

History Mysteries™ and American Girl™
are trademarks of Pleasant Company.

PICTURE CREDITS
The following individuals and organizations have generously given permission
to reprint illustrations contained in "A Peek into the Past": p. 157—©Corbis; pp. 158-159—
©Corbis/Bettman-UPI (Roosevelt); *J and L's* by Theodore Allmendinger, courtesy Greater Latrobe
(PA) Senior High School (factory); Franklin D. Roosevelt Library, #NLR-PHOCO-65702(40) (girl);
pp. 160-161—Library of Congress, #LC-USW3-9700-D (scrap pile); Culver Pictures (poster);
©Corbis/Bettman-UPI (grocery); State Historical Society of Wisconsin, neg. #(X3)52130 (ration
coupons); Franklin D. Roosevelt Library (worker); Popperfoto/Archive Photos (air-raid shelter); pp.
162-163—from the book *Victory at Sea* by Richard Hanser (ship); National Archives, #111-SC-345-
140 (mail call); Blethen Maine Newspapers, Inc. (children); p. 165—Bill Sauers Photo.

Cover and Map Illustrations: Dahl Taylor
Line Art: Greg Dearth
Editor: Peg Ross
Art Direction: Jane Varda
Design: Laura Moberly and Kim Strother

Library of Congress Cataloging-in-Publication Data

Ayers, Katherine.
Voices at Whisper Bend / by Katherine Ayers. — 1st ed.
p. cm. — (History mysteries)
"American girl."
Summary: In their Pennsylvania town in 1942 twelve-year-old Charlotte
and her classmates collect scrap metal for the war effort only to have it disappear
from the school basement.

ISBN 1-56247-817-6 (alk. paper). ISBN 1-56247-761-7 (pbk. : alk. paper)
1. World War, 1939-1945 — Pennsylvania Juvenile fiction.
[1. World War, 1939-1945—United States Fiction. 2. Pennsylvania Fiction.
3. Mystery and detective stories.]
I. American girl (Middleton, Wis.) II. Title. III. Series.
PZ7.A9856Vo 1999 [Fic]—dc21 99-24456 CIP

for Elena, for Rachel
my daughters, my friends

TABLE OF CONTENTS

CHARLOTTE'S WORLD

Pennsylvania in 1942

CHAPTER I

BOATS

How was school, honey? Did you do all right on that history quiz?" Ma stood at the kitchen sink, peeling vegetables for homemade soup.

"The quiz was postponed," Charlotte began. "We had—"

"We had an air-raid drill," Robbie interrupted. "A long, scary one. And I got stuck sitting between two girls. Phewie!" He waved his hand in front of his nose.

Charlotte pushed back from the kitchen table where she was mixing black, blue, and white paints in a can. "You stop that right now, Robbie Campbell, or I won't paint your dumb tugboat for you."

"But, Charlie, you promised," Robbie protested.

"Spit on your hand and swear then, buster," Charlotte said. "Repeat after me. Girls do not stink."

Robbie raised a grubby hand, palm facing toward her. "Some girls do not stink. Is that good enough?"

He wrinkled his nose and Charlotte held back a laugh.

"Why don't you quit while you're ahead, Robbie?" Ma said with a grin. She turned to look at Charlotte. "Was the drill a bad one?"

Charlotte shrugged. She swirled the paint in the can with a wooden stick, making the white disappear into the darker colors. "Like Robbie said, it took a long time."

"Did many kids get upset this time? Did Betsy?" Ma wore her serious look. Betsy Schmidt lived next door. She and Charlotte had been best friends forever. So had their mothers.

Charlotte didn't want to be disloyal to her friend, but she couldn't lie, either. "Betsy cried some. So did a few other kids. The Cussick twins always pray during the drills. I know that should make me feel better, but instead I feel worse. Like we're really in trouble and it's not just practice."

"I wish we lived out in the country," Robbie said. "Even those mean old Germans wouldn't bomb cows."

"I'm sure they don't plan on bombing schoolchildren, either," Ma said. She sat between Charlotte and Robbie at the table and took their hands in hers. "You both know it's a precaution, don't you? The school turns out the lights just in case—so it won't look like a war factory from above and become a target like the steel mills are. But you're not to worry. German warplanes haven't crossed the Atlantic Ocean yet, and we pray they never do."

Charlotte nodded. But sometimes it was hard not to worry. In a factory town like Braddock, the air-raid drills came once a month, with blaring sirens, and quite a few kids got upset. Teachers postponed tests and homework afterward.

"I'm glad Pa works on the *Rose,*" Robbie said. "If he sees a German warplane, or even hears one, he'll rev up his engines and zoom away so fast his wake will smack the shore like ocean waves. *Vroom!*" Robbie lifted his home-made wooden tugboat and put her through maneuvers that would capsize the biggest tug on the river. "I guess we're luckier than Betsy, aren't we?"

Ma nodded. She didn't say the words, but Charlotte knew what she was thinking. Betsy's father worked at the Edgar Thomson, the steel mill upriver. Now *that* was a target. Huge brick chimneys soared into the sky, blowing out smoke and shooting flames all day and all night. They could never douse the lights of the steel mill, nor hide those tall chimneys from a bomber. All along the Monongahela River from Pittsburgh to West Virginia, mills were belching out smoke and flame, proud to be helping the war. Targets, every one of them.

Robbie nudged Charlotte's arm. He sailed his tug right under her nose. "Are you going to mix all day, or are you going to paint?"

Ma smiled again, and returned to her vegetables.

Charlotte shook her head. Were all nine-year-olds so

impatient? "Hand it over. Is this color close enough to the *Rose?*" She daubed the stirring stick on the newspaper that covered the kitchen table.

"Not bad, for a girl."

"I'll paint *you* if you don't watch out." She took the boat from him and waved a dry brush at his right cheek.

The color she'd concocted pleased her. The main deck, hull, and engine room of Pa's tug were the same dark blue-gray she'd mixed. The engine house rose up high above it, a scrubbed, clean white. And Pa had chosen bright blue for the stacks. Robbie had done a pretty good job with the model. Of course, he'd had help. Their older brother Jim had taught him how to use the chisel and plane and how to get the size right.

"I want to make barges too, Charlie, but I can't figure out what wood to use. Everything we've got is too thick. And with Jim gone and Pa so busy, I don't have anyone to help me with the saw."

"I know." Charlotte dipped her brush and began to smooth paint on the wooden hull. She kept her eyes focused on the brush and the pine boat. She didn't want to look at Ma's back, which was sure to be stiff at the mention of Jim. "How about an orange crate? Bet you could find an empty one at the market. Those boards are real thin. You'd just have to watch out for splinters."

"I got sandpaper. I'm a good sander. And I could paint rocks black and glue them on the barge, for coal." He stood. "Can I go now, Ma? Can I try the market?"

"Isn't it still raining?" Ma asked. She lifted one of the kitchen curtains aside.

"Just April showers. I won't melt. Please, Ma?" He was hopping up and down on one foot.

Ma nodded. "Okay. But just to the market and right back. No sightseeing today, mister. And dry your feet when you get home."

Robbie dashed out the back door. Charlotte continued to paint. She felt Ma's hand on her shoulder. "It's nice of you to help your brother with his boats."

"This size boat I can handle," Charlotte said.

Ma nodded, a faraway look in her eye. "He misses Jim a lot."

"He's not the only one, Ma," Charlotte said. She set down the paintbrush and boat, stood and leaned into Ma's shoulder. "Where do you suppose he is right now?"

"God only knows," Ma said, scrubbing hard at a carrot. "God and the admirals."

Later that evening, Charlotte sat close to the radio and listened hard to the President's voice as he told the country bad news. Robbie lay on his stomach on the carpet next to her and rested his chin in his hands. As usual, his dark hair stuck up in messy tufts. Across the room, Ma sat close to

Pa on the sofa, still wearing her apron. She stared at the radio as if Mr. Franklin Delano Roosevelt himself were going to step out of that wooden case and sit down on the green rocking chair where Jim used to sit, to tell them how badly the war was going.

Charlotte traced the large tan roses in the carpet as the President's crackling voice reviewed all the battles lost to Germany and Japan. Then his voice softened, and she listened harder.

"As we here at home contemplate our own duties, our own responsibilities, let us think and think hard of the example which is being set for us by our fighting men."

They're on my mind all the time, Charlotte answered him silently.

The President continued. *"Our soldiers and sailors are . . ."*

They're our brothers, Charlotte thought, like Jim. Back in December when America joined the war, he'd gone in and talked to Mr. Butler at the draft board. Mr. Butler had suggested that Jim would make a swell sailor, what with helping on Pa's tug most of his life. So Jim had enlisted in the Navy and traded the Monongahela River for an ocean somewhere.

Charlotte blinked and turned toward Ma for comfort, but Ma's eyes looked swimmy. Next to Ma, Pa sat with his hands clenched into fists.

The President's words brought pictures to Charlotte's mind, pictures from the newsreels. She'd seen the map of

France covered by a big black swastika. Seen the long lines of German soldiers marching in their heavy black boots. Seen a huge ship take a hit from a torpedo and roll over into the ocean, dumping all the sailors overboard to die.

Mr. Roosevelt's fighting men were boys—brothers and sons, cousins and neighbors.

"They are the United States of America. That is why they fight. We too are the United States of America. That is why we must work and sacrifice.

"It is for them. It is for us. It is for victory."

On the radio, a band began to play. Robbie stood up and saluted the President. Pa switched off the set.

Ma straightened. Charlotte watched her blink a couple of times, like she had a speck of dirt in her eye. Then she cleared her throat and turned to Charlotte and Robbie. "Your schoolwork done?"

"Yes, ma'am. But I got sanding and gluing to do." Robbie saluted again and marched off to the kitchen and his model boats.

"What about you, Charlotte?"

"Yes, Ma. There wasn't much schoolwork because of that air-raid drill." Charlotte could tell that Ma wasn't really worried about science or arithmetic—she just didn't want to think about the war anymore.

"Then how about a game of dominoes, Lottie?" Pa asked Charlotte. He rolled up the sleeves of his plaid shirt, like he was ready for serious business.

Charlotte got out the wooden box of dominoes and took a seat on the floor next to a flat-topped trunk. Pa gathered pencil and paper from the lamp table and sat across from her.

As they turned the dominoes face-down and mixed them, Charlotte was still running the President's words over in her mind. He hadn't just talked about faraway battles; he'd spoken about people here at home, too. How they had to help the soldiers and sailors win the war. She spoke to Pa softly, so as not to bother Ma, who had pulled out her sewing basket and was threading a needle. "Mr. Roosevelt was talking about us tonight, Pa. How we all have to work hard and sacrifice."

"Yep, that he was."

"But, Pa, I don't understand. How can we help?"

Pa smiled at her. "Folks around here are already doing what they can. The mills are running night and day."

"I know," Charlotte sighed.

"And not just in Braddock," Pa said. "Up and down the Mon valley, we're pouring more steel every day. Makes a person proud."

"I know, Pa," Charlotte said again. "You're doing a lot, too. Running extra trips on the river so the mill won't run out of coke and coal and ore." Charlotte glanced toward the sofa. "Even Ma, she's over there patching a dress so more cloth can go for uniforms, but . . ."

Pa took her chin in his hand. "What's bothering you, sweetheart?"

"What about me, Pa? Mr. Roosevelt said every man, woman, and child. I'm twelve. How can I help fight the war? Jim's doing so much . . ."

"You're already saving your money and buying defense stamps. And you've helped your ma plant a victory garden."

"That's not enough."

"Wait till summer comes. You'll be weeding and watering, you and your brother. And you can help Ma with the canning and pickling." Pa reached into the boneyard for his seven dominoes.

"I did that before we went to war, Pa. I want to do something real." Charlotte picked her dominoes and set them up, checking the faces.

Pa held up a domino and grinned. "Ah, I got double eights. Unless you got the nines . . ."

"No. You go first, Pa." Charlotte sighed again. The only double she had was the double zero. Nothing. And that's about how useful she felt.

Before she went upstairs to bed, Charlotte stood beside the front window and looked out. Just another damp April night. She touched each point of the blue cloth star that hung in the window. Jim's star. Ma had hung it up the day he left for the Navy, like every mother did who sent her son to war. But where was Jim now? How was he? Was it bedtime where he was, or morning? Dark or sunny?

With one finger, Charlotte planted a kiss on the top point of the star, just as she did every night at bedtime. "Good night, Jim. Wherever you are, sleep well."

Upstairs, Charlotte pulled on her nightgown, but she didn't feel sleepy. The President's words and the wail of the air-raid siren still echoed in her mind. She stood near the window and looked outside again, across the backyards. Upriver, the sky glowed orange-gold from the furnaces of the Edgar Thomson. Straight ahead, she could see a small piece of the Monongahela. With all the rain, the water would turn brown and muddy, and the current would pick up.

Charlotte shivered as she remembered another time when the river had run fast, filled with spring rains. Sometimes it felt like only yesterday, instead of years ago, when she'd run too fast along Pa's wet deck and slipped into the Mon. She couldn't forget how that oily brown water had closed over her head and she'd sunk down, down, into murky nothingness. When she'd tried to open her mouth to call for help, cold, choking water had rushed in, ripping like icy knives into her lungs. But Jim had been there to fish her out. He and Pa had pounded her chest and got her breathing again. She'd been all right after that, except when the memory came back in the middle of the night.

Nights like that, she missed Jim the most. He'd been there, he understood—she could knock on his door and he'd listen and then tell her stories until she felt all right again.

She hugged her arms, suddenly missing Jim with
a fierce, cold ache. Why did she still want to go cry
on her big brother's shoulder? After all, hadn't the
accident happened a long time ago? Hadn't she out-
grown all that?

As far as the rest of her family knew, she was fine.
And most of the time, she was. Most of the time, she
figured she was just a cat, a critter that didn't much like
the water. But a critter with nine lives. She'd used up
one of her nine that spring day when she was five and
slipped off the tug into the Mon.

Enough, Charlotte, she scolded herself. She'd be as
cranky as a cat if she didn't get to sleep soon. And there'd
be that postponed history quiz first thing in the morning.
A good grade would help her final report card. She
climbed into bed and pulled the blankets up to her chin.
Warm and dry, I'm warm and dry. Maybe if she said the
words often enough, she'd believe them. She closed her
eyes and waited for sleep.

⚜

In the night a dream came.

Charlotte sat up in bed, wide-awake and sweating as
bits of the dream still clung to her mind. There she was
in rough water, huge waves swelling and sinking all around.
Through the darkness, she could see Jim balancing near a

ship's rail. Then a lurch and a wash of seawater and Jim disappearing.

"Just a dream, a nightmare," Charlotte whispered to herself. She wiped sweat from her face with a corner of the sheet and took a deep breath. But the palms of her hands still stung where she'd dug her fingernails in, trying to hold on to that phantom ship's rail, and trying without success to sight her older brother in the whirling black water.

CHAPTER 2
SCRAPPERS

The next morning Charlotte knelt in the damp grass, petting a pale gray cat. He was one of the dozens that belonged to old Mrs. Dubner, who lived next door in the corner house. The cat's fur was matted and rough with burrs. Charlotte pulled a couple out. "Looks like you had a bad night too, kitty," she said. "Hope you didn't have bad dreams."

"Hey Charlotte!" Betsy called from her doorway on the other side of Charlotte's house. Betsy hurried to the sidewalk, pulling on a sweater, her pale brown pigtails bouncing. "Sorry I'm late again. Why are you petting that nasty cat? He probably has fleas. He looks like he's been in a fight."

"He just needs a good brushing," Charlotte said. She stood and stepped carefully across a wide crack in the sidewalk. "Betsy, did your family listen to the President last night?"

"Sure. Everyone here at home's going to have to pitch in. I'm buying an extra war stamp this week. How about you?"

Charlotte shrugged. "Buying a measly war stamp doesn't seem like much. Not with what our brothers are doing." They turned off Talbott and headed north, toward Braddock Avenue. Once they crossed Braddock, the climb would start, but for now the hill still lay in shadows, waiting to burn their leg muscles.

"We could lie about our age and get jobs at the mill," Betsy suggested. She pulled her shoulders back. "We're both tall."

Charlotte laughed. "They'd never believe us."

"What about the Red Cross? They'd let us help."

"Rolling bandages? Little old ladies do that." Charlotte shook her head. She and Betsy crossed Braddock Avenue, passing by all the stores and businesses, and began the long uphill climb. "I wish we could do something interesting," she continued. "Like being spies."

"Are you kidding?" Betsy huffed as she spoke. She wasn't much of a climber.

"Come on, Bets. We could do it. Nobody would ever suspect a couple of kids. We could sneak places and overhear war secrets."

Betsy shoved her shoulder. "You're nuts, Charlotte Campbell. What war secrets are we going to hear in Braddock, Pennsylvania? Nope, unless your brother can smuggle us onto a Navy ship and slip us into Germany or

France, we're not going to hear anything more interesting than Mrs. Dubner swearing at her cats."

Charlotte felt the familiar burn in the back of her calf muscles and picked up speed. The best way to make your legs stop aching was to get to school fast. She kicked at a stone and sent it flying across the street. "Mrs. Dubner does swear a blue streak. I caught Robbie using some of those words on Monday. Now he owes me."

Betsy shook her head. "Ma says she's a disgrace to the neighborhood. If she'd just clean her yard and porch, she wouldn't have to holler. Those poor cats are always bumping into trash and knocking cans over."

"She's old, Bets. And there's so much junk, it would take a whole company of soldiers to clean her place." Something glinted on the sidewalk and Charlotte stooped to pick it up.

"What'd you find?"

"Nothing. Just a bottle cap." She drew back her arm, ready to pitch it, then stopped stock-still. "Hold on a minute. Look at this." She showed the cap to Betsy. "What's it made of?"

"I don't know. Steel? Tin, maybe. Why? What are you thinking up, Charlotte?"

Charlotte smiled. She tossed the bottle cap into the air and caught it. Then she polished its smooth silvery top on her skirt. "That's it. That's what we're going to do for the war."

"Pick up bottle caps? Why? So we can throw them at the wicked Germans? That's about as dumb as being spies."

Charlotte turned and pointed upriver toward North Braddock. Huge billows of black smoke drifted across the morning sky from the giant mill chimneys. "Look, Bets, they're making more steel every day. People are having scrap metal drives all over the country, so mills like the Edgar Thomson can melt down the old metal and pour new steel for ships and planes."

"Scrap metal. Sure, we could collect that—steel and tin and aluminum! Charlotte, you're a genius."

"We'll get our class to help. Mrs. Alexander will go for it. She's been making us write all those paragraphs about freedom and the USA." Charlotte speeded her stride again. Uphill, the early bell rang.

"Slow down," Betsy said. "You're always in such a hurry, Charlotte. We've got five minutes. This hill's a killer."

"Come on, I want to talk to Mrs. Alexander right away. Before school starts." Charlotte stuck the bottle cap into her skirt pocket. Maybe she was in a rush, but today she had a good reason.

"I'll hurry, but if I pass out on the sidewalk, you'd better pick me up." Betsy's cheeks were red and she was huffing and puffing.

Charlotte's lungs burned too, but they only had a block left to walk. "I'll tell you what we'll be picking up. Old wheels and bent pots."

"Sounds like work," Betsy said. "But down by the river it wouldn't be so bad. You see a lot of old junk there. 'Course, we'd have to be careful. The banks can be steep."

Steep and slippery. Charlotte shuddered. "I've got a better idea. We'll start our drive right in old Mrs. Dubner's backyard. Just you wait, Bets. We'll be the best scrappers in Braddock."

Charlotte placed her right hand over her heart and recited the Pledge of Allegiance. On mornings like this one, when the President had just given a speech, it seemed like everybody stood a little straighter and spoke a little louder. Even her teacher wore a dark blue suit that looked military. Charlotte held her shoulders back the way Jim had taught her to do once he joined up. She wished that the flag hanging over the blackboard was bigger, and less faded.

Then Mrs. Alexander nodded for them to sit down. She perched on the edge of her desk. "Class, may I have your attention, please? Before we begin this morning's current events reports, Charlotte Campbell would like to speak to all of you."

Heads turned. Charlotte's stomach did somersaults. She stood and cleared her throat. "Um, I guess you all heard the President last night. I'd like to do something for the war. Not just buy stamps. Betsy and I got an idea.

We could start a metal drive, right here in Braddock. What do you think?"

Her cheeks burned. She slipped into her seat, fiddling with the bottle cap. Around the room she heard whispers. What would they say? Would they do it? Amazingly, most of the class liked her idea.

Then Sophie Jaworski raised her hand. "But what about lockjaw, Mrs. Alexander? You can get it from rusty metal."

Charlotte rolled her eyes at Betsy. They both knew what really worried Sophie—getting dirty, or, heaven help her, breaking a fingernail.

"Good question, Sophie. We'll have to be very careful."

Paul Rossi wanted to collect everything—rags, rubber, and paper, as well as metal—but Mrs. Alexander didn't agree. "Let's save something for the seventh and eighth graders to work on. I'll speak to their teachers. Now, on to current events."

Several kids reported on the President's talk, which seemed odd to Charlotte. Every family in America listened, so why tell what people already knew?

Sophie Jaworski pulled her news from the fashion pages as usual. "Hemlines Go Up to Save Fabric for Our Soldiers." It was war news, but barely. That girl!

When it was Paul Rossi's turn, he got out a newspaper clipping and read the headline. "'Woman Found on Church Steps.' Did you see this?" he asked. "It was in the morning paper. They found a dead woman on the steps of

St. Stanislas Catholic Church in Pittsburgh. She was wearing her nightgown and wrapped in a torn blanket. Nobody knows who she is. Nuts, isn't it? I've heard of people falling asleep in church, but this one never woke up."

When he sat down, a lot of the boys were grinning. Some laughed out loud and Mrs. Alexander had to shush them. How dare they laugh? It made Charlotte want to cry. The poor woman, left there like nobody cared about her.

Charlotte scowled. That Paul Rossi, he was always digging up creepy stuff from the newspapers. Murders and bodies and escaped convicts. What kind of person enjoyed reading about such things? She wished he lived in a different state.

After current events, they planned the scrap drive. Mrs. Alexander spoke to other teachers at lunch. By the end of the day, Charlotte's idea had caught fire in the whole school. The principal visited her class and explained what each grade would do. "Thanks to Charlotte, the sixth grade will become scrappers," he said. "The seventh grade wants to run a newspaper drive and save some trees for building barracks. We'll store the metal and the papers in the school cellar. And the eighth graders will roll old tires to the riverbank, where they'll be loaded on a barge and sent to a factory to make new tires. Younger students in first through fifth grades will help their older brothers and sisters." He shook Charlotte's hand before he left.

❧

Back at home, Charlotte changed out of school clothes and rushed to meet Betsy in front of old Mrs. Dubner's house. Junk littered the small front yard and the porch. The only thing that kept the trash from spilling into the Campbells' yard was the tall wooden fence Pa had built between the yards. If the old lady's house had ever been painted, you couldn't tell what color, for it had faded to a soft, peeling gray.

"You knock," Betsy said. "I'm too nervous. What if she says no?"

"I'll knock, but we'll both ask her. That way she can't say no." Charlotte knocked, and the old lady answered as a pair of cats wove themselves around her thin legs. She wore a long, baggy dress and what looked like men's socks and slippers.

"We're having a metal drive," Betsy began.

"It's for the war," Charlotte added. "We wondered if you had any old stuff you didn't need." She pointed toward a rusty wheel in the front yard. "We could haul it away for you if you wouldn't mind."

Mrs. Dubner bent to pick up a gray-and-white cat. She scratched its ears. A light wind blew raggedy strands of white hair into her wrinkled face. "You'd clean my yard for me? How much?"

"For free," Charlotte said. "We're collecting metal.

We'll haul off things from your house too, if you'd like."

"The yard and the house too? For nothing? If that ain't a bargain. Sure. You gals help yourselves to all the junk you want. Ain't nothing out here I need." She closed the door.

"Let's start in the front yard," Betsy suggested. "The whole street will look better once we clean that up."

Charlotte nodded. "Fine with me."

She borrowed Robbie's wagon. Betsy brought three bushel baskets from her house, and they set to work. By suppertime, they'd filled them with tin cans and dented pails. They'd even piled two tires on the sidewalk for the eighth graders to pick up.

"See you tomorrow," Betsy said. "I'm tired and starving."

Charlotte grinned. "You're not too clean, either. Good thing there's nobody around with a camera, or they'd black-mail us for sure. See you tomorrow."

Charlotte let herself in the back door and scrubbed her hands before supper. She could hardly wait to tell Ma and Pa about the scrap drive. But first she carried steaming bowls of beef stew to the kitchen table as Ma poured milk for everybody. Then the family sat, and Charlotte waited for Pa to say the blessing.

"Guess what," she said as they began to eat. "I'm helping with the war."

"The whole school is helping," Robbie interrupted. "And it was Charlie's idea. Not bad, for a sister."

Pa smiled as Charlotte explained.

Ma looked thoughtful. "I'm proud of you, Charlotte." She paused for a moment, straightened her napkin, then looked up at the family. "I want to do my part too. I'm considering going to work."

"Work?" The word stuck in Charlotte's throat.

"What? Where?" Pa asked.

Ma rubbed her chin with her knuckles. "At first I thought I'd go down to Pittsburgh, to the Heinz plant. They put out a call for workers, and I thought maybe I could make rations for the troops. Might even end up fixing meals for our Jim."

"Did you get a job, Ma?" Robbie asked. His eyes were round.

"Not at Heinz. I phoned up first. They aren't looking for cooks. Turns out they've converted half their plant to make plywood for airplane parts. Besides, the plant's a long ride from here. So I decided to stop at the mill here in Braddock and see if they could use me."

"The Edgar Thomson?" Pa asked. Charlotte could tell from the look on his face that he was as surprised as she was.

Ma nodded. "They're making plate steel. A lot of it goes into ships for our Navy. I said I could start Monday."

"Wow, swell, Ma," Robbie said. He saluted her and then Charlotte. "All hands! Now everybody's helping Jim win the war."

Ma's cheeks turned pink. "James, what do you think?" she asked Pa.

He turned a serious face toward her. "I've hardly had a chance to think. What would you be doing in that mill? A lot of those jobs are heavy work, Mary. And dangerous."

"They seem to think they could train me to operate a crane."

Pa didn't speak right away. When he did, it sounded like he was picking out each word. "If . . . if it's what you want . . . I'll be proud. Proud of both my gals." He smiled at Charlotte. "You collect the metal, and your ma here will turn it into battleships."

Ma cleared her throat. "One thing," she began. "I know you'll be busy in school, Charlotte. And now this metal drive. But I'll need you to help with the housework, start supper for the family, and watch Robbie, especially when your pa's on the boat."

"Sure, Ma," Charlotte said, but her tongue felt like lead. She needed to spend every free moment hunting scrap metal. How could she help win the war if she had to do Ma's jobs too?

CHAPTER 3
CONFETTI LETTER

"Seaman First Class, Robert Michael Campbell, reporting for duty, sir."
Supper was over. Charlotte was washing dishes and trying to figure out how to collect as much scrap as she could before Ma started at the mill. Robbie saluted, then reached for the dish towel.

"Cut it out," Charlotte grumbled. "You're not in the Navy."

"Not yet," Robbie said. "But when I'm old enough, I'm going to be a sailor, same as Jim. On a battleship."

"Who says he's on a battleship?" Charlotte asked. She scrubbed at a sticky spot on a plate. "He might be on a destroyer, a patrol boat, convoy duty. We don't know. We don't even know which ocean they've sent him to."

"Wherever they sent him, I'm going too." Robbie stuck out his chin.

Charlotte knew she'd never win that argument. She

changed the subject. "For now, how about becoming Landman First Class?"

Robbie groaned. "Not more gardening. We already dug Ma's victory garden. There's not much left of the backyard."

Charlotte lifted the skillet into the sudsy sink. "I'm not talking about gardening, buster. How about helping Betsy and me collect scrap at Mrs. Dubner's?"

Robbie whirled his dish towel above his head. "You mean it? You want me in your crew? Aye, aye, capt'n. When's my first job?"

"Tomorrow morning. We've got a heavy load to haul up the hill."

Robbie threw the dish towel on the back of a chair and rubbed his hands together. "How about collecting more junk right now? The dishes are done, and I'm good at finding stuff."

And he was. Before it got too dark to see, he and Charlotte had cleared half of the old lady's backyard and piled up three more heaps of junk. That night, Charlotte was too tired for dark thoughts or bad dreams.

Everybody in Charlotte's class brought scrap metal to school the next day. Mr. Willis, the janitor, stood at the door to the school cellar to help them stack it. He was a skinny man with thinning gray hair, and he didn't talk much because he had a bad stutter. He always smiled at Charlotte, though, and he gave her a big grin when he saw her full wagon. "N-nice, Missy," he said, pointing to the back corner where kids were busy unloading.

"Great idea, Charlotte," one of the boys said. "My ma says the town of Braddock has never had so many clean basements. She's treating my pals and me to the movies on Saturday for all the work."

Charlotte smiled. Scrap for the war *and* clean basements. That was a good deal.

⚓

Over the weekend, Charlotte, Betsy, and Robbie gathered even more scrap, finishing Mrs. Dubner's yard and starting on her cellar. They carried another large haul to school on Monday morning, and all that day Charlotte counted the minutes until school let out and they could get back to work at Mrs. Dubner's.

When she reached home Monday afternoon, Robbie met her on the back porch, as anxious to start as she was. "Hey, Charlie, do you think we could use Pa's gardening wheelbarrow? We could haul more."

"We'll ask Ma," Charlotte said. But when she reached to turn the back doorknob, it wouldn't move. Then she remembered. Ma wasn't home. She'd started her job at the mill today. Charlotte pulled on the string that hung around her neck, fished out a key, and unlocked the door.

Robbie rushed inside and headed upstairs, but Charlotte stepped into the kitchen slowly. It didn't feel right, coming home to a locked-up house—it felt cold and empty. Charlotte shut the door and glanced around the quiet kitchen. Ma had left a note on the table. Charlotte leaned over and read it.

Dear Children,
 Please finish all your schoolwork before going outside. My shift goes until four o'clock and I'll take a while to walk home, so don't expect me before four-thirty or five. Don't forget to change into play clothes.

Love,
Mother

Charlotte looked up as Robbie bounced back into the kitchen and headed for the door. "Schoolwork first," Charlotte told him.

"Aw, come on, Charlie," he grumbled. "I want to get more stuff from that cellar. Ma won't know if I do my arithmetic now or later."

"Schoolwork first," she repeated. "Orders from the first mate."

He frowned and his shoulders slumped. "Aye, aye."

"I'll help if you get stuck with your multiplication," Charlotte offered. "Do the easy ones while I work on current events. Then we'll go to Mrs. Dubner's."

Charlotte nudged Robbie into a kitchen chair, then seated herself and unfolded the newspaper to check the headlines. "Two Convoy Ships Sunk in Shipping Lanes off Florida Keys." "Destroyer Crippled by Bombs in North Atlantic." Bad news for the Navy, and that meant bad news for Jim. She tried to ignore the sick feeling in her stomach and turned to the inside pages. "Three Men Hold Up South Side Bank." Great. That was a Paul Rossi article. She didn't need to read it—he'd tell all about it tomorrow. "Sugar Rationing to Begin, Meat Will Soon Follow." She clipped the column. That was an article she could tell about without crying in front of her class.

She and Robbie finished their work and repacked their books. They changed quickly and headed next door for Betsy.

"The cellar again?" Betsy asked as they turned up the sidewalk toward Mrs. Dubner's. "I wish we could work outside today. That sun feels so good. Spring's really here."

Charlotte nodded. "Come on, troops. To the cellar, spring or not. All the outside trash is gone." Charlotte knocked on the back door, then led the way down the rickety steps and found the string that worked the bare lightbulb. A moldy, damp, earth smell filled her nose. Deep in the shadows, spiderwebs hung as thick as curtains.

"Clear the decks," Robbie warned. He grabbed a broom and attacked the spiderwebs, covering himself in sticky dust.

Charlotte pried open a door off to one side, revealing a little room packed to the ceiling with old newspapers.

Betsy peered over her shoulder. "Hey, my cousin Pete's in seventh grade," she said. "He and his friends could haul these papers away for their drive. Shall I go find him?"

"Good idea. There's plenty of metal over there for us." Charlotte pointed to where Robbie had swept away the spiderwebs. As Betsy left, the two of them started clearing out the corner.

"Here's a lunch pail. Nice one too, except the catch is busted." Robbie tossed it into a bushel basket.

"Hey, look at this," he said. "Did Mrs. Dubner ever have a kid?" He lifted out a bent and twisted frame with four wheels. The bottom and sides were in shreds, but once, a long time ago, it had been a baby buggy. Robbie shoved it along the cellar floor, but one of the wheels was stuck so it wouldn't roll. "Did she have a kid, Charlie, or did she use the buggy for one of her cats?"

Charlotte ran her hand along the cold handle of the baby buggy. Her right thumb caught on a rough spot where rust had eaten away at the metal. She shoved the buggy toward Robbie. "I don't know. Add it to the stack."

The idea of Mrs. Dubner being somebody's mother felt strange. For all of Charlotte's life, the woman had been the neighborhood's odd person. She wasn't actually loony, but close to it, with her ancient, baggy clothes and her untidy wisps of hair. Charlotte had never imagined her having children. Had Mrs. Dubner just picked up the old buggy on the street and brought it home?

Charlotte didn't have time to think about it. Betsy arrived with her cousin and three of his friends. The older boys kept up a loud parade from the cellar to their wagons and wheelbarrow waiting on the sidewalk. Funny, Charlotte thought. Old Mrs. Dubner was doing her part to win the war without planning it.

"Wow! Look, Charlie. Bones!" Robbie bent over a rusty washtub.

A shiver ran up Charlotte's spine. "Don't be ridiculous. April Fools' is over."

"I'm not fooling," he said. "Come see."

Charlotte stooped and peered into the washtub. Betsy stood behind her. "He's right, Charlotte, those do look like bones. Tiny ones."

"Bet it's from a cat," Robbie said. "She has so many she wouldn't miss one."

"More like a kitten, from the size of the skull," Charlotte said, pointing. A sour taste rose to her mouth. Sometimes when you looked for one thing, you found something else. Something you'd never want to find.

"I'll fill up the washtub with junk and take it outside," Robbie offered.

Charlotte suspected he'd save the kitten bones first and sneak them into his room. Fine. She'd stay away from his room.

"Okay," she said. "After that, how about we quit for the day?"

❧

When Ma came home she didn't even look like herself; her cheeks were smudged and she wore dirty overalls and a cap. First thing, she filled the tub for a long soak. Then she lay on the sofa and called out instructions for warming up the supper she'd made the day before.

That evening, Charlotte felt like she'd been drafted to fight on the home front. The kitchen became her battlefield, the old creaky stove, her enemy. She did her best with the cooking, but as the week wore on, she scorched potatoes and left hamburgers raw in the middle.

The newspapers had warned that rationing would begin any day, so people rushed to the stores to stock up on supplies before rationing started. That week, Charlotte stood in line twice for sugar and could only buy five pounds.

Still, whenever she had a few spare minutes, she rushed next door to work on Mrs. Dubner's cellar. By Friday, Charlotte was nearly as tired as Ma.

Her tiredness slipped away when Mrs. Alexander made an announcement late on Friday afternoon. "Congratulations, boys and girls. In just one week, this class has filled a room in the school cellar with metal. On Monday afternoon, a truck will come. All of you sixth graders are invited to stay after school to load the truck. Then we'll follow it down the hill to the scrap yard next to the Edgar Thomson. If you wish, you may stay and watch as magnets sort out iron and steel for the mill furnaces."

The kids cheered. "Hurray!" "Swell!" "The scrap drive was a great idea, Charlotte." Her face broke into a smile so wide it hurt. Yes, she really was helping with the war. They all were. Victory!

Charlotte grinned all the way home.

Robbie stood waiting at the back door. "What's wrong with your face? You break it?"

"I'm feeling good, buster. There's a big truck coming Monday to take our scrap down to the mill, and we get to go along. Besides, Ma has a weekend coming and Pa's due home early for once." Charlotte reached into the mailbox and pulled out a letter—a flimsy envelope with a special postmark.

"Look! From Jim!"

"Open it, open it right away," Robbie begged.

She fingered the envelope, tempted. Then she shook her head. "No. Ma and Pa need to be here. It's addressed to them."

"Come on, Charlie." He reached for the letter. "We'll glue it back. They'll never know."

"No. This paper is awful thin. It could tear. Hands off, buster."

She carried the letter inside and propped it up on the kitchen table, where Ma would see it first thing. Instead of a nice note like she'd left on Monday, this morning Ma had simply made a list—*schoolwork, dust, sweep, mop kitchen and bathroom.*

Robbie eyed Ma's note and tried to duck down the hall.

Charlotte grabbed the back of his shirt. "We've got work to do," she told him. "I'm not doing it all."

"But it's the weekend."

She pointed to the letter on the kitchen table. "You think Jim gets weekends off? *Sorry, Captain, can't swab the decks. It's the weekend.*"

Robbie frowned and slumped. "No. But . . ."

Charlotte grinned at him. "Come on, sailor. Time to make this place shipshape."

Between them, they pulled the house into order before Ma came home. She arrived dirty again, and she looked tired, with gray patches under her eyes, but when she saw Jim's letter a smile lit up her face. She scrubbed her hands fast, then peeled the letter open carefully. As Ma began to read, Charlotte noticed holes where the Navy censors had cut out words.

Dear Folks,

Hope this finds you all well. We sure are busy. Keeping a ▓▓▓▓▓ *ship in fighting trim is a lot more work than on Pa's tug. And the water—I can't say where I'm serving, but the water stretches for miles on all sides. The sky goes on forever.*

When we first came aboard, a few fellas turned green and hung over the rails for a while, but those high-water days on the Mon tamed my stomach so I didn't embarrass myself. My legs handle the ship's roll just fine.

My shipmates are swell. We've had our moments, but we're mostly okay. A lot of the guys on my watch are jokers, so there's always somebody to cheer a fella up if he's feeling blue or missing his girl. We got one real young kid who lied about his age to join up, so we're watching over him pretty close. Funny, we come from all over, and we haven't known each other long, but somehow we're more than just pals. Almost like brothers, I guess.

Sea rations are nothing to brag about, but every so often we get a load of ▓▓▓▓▓▓▓▓▓▓, *a pleasant change. Sure do miss Ma's cooking, though.*

Buster, keep your nose clean. Practice your salutes and follow orders. If you ever join the Navy you'll find out just how many orders a fella can get in one day.

Lottie, hope you're helping Ma and Pa like you promised. Don't grow up too fast while I'm gone. Wait

*till I get home to invite fellas over, so I can inspect all
your admirers and toss out the stinkers.*

*Ma, Pa, keep the home fires burning. I can't tell you
how often I close my eyes and see all of you sitting around
the kitchen table. That's what we're fighting for—home,
peace, freedom.*

*Love to all, your son and brother,
Seaman First Class,
James Henry Campbell, USN*

"Thank God." Ma wiped her eyes.

"Darn confetti letter," Robbie said. "How come they
cut out holes this time?"

"He couldn't tell us what kind of ship he's on,"
Charlotte said. "You know that."

"Sure, but they cut out words when he was talking
about food. How come that's a big secret?"

"I don't know," Charlotte said. "Ma?"

Ma looked over the letter again. She blotted her eyes.
"I'm not sure. If I had to guess, I'd say whenever they come
near land, they bring on fresh provisions. If it's pineapples,
he's in the Pacific. Salmon or herring would mean the
North Sea; oranges and lemons, the United States shipping lanes near Florida. So it's classified information."

"I hate those secrets," Robbie grumbled.

"I know," Ma said. "But it's for safety. And we all want
him safe." She turned to Charlotte. "House looks nice,

honey. I'll go run my bath and soak off some of this soot. Then when your Pa gets home, we'll walk uptown and get ourselves some supper. You've cooked plenty this week."

"Burned plenty, too," Robbie said after Ma left. "I think Jim's in the Pacific. It's where I'd want to be. Those tropical islands."

Charlotte bit her lip. "I don't like to think of him so far away. The Atlantic's a lot closer."

"And a lot colder," Robbie argued. "I vote for the Pacific."

"We don't get to vote." Charlotte shook her head. She wasn't about to remind Robbie of all the terrible battles fought on those Pacific islands. But she knew them by heart—Manila, Corregidor, Bataan. The names rumbled through her mind like heavy slag trucks.

They stayed with her, through supper and hot fudge sundaes and beyond, into the night. And in spite of Charlotte's good-luck touch on Jim's blue star, the dream came again. Like before, Jim stood near the ship's rail. Then in an instant he was washed overboard. This time waves grabbed Charlotte too, forcing her to follow Jim.

She thrashed against the icy sea, kicking and pushing, but the swells knocked against her again and again, dragging her under. She struggled to breathe, but instead of air, she drew in water that stung her choking lungs. She coughed and tried to breathe but she was too heavy. She couldn't rise high enough, couldn't get out from under the swells rising up and up on all sides. And then she awoke and could breathe again, but her chest ached, and in her mouth the oily taste of river water lingered. *Odd—river water, not salt.* She sat up, startled, and pounded on her chest to clear it. Nothing came out except a raspy cough. She touched her hair, but it was dry. Still, the burning in her lungs felt so real, and the peculiar taste of river water so sour in her mouth.

She sat still in the darkness, trying to calm herself. What was going on? Had the dream of Jim somehow gotten mixed up in her mind with her own accident on the river? Why wouldn't that old memory go away? Sometimes she forgot about it for long stretches of time, but sometimes, like tonight, when the memory of river water tasted strong in her mouth again, it felt like it had all just happened yesterday.

CHAPTER 4

PERSONS UNKNOWN

Charlotte crammed a week's worth of chores into the weekend. She helped Ma with cleaning and laundry and finished most of her schoolwork.

Still, she and Robbie and Betsy managed to collect another load of scrap to haul to school on Monday. The truck was coming, after all, and Charlotte was determined to send it to the mill full of metal.

On Monday morning, Charlotte and Betsy took turns shoving Pa's wheelbarrow filled with metal uphill toward school. Robbie hurried along behind, pulling a heavy load of bent pots and pans in his wagon. Along the sidewalks, other kids carried, dragged, and hauled junk they'd found. Boy, would they fill up that truck.

"Wait till the kids see this. I bet we got the most metal of anybody," Betsy said. "This wheelbarrow's so heavy, my arms are about to fall off."

"Thanks to Mrs. Dubner," Charlotte said. "If her house hadn't been so full . . ."

"Well, it's empty now," Betsy said. "It almost looks nice."

"And don't forget the tulips she gave us," Charlotte said. "Until we cleaned up her yard, those tulips were buried." She shoved the wheelbarrow along the sidewalk and steered it toward the school.

By the time they reached the cellar door, the last bell was ringing and kids were hurrying inside. Was everybody late today? The cellar door was shut, and kids had left baskets and piles of scrap all around instead of hauling it inside. And where was Mr. Willis? She tried the door, but the knob didn't turn. Maybe he was late. Of course, if he hadn't opened the cellar, the kids couldn't put their scrap inside.

"Let's just leave our stuff out here with the rest," Charlotte said. "Maybe we can put it away at recess."

Betsy tugged on her arm. "Come on, wasn't that the last bell? Mrs. Alexander gets mad if we're late."

"Right, Bets. See you after school, Robbie."

When Charlotte and Betsy got to the classroom, Mrs. Alexander looked mad, all right. She stood stiffly beside her desk, frowning. Instead of the usual bustle, kids spoke in whispers. *This couldn't be my fault, could it?* Charlotte wondered. *The whole class wouldn't be acting strange just because Betsy and I were late.* What was going on?

"Do you think it's bad war news?" she asked Betsy. "I didn't hear anything on the radio."

"I haven't heard anything either." Betsy shrugged and looked puzzled.

An uneasy feeling stirred in Charlotte's stomach. If it was more serious than lateness, and it wasn't the war, what was it?

Mrs. Alexander looked around the room, and it felt like she was peering right into Charlotte's mind. Did the teacher know she hadn't finished her arithmetic and was planning to work on it during reading? "Boys and girls, be seated please. I have some very unpleasant news to report."

Kids slid into their seats without noise. It sounded like Mrs. Alexander's news was worse than unfinished fractions.

"Sometime between Friday afternoon and this morning," Mrs. Alexander said, "a person or persons unknown entered the school cellar."

No, Charlotte thought. Please no.

"He, she, or they removed all the metal that this class has collected. From what we can gather, it might be worth a pretty penny if someone tried to sell it," Mrs. Alexander went on. "The principal informed the mill, and today's delivery has been canceled."

"Wow!" "That stinks!" "Doggone!" "No fair!" Voices bubbled up around her, but Charlotte couldn't say a word. Who could have done such a thing?

She looked around. She liked most everybody in her class. Oh sure, Sophie Jaworski could be a pill, but she wouldn't have done this. She'd have gotten too dirty.

Charlotte had watched what Sophie brought in for the drive. One or two tin cans each day, scrubbed as clean as Ma's dishes. And everybody else had worked hard. The Cussick twins had brought in nearly as much scrap as she and Betsy had. Some boys who lived near Braddock Avenue had even collected from the stores. It couldn't be somebody in the class.

Then her eyes fixed on Paul Rossi. His dark hair was overgrown as usual, and he brushed it back from his eyes in a way that looked sneaky to Charlotte. That boy was always getting in trouble. Look at those stories he brought in from the newspapers. He loved crimes and criminals. And stealing was a crime.

"Class, class, please. Settle down." Mrs. Alexander blinked the lights and the room grew quiet. "I'm glad to see that you're all as distressed as I am. This is a deplorable incident, and we will discover the culprit. In the meantime, we need to make a decision—shall we discontinue our scrap drive until the thief is found, or shall we redouble our efforts and make sure to improve our security?"

"Keep going, keep going." The class burst into noise again.

Mrs. Alexander raised her hands. "We'll take a vote. All in favor of continuing to collect metal, please raise your hands."

Every hand shot in the air. Charlotte had never been prouder of her friends.

At recess, even though it was a sunny day and made for games, most kids stood around in clumps. Charlotte and Betsy stood close to the low red-brick wall that enclosed the school yard, whispering. "I feel so bad," Betsy said. "We'll never find as much junk as we did at Mrs. Dubner's."

Before Charlotte could answer, a commotion across the school yard caught her attention. She folded her arms across her chest and frowned. "Look at him, look at that Paul Rossi."

He stood on the seesaw, right in the middle, with his arms flung out. He shifted from side to side, banging the wooden ends down.

"Showing off as usual," Betsy said. "Don't bother with him."

"But don't you see, Bets? Everybody else is talking about the theft. Paul's acting like nothing happened. That's suspicious."

"No, that's Paul. He's a goofball. Hey, Charlotte, do you have to fix dinner for your ma today, or can we start cleaning out my attic for scrap?" Betsy pointed across the yard to the cellar door. "I'd like to refill that room with metal as quick as we can."

"Sure, we can work this afternoon. Ma already fixed a casserole. But Bets, I don't just want to collect more metal. I want to find the scrap we already collected and get it back."

"You think we could find it?"

"I don't know. I'm just so mad! I *hate* what's happened. Stealing's bad enough. But stealing from the war is like *treason.*" Her fingers curled into a fist and she smacked it against the rough red bricks. "I'd like to find the person who did this. I'd show him."

Charlotte glared at Paul Rossi, who now hung from the monkey bars. She hadn't noticed before, but he had a bruise on one cheek. From sneaking around in the dark? "There's got to be a way . . ."

"A way to *what*? Charlotte, what are you up to?"

"I'm going to figure out how to catch our thief, that's what. We'll bait a trap, then we'll stand guard and catch him red-handed."

"You're nuts, Charlotte Campbell. You've been reading too many of your ma's mysteries."

But by the time school let out, Charlotte had a plan. She and Betsy talked about it all the way home, figuring out the details.

As they were saying good-bye, Robbie caught up with them. "I know how we can catch the thief!" he said.

Betsy and Charlotte laughed and rolled their eyes at each other. Betsy headed home.

"Stop making faces, Charlie. I do know how to catch him. I have a plan. And it's perfect."

"Let me unlock the door first, buster."

"But, Charlie, it's a great idea. It's sure to work."

Inside, he raced for the bathroom, but he was bouncing with excitement when he got back. "You know down at the mill, how they have those giant magnets?"

"So?" Charlotte set her books on the kitchen table.

"Okay. We need to get one of those magnets. And we'll carry it around and when we feel a tug, we've found the thief's hideout."

"That's ridiculous. Do you know how heavy those magnets are? Your whole class couldn't lift one. It takes a crane."

"We could too lift one. I'm gonna ask Ma. She'll get one for us from the mill. Just you wait and see, Charlotte Campbell. You're not the only person around here with a brain."

❧

The next morning before school, kids again stood around talking quietly about the theft. Charlotte and Betsy stood close together in a sunny corner next to the low brick wall whispering, polishing their plan. "It's good we hadn't started cleaning out our own houses yet. We'll have lots of stuff for bait."

Charlotte pointed to Paul Rossi. He and some other boys were smacking each other's hands. It looked like a game of some sort. "Him. I know he's the one. So all we have to do is make sure he hears us talking about all the junk we've still got in our cellars. How we'll put it outside ready to haul tomorrow night. Then we stay up late and watch. When he shows up to steal it, we catch him."

"Catch who?" Sophie Jaworski asked. "That teacher?"

Charlotte's head snapped up. How had Sophie sneaked up on them? "What teacher?"

Sophie lowered her voice. "Mr. Costa. You know the one. He's new this year. Teaches science to the eighth grade."

"How do you know him, Sophie?" Betsy asked.

"I don't. But my sister has him. He's mean. He really stinks. She and her friends think he's the one. I listened outside her door last night. One of Helen's friends says Mr. Costa could be working for that Italian dictator guy, you know, Mussolini. Mr. Costa is Italian."

"So's Paul Rossi," Charlotte whispered to Betsy. "Could be they're working together."

Betsy shook her head. "A teacher? Come on, Sophie."

"I'm telling you, Helen and her friends have it all figured out. You know how that history teacher, Mr. Debevec, has signed up for the Marines, and Mrs. Alexander's son is training to be a Navy pilot?"

"What's that got to do with Mr. Costa?" Charlotte asked.

"Well, he's young like them, and he's not married either. So how come he didn't sign up to fight?" Sophie lowered her voice to a sly whisper. "Maybe he's a traitor.

Or maybe he's just a yellow-bellied slacker. Either way, he's rotten enough to steal our metal."

"Gosh, Sophie," Betsy said. She shook her head. "Do you really think a teacher would steal the metal?"

"Somebody did. That scrap didn't walk away by itself. So my sister and her friends are gonna keep their eyes on Mr. Costa. Shh." Sophie put her hand to her lips and pretended to turn a key, then walked toward another group of girls.

"That Sophie, she's nuts," Charlotte said. "She's blabbing to the whole school, but she wants us to keep quiet. Besides, it's got to be Paul Rossi."

"I don't know, Charlotte," Betsy began. She stopped talking as two big eighth-grade boys came right up to her.

"You Betsy Schmidt?" one asked.

His voice had an ugly sound. Charlotte reached for her friend's hand and Betsy took it.

"Yes. I'm Betsy."

"We're watching you. Me and my friends, we're gonna keep you in our sights all the time. You and your Kraut family."

"Wait a minute," Charlotte said. "What do you mean, *Kraut?*"

The boy sneered at her. "Lousy German. Stinkin' Nazi. You understand them words?"

"But Betsy's not—" Charlotte began. Betsy squeezed her hand tightly.

The other boy stuck his finger right under Betsy's nose. "You tell us. If you ain't a Kraut, where'd you get your last name?"

"My great-great-grandparents came from Germany. But that was a long time ago."

"See." The first boy glared at Charlotte. Then he turned his attention to Betsy. "It's just plain rotten, how they let scum like you into the U. S. of A. Don't make another move, or you'll be sorry."

"Who are you calling scum?" Charlotte demanded. "You leave Betsy alone. Her brother's fighting for the U. S. of A."

She tugged Betsy's hand and they ducked away from the boys toward the door.

Betsy's face had turned pale and her blue eyes looked wet.

"Come on, don't listen to them," Charlotte said. "They don't know anything. The one in the blue sweater, Frankie Zalenchak, he's a bully, always picking on younger kids. And that Danny Merkow just sticks with Frankie because he likes to sound tough."

"But they called me a Kraut, Charlotte. I can't help my last name." The tears spilled over and Betsy rubbed at them with her fists.

Charlotte flung her arm around Betsy's shaking shoulders. "They're crazy, Bets. Your family's been in America for a long time. If anybody's a foreigner here, they are."

She turned and glared at the boys, but they had their backs to her and couldn't see.

"Oh, no. Look, Charlotte. They're going after my cousin Pete. They got into an argument with Pete last week, and now it's starting up again. He's got a temper. They're going to get him in trouble. Charlotte, we've got to—"

The bell rang, and just in time. Another minute and war would have erupted in the school yard.

As they marched back to their classroom, they passed the cellar door. Mr. Willis knelt on the floor with a screwdriver in his hand. As she stepped closer, Charlotte could see that he was installing a new lock on the door. Well, good.

"Look, Bets," she whispered. "The new metal we collect will stay safe. We'll collect so much, nobody will dare say another word about your last name."

Betsy shook her head like she didn't believe Charlotte. "What if they talk to their parents? What if somebody says something to my dad at the mill? He's got a temper just like Pete's."

"All the more reason for us to collect the most metal of anybody. And find the real thief. Once we catch him, we'll be heroes. Come on, we'll drop the first hints now, when we get close to Paul Rossi's desk."

"I don't know," Betsy said.

"Well, I do." Charlotte stepped quickly past Sophie and the Cussick twins. She was practically leaning on

Paul's desk. "Okay, Betsy, let's stack it all in my back alley tomorrow night. Wednesday," she added loudly, just in case Paul wasn't listening the first time. "We'll have a ton of metal by then. We'll show them. Nobody can beat the team of Campbell and Schmidt."

CHAPTER 5
SUSPICIOUS CHARACTERS

The commotion didn't stop when Charlotte got home. Robbie and his friends had been busy, too. "I got two ideas about the thief," he announced to Charlotte. "Two real good ones."

"Oh, come on," Charlotte said. "You're in fourth grade." She unlocked the back door. How did nine-year-olds come up with suspects?

"Just 'cause we're smaller than you doesn't mean we're dumb." He stomped inside behind her and slammed down his books on the kitchen table.

"Okay, who's on your list?"

"I'm not gonna tell."

Oh, great. Mr. Stubborn. "Please, Robbie. You were good at finding scrap. You might be good at finding the thief, too."

"You mean it?"

"Come on, tell me. Who knows, if you're right, we might catch the thief in the act. How about that?"

He grinned. "Okay. Most of my class thinks one thing. But I'm not ready to make up my mind yet. I'm still looking at the clues."

"What clues? Who does your class think took the metal?"

"Wagon Willie."

"What?"

"You heard me. Wagon Willie. You know, the janitor."

"You mean Mr. Willis? Why would he . . ."

"He already goes around collecting stuff. All summer long, he pushes that big wagon of his around the streets collecting stuff to sell."

"And you think he took our metal?"

"I'm not sure yet. But he could have. He's always around school. Some kids say he sleeps there. And he's, you know, strange."

Charlotte shook her head. "He just has trouble getting his words out sometimes. I don't think he'd steal. He's always nice to us." She frowned. She'd known Mr. Willis ever since she'd started school. A lot of kids made fun of him, but Charlotte thought he was nice.

Once in second grade she'd gotten sick in the hall and he'd cleaned it up. She'd said she was sorry, but Mr. Willis had shaken his head and smiled. "N-n-no, Missy. Can't help getting sick. F-f-feel better."

And she had. No, Mr. Willis couldn't be the thief. She refused to believe it. "You said you had two good ideas, Robbie. Who else?"

"There's this kid in my class, Tommy Stankowski. I don't like him anyway. He's always dirty and he talks rough."

"You think a fourth grader took all that stuff? Impossible. It's too heavy."

"Okay, maybe it's a long shot, but he could have had help. Listen, Charlie, he brought a lunch pail to school that looked exactly like the one we found in old Mrs. Dubner's cellar. It was even busted in the same place."

"That's ridiculous. Half the kids in school have metal lunch pails. And I bet a lot of them are broken. Nope, *I'm* betting on Paul Rossi, buster. And we're going to set a trap to catch him. Want to help?"

"A trap? Sure."

As soon as Charlotte had changed clothes, she headed to Betsy's house and knocked on the door. Mrs. Schmidt answered. "She's not feeling too good, Charlotte. And to tell you the truth, neither am I. She'll see you tomorrow." Betsy's ma looked tired and didn't even try to smile.

Charlotte couldn't blame her. The way those eighth graders had gone after Betsy, it was wicked. She told Robbie about it when she returned home and they started down the steps to their own cellar.

"For real? Some guys said Betsy was the thief? And called her a Kraut? That's dumb."

"You want more dumbness? Sophie Jaworski thinks one of the teachers did it."

"Which one? How come?"

"Mr. Costa, because he's got an Italian name." A shadow of guilt flitted across Charlotte's mind. She'd said the same thing about Paul Rossi. That maybe he and Mr. Costa were in it together because they were Italian. Her cheeks felt hot as she remembered.

Well, that wasn't the real reason she suspected him, she told herself. With all those crime stories, he made himself look guilty. "Come on, Robbie. Let's start in the back room. The more metal we collect, the better trap we can build."

Instead of hauling the day's collection to school the next morning, Charlotte and Robbie stacked it in the alley behind their house. Bait.

She pointed it out to Betsy on the way to school.

"That's nice, Charlotte," she said. Her voice was quiet.

"You're still upset, aren't you?"

"Wouldn't you be?"

"Yeah. But you can't let those dumb boys get to you. They don't have one brain between the two of them. Come on, let's get to school fast. So we can talk real loud about our stash of metal in front of you-know-who. If we catch him, that'll take care of Zalenchak and Merkow."

"Yeah, maybe." Betsy still didn't sound convinced.

That made Charlotte even more determined. She walked faster. When they got to the school yard, the early bell hadn't even rung and kids were milling around. Charlotte spotted Paul Rossi and headed toward him, dragging Betsy along.

"Hi, Paul," she said. "Find any pots and pans lately?"

"Some. How about you?"

"Lots. We found so much, we can't carry it," Charlotte said. "We'll have to wait till Betsy's pa can drive it to school."

"Oh yeah?"

"Yeah. And we'll have even more by tomorrow. If you don't believe me, just take a look in the alley behind our house."

"Maybe I will and maybe I won't. You know, you've got to watch out for dark alleys. Two guys busted out of jail yesterday down in Pittsburgh. They could be headed this way. Don't say I didn't warn you." He raised his eyebrows, then walked away.

Charlotte frowned. The early bell rang and Betsy tugged on her sweater, pulling her toward some girls in their class who were stretching out a jump rope. "Come on, you two," they called. "You want to try double Dutch?"

"Sure," Betsy said.

Sophie Jaworski turned and stopped them as they got close to the girls with the rope. "Charlotte, Betsy, what's going on? I saw you talking to that Paul Rossi. If I didn't know better, I'd think one of you had a crush on him."

Betsy shook her head. "Not me."

"Me either," Charlotte said. She stuck out her tongue and wrinkled her nose. "He's the worst boy in our class."

"That's what I've always thought," Sophie said. "Still, you went over to him. You better watch out, Charlotte. People will talk . . ."

"Forget it, Sophie. I've got better things to do." Charlotte and Betsy joined the group of girls and took turns jumping.

When the bell rang again, Charlotte and Betsy shoved through the crowd and up the worn stone steps into the main hallway, where little kids' drawings of spring flowers decorated the walls. Sophie's words still bounced around in Charlotte's mind. A crush on Paul Rossi? She couldn't get far enough away from Sophie and her crazy ideas. As they reached the door to their classroom, Frankie Zalenchak and Danny Merkow practically knocked them down.

"Watch where you're going, you big bullies," Charlotte called after them.

Betsy turned to Charlotte, a worried look in her eyes. "What are they doing here? The eighth graders use the stairs at the other end of the hall. I don't like this one bit."

"You can't let them get on your nerves, Bets. If they see you're scared, they'll bother you more. Come on, Mrs. Alexander is waiting for us."

When she walked into her classroom, Charlotte sniffed. Something smelled funny. The smell grew stronger as she and Betsy moved down the row toward their desks. "Hey, what is that smell, anyway?" she asked.

She was about to slip into her seat when she caught sight of Betsy, pale like somebody had painted her face with flour.

"No! Oh, Charlotte, no!" Betsy dropped her books and covered her eyes.

Charlotte stepped closer and looked into Betsy's opened desk. The smell hit her nose like a stink bomb. Somebody—two somebodies, Charlotte figured—had dumped a big can of sauerkraut all over the inside of Betsy's desk.

❧

The sixth grade got to play dodgeball for an hour that morning while Mr. Willis cleaned up the mess and brought in a new desk for Betsy. Frankie Zalenchak and Danny Merkow got kicked out of school for the rest of the week.

Mrs. Alexander asked Betsy if she'd like to go home, but Betsy refused. "I didn't do anything wrong," she said. "I'll stay."

"Good for you," Charlotte said. "You're not letting those bullies turn you into mush."

And Betsy didn't. For a soft-looking girl, with rosy cheeks and pale brown hair, Betsy flung the ball that morning like she was training for the dodgeball Olympics. Charlotte felt sorry for the kids in the middle.

By lunchtime, the whole school was buzzing about the sauerkraut incident. The sixth and seventh grades stuck up for the Schmidt family, angry that Betsy and her cousin Pete were being treated like enemies. The eighth grade was split. The boys stuck with Zalenchak and Merkow, but the girls thought they were bullies. Besides, according to Sophie, the eighth-grade girls still believed that Mr. Costa was the thief.

"They're going to get some evidence on him. This week," Sophie promised. "They have plans, but I couldn't hear what. I'll keep spying on my sister and her friends to see what they're up to."

Charlotte shook her head. Anybody who thought she had a crush on Paul Rossi couldn't be trusted. She'd keep to her original plan and make sure Paul heard again about the big pile of metal she'd collected. She'd catch him tonight, red-handed, and prove Betsy innocent in the bargain.

෴

Late that night, she sat in the dark and peered out her bedroom window. In the distance, factory lights lit up the riverbanks as the Mon flowed on, a wide black ribbon, smooth and treacherous, broken only by the tiny star-points of buoy lights.

She shifted her attention back to the dark alley below. Among the shadows, she could just make out the heap of scrap she and Robbie had carefully piled up, ready to come crashing down at the slightest touch. Next door, Betsy was awake and watching, too. They were probably the only people awake in the whole neighborhood, Charlotte thought. But they were ready. They each had a flashlight for signaling. Charlotte had borrowed Jim's baseball bat and propped it right next to the window.

At about eleven, Charlotte heard a loud, clattering clank. The thief! She pressed her nose to the glass, but all she could see were black trees, spidery bushes, and the shadowy pile of bait. She flashed her light out the side window twice, toward Betsy's house, and waited. No reply.

Had Betsy fallen asleep? Charlotte signaled again. Nothing. Maybe she should get Robbie. But he slept like a stone. And she didn't dare wake Ma or Pa . . .

Charlotte's mouth went dry. This couldn't be happening. She and Betsy had made plans to catch the thief together. Now she was all by herself. She peered out the window.

What if Paul wasn't working alone? What if it wasn't even Paul out there? Suddenly his warning popped back into her head. Watch out for dark alleys, he'd said. Hadn't two men just broken out of jail in Pittsburgh? Would they come to Braddock?

No, of course they wouldn't. Besides, if her trap was working, she couldn't give up the chance to catch the thief red-handed. Heart pounding, she tucked the flashlight under her arm, grabbed the baseball bat, and eased open the door to her room. On tiptoe she made it to the top of the stairs, then crept down through the inky blackness and into the kitchen. With shaking fingers, she eased open the back door. The night air chilled her face; as she tiptoed out to the porch her bare feet felt damp. One step at a time, she inched toward the alley.

Something hissed. Then something yowled and brushed her leg. She jumped backward. With a crash, two silvery cats sprang from the scrap pile and bounded over the fence into Mrs. Dubner's backyard.

A light went on there, and Charlotte heard a voice. "Hush, you silly rascals. Hush now. There, that's better."

Cats! Crazy old Mrs. Dubner's cats. There should be laws to keep people like her from acting so strange and scaring the neighbors, Charlotte thought.

She took deep breaths and tried to make her heart stop racing. Cats, just cats. She flashed her light on the alley, to make sure. All she could see were an old cast-iron sink, a rusty bucket, and a mess of tin cans. She re-piled the metal and crept carefully back to her room to watch. Paul Rossi might still show up tonight, she told herself.

It took half an hour for Charlotte's heart to return to its regular speed. In another half hour, she was yawning.

Sometime after midnight, she gave up and crawled into bed.

At first light, she tumbled out of the covers and checked the window. Her scrap pile sat in the alley, undisturbed. Darn it, anyway. Why hadn't that rotten Paul Rossi snapped up her bait? She fell back into bed and tried to make a new plan as she waited for the rest of the family to wake up.

❧

No brilliant ideas came that morning, not in bed, not at breakfast, not on the way to school with Betsy. When she reached the school yard, more bad news waited.

"Somebody came back to the cellar last night," Marnie Cussick announced. "Teachers are in there now, looking around."

"Somebody stole our scrap again," her sister said. "It's wicked and rotten."

No! Charlotte felt like somebody had set her on fire. She shoved her way through the crowd of kids gathered near the cellar door, to where Paul Rossi stood alone, watching the angry faces. "Now I know why you didn't grab the scrap from my alley. You had other plans last night, didn't you?"

"What are you talking about, Charlotte? You calling me a thief?" He stared at her hard, without blinking.

"What if I am?" She stepped closer to him. "You skip school sometimes. Don't deny it. And you're always getting sent to the principal and bringing in those crime stories."

"So what? That doesn't mean I'd mess with the war. I'm no traitor. I got two brothers in the Marines."

Betsy came up behind her and took Charlotte's hand. "You have brothers in the war, too? I didn't know that."

Charlotte stepped back. She hadn't known it either. She swallowed. "But still . . . where did you get that bruise on your cheek?"

"Mind your own business." He swiped his cheek and glared as the bell rang, ending the argument but not Charlotte's suspicions.

Still, to be fair, right after the Pledge of Allegiance she made a complete list of people who might have stolen the metal—Paul Rossi, Mr. Costa, Mr. Willis, even that little kid in Robbie's class. She refused to put Betsy's name on the list. But at the bottom she wrote down Zalenchak and Merkow. Were they smart enough to accuse Betsy so nobody would suspect them? Sure. So maybe they should take Paul's spot at the top of her list. Maybe, and maybe not. Either way, she'd have to set another trap. A better one.

She slipped the list into her history book so Mrs. Alexander wouldn't think it was a note and read it out loud. A good detective couldn't let her suspects know what she was up to, could she?

CHAPTER 6
STITCHES

After lunch, the little kids were going inside as Charlotte's class was heading out. Robbie popped out of line and stuck a note in her hand.

Charlotte. Rick Maloney found an old dump. Buried treasure, lots of cans, up at the end of Second Avenue. Let's go after school. Robbie

Charlotte had on her oldest skirt, one that was too tight, anyway, so Ma wouldn't mind if she worked awhile without changing. They'd lose half an hour if they went home first. "Okay. Meet you there," she called as Robbie's class marched inside.

After school, she and Betsy walked along Second Avenue. The neighborhood was west of theirs by a few blocks, but it looked about the same. All the houses in the flats along the river were lined up in rows, with small yards and alleys along the back. If you wanted fancy in Braddock, you had to climb the hill.

At the end of Second Avenue, Charlotte could see a weedy, junk-filled vacant lot with several small boys hard at work. On the sidewalk they'd lined up buckets and wagons and filled them with old rusty cans. Robbie and his friend Rick stood in the middle of the vacant lot wrestling with what looked like a door from an old car.

"That's real heavy. Let us help," she offered.

She stepped carefully around an old icebox and some broken bottles. Robbie was grabbing the top of the old car door. Rick tugged at the handle.

"We need to move this old tire out of the way first," Betsy said. "It's jamming the door."

Charlotte bent to grab the tire. Nasty, greenish water dumped out when she and Betsy lifted it. "Come on, let's roll this to the sidewalk for the eighth graders' tire drive. Even if we're mad at them, the tires will help the war."

When they got to the sidewalk, Charlotte let the tire flop down. As she straightened her back, she found herself looking at Paul Rossi. "What are you doing here?" she asked in surprise.

"What, is there a law against standing on the sidewalk? I live nearby. What about you?"

She shrugged. "Just collecting scrap. My brother and his friends—"

"Hey, that's a big door they're lifting. Want some help?"

No, Charlotte wanted to say. You'll only steal this too. But if he really did have brothers in the Marines, would he? Besides, Robbie and Rick were getting nowhere with that door.

"Okay. The door is pretty heavy."

Paul, Charlotte, and Betsy stepped back around the icebox. With five kids lifting, they freed the car door and lugged it to the sidewalk.

"Let her down easy," Paul said. "One, two—"

Something must have slipped. Charlotte held tight to the door bottom, but the top clanked to the ground.

Robbie reached and tried to stop it, then yelled. "Oww!"

"What?" Charlotte dropped the door and grabbed for Robbie's hand. Blood dripped all over the sidewalk. "Gosh, Robbie! Oh, geez. Somebody help us."

Before she could even think what to do, Paul Rossi had ripped off his shirt and was wrapping it tightly around Robbie's hand. "Come on, kid. We'd better get you to the hospital."

"Wait! Our doctor's office is right up on the avenue. It's closer," said Charlotte, staring at the shirt. Blood was soaking through. Robbie's blood. The muscles in Charlotte's legs went soft and she swayed. Betsy grabbed hold of her and put an arm around her waist.

"Lead the way." Paul picked up Robbie. "We'll make better time if I carry you," he said. "And you can holler if you want. I sure would."

৩৵

"Five stitches." Robbie waved a white gauze hand under Charlotte's nose.

She ducked back. It looked like a mummy's hand from a creepy movie.

"It's neat," he bragged. "I'd show you, but they wrapped my hand up so you can't see."

"I . . . I'll see it later. Can we go home now?"

"Did they give you a tetanus shot?" Paul asked. "Last time I got sewed up, they poked me with a needle big enough for a horse."

"Right here." Robbie pointed to his left arm. "I told them to save the shot for a soldier, but they said they had plenty."

Beside her, Betsy shivered. "I hate shots."

"Me too." Charlotte studied Robbie's face. He was grinning, but his skin looked pale. "Can you make it home?"

"I'm no baby."

"I'll come too," Paul offered.

Charlotte shook her head. "Thanks, but . . ."

"No trouble. Those shots can make you pretty woozy."

A nurse gave Charlotte a sheet of instructions for Ma and explained how to clean and wrap Robbie's hand. He'd need to come back in a few days so they could take out his stitches.

They walked home slowly. At every corner, Paul made Robbie stop and sit down on somebody's steps and rest before starting the next block. Charlotte wanted to hurry home so she could wash the blood off her hands and clothes, but Paul seemed to know what he was doing.

When they finally got home, Robbie flopped onto the sofa. Charlotte headed into the kitchen to wash up, and Betsy followed her.

"Robbie's pretty pale," Betsy began. "You don't look so good either, Charlotte. You want me to get my mother?"

Charlotte checked the kitchen clock as she scrubbed the blood off her hands. Ma would be home soon, and they'd have some explaining to do. She shook her head. "Thanks, Bets, but we'll be okay."

Betsy left by the kitchen door. Charlotte dried her hands and slipped into the living room in time to see Paul stick a pillow under Robbie's arm. "Keep it high," he said. "Won't hurt so much."

"How do you know all this stuff?" Charlotte asked.

Paul seemed startled to see her. "Me and my brothers, we've been stitched some. No big deal."

Suddenly it was a big deal to Charlotte. She'd accused Paul Rossi of stealing, and then he'd turned around and taken care of Robbie. He'd behaved real nice, too, not tough like he acted at school.

"I'm sorry," she began. Her cheeks burned, but she refused to let that stop her. "What I said in school. I was wrong. You're not a bad guy, a thief."

Paul shrugged. "Don't make a fuss, Charlotte. At school now, with everybody accusing people . . . Well,

when I think about my brothers off fighting, it makes all
this seem cheap."

"You're not mad at me?"

"I was. But geez. Your folks will light into both of you
tonight. That's enough for one day." He slapped Robbie
on the shoulder and stuck out his hand to Charlotte.
"Pals? I'll help you haul stuff to school if you want, since
he's on the wounded list."

Charlotte shook his hand. "Thanks." As he left, she
stared after him. Who'd have thought she'd ever be pals
with Paul Rossi? Or that he could be nice?

Half an hour later, Ma came home. After she checked
Robbie's hand and made sure he was okay, she glared.
"No more collecting metal for you, buster. You either,
Charlotte."

"But, Ma . . . It's for the war."

"It's too dangerous," Ma said. "I've got enough on my
mind, worrying about Jim."

"But, Ma, it's for Jim. Could I please keep working?
I'll be really careful. I'll wear gloves."

"I'll think about it. But neither of you picks up as
much as a tin can until I decide. Hear me?"

"Yes, Ma."

"Buster?"

Robbie didn't reply. He'd fallen asleep.

❧

With Robbie's hand needing to heal, all the chores landed on Charlotte. Ma probably didn't mean it as a punishment, but it felt like one. Washing clothes on a rainy Friday afternoon, then pinning them up in the cellar to dry—that wasn't Charlotte's idea of a weekend. Neither was cleaning and ironing all day Saturday. But she couldn't complain; Ma worked twice as hard.

When Sunday dawned, it was the third rainy day in a row. Charlotte made her way to the kitchen, where her parents read the paper over coffee.

"I've got a sweet roll still warm in the oven for you," Ma said. She stood and gave Charlotte a hug. She pointed to Robbie, who was reading the funny pages. "Had to hide it from that brother of yours. Something about stitches seems to make fellas hungry."

"Thanks, Ma. I'll help you with the cooking after church. It's a mean day outside."

"Bad weather or not, I've got lines to check," Pa interrupted. "That Rowley boy just joined the Army, so I'm down a deckhand." He turned to Charlotte. "I need you on the *Rose* this afternoon."

Her stomach tightened. "But, Pa, can't Robbie help?"

"He'd get his bandages all wet."

Robbie looked up from the comics. "I want to go. Please, Pa. I'll be careful. I can wrap my hand."

"You can come if you want, but you can't work. You'll just keep us company. Lottie, I really need you today."

Pa folded up his paper and went to dress for church.

That morning in church, Charlotte prayed as she always did—for the war to end, for Jim and all the soldiers and sailors to come home safe. She added a couple extra prayers at the end.

"Please, God, forgive me for letting Robbie get hurt. And for thinking and saying bad stuff about Paul Rossi." She closed her eyes tighter. "And if I have to help on the boat, could it maybe stop raining?"

Either God wasn't listening, or he'd decided that a little rain was good penance, for the clouds only got grayer as afternoon came and she, Pa, and Robbie walked to the docks. Since the war had started, Sunday was about the only day the docks were quiet. Still, there were signs of activity inside the nearby mill buildings. Charlotte shivered and wished she could help indoors instead of on the tug in the rain.

They neared the mooring where the *Rose* bobbed in rough water, shedding rain like an oversized duck. The *Rose* wasn't a big tug like the ones that hauled long strings of barges from the Great Lakes to New Orleans. But she wasn't small, either. The engines took up most of her wide belly, the pilothouse sat above the front, and tall exhaust stacks poked up behind, making her nearly as high as she was long. With her blunt nose hitched close to the dock, she looked clumsy and bulky, but on the water with a barge or two in tow, she was shipshape enough. If a person cared for ships.

Pa climbed aboard and held out his hand, first to Robbie, then to Charlotte. She looked down as he swung her onto the deck. High water, rushing and brown with all the rain. The worst time to be on the river.

"We need to check all the lines and all the cables," Pa said. He unlocked the door, which led up to the pilot-house and down to the engine room. "Let's get oilskins on so we don't get completely soaked." He opened a storage locker and pulled out three yellow slickers, then went below to the engine room.

Charlotte shrugged into the oilskin, which felt chill and clammy. She stared out at the choppy river. Raindrops pocked the surface, and gusts of wind whipped up waves. A metallic, oily taste came to her tongue.

Robbie scowled at her. "What's the matter, Charlie? You scared? Come on, you can swim, even if it took you forever to learn." He made it sound like he was the older one and she was a dumb little kid.

"I'm not scared. I just don't like high water." Charlotte frowned, remembering. After the accident, Jim had dragged her to the Carnegie Library's big indoor pool after school for months. "No sister of mine's gonna drown," he'd said. He'd been real patient with her, though. All along, he'd told her it wasn't her fault she was a sinker, too skinny to float. And finally, she'd learned. But swimming in a pool wasn't the same as facing high water on the river.

She looked at Robbie's sturdy, solid shape. He and Jim

took after Pa, born loving water and swimming like fish. She, on the other hand, had gotten Ma's long, lean bones. Heavy bones.

Pa returned from the engine room below.

"Can I use the spyglass, Pa? While you and Charlie check lines?"

"Don't see why not. Go on, sit up in my chair and keep watch. We'll snap on the radio, too. You holler down if you spot trouble."

Trouble? Charlotte looked around at the surging river. She followed Pa to the front, where several thick ropes lay in neat coils. On the port side, he lifted one, stretched it out, and rewound it, carefully checking for worn spots. It was important work, Charlotte knew, even if she didn't like doing it. A frayed rope could mean a lost barge. She knelt on the starboard side and checked her first coil.

The lines were soaked with rain, and cold. The wet made the twisted hemp swell up even thicker than usual. Her fingers ached by the time she'd re-coiled the first one. Heavy work, but at least she didn't have to look at the river. She glanced up to the window of the pilothouse. Robbie had Pa's spyglass out and was studying the southern riverbank. She moved to a second coil, then a third.

The front lines and cables were all strong, so she and Pa moved to the stern, where Pa found a mooring line unraveling in the middle. She helped him secure a new line, holding the thick hemp rope as he worked the knots.

"Hold tighter, Lottie," he said. "You're letting her slip."

"It's hard, Pa. My hands are cold."

"Put on gloves then. Should be a pair in your pockets. If this knot gives, a whole string of barges could drift off. You know that, girl."

Charlotte pulled on the heavy leather gloves. They were damp and too large, but they did make the rope less slick.

Pa slipped the last loop into place and tested the line. He nodded. "Good and tight. Thanks, Lottie."

Great, they were done. Charlotte could go home now and get warm and dry. This hadn't taken too long, after all. Just then she heard a shout.

Above her head, Robbie leaned out of the pilothouse window, waving his arms. "Pa, Charlie! Trouble on the river. Barges loose upstream! On the radio they're calling all the tugs to help!"

"Not us. We can't . . ." Charlotte began, but she knew better. When trouble came on the river, all hands pitched in. There wasn't much worse trouble than loose barges. If the barges were fully loaded, they could ram and destroy anything in their path. "Oh, Pa," she cried.

But Pa didn't hear. He'd already run for the stairs and the radio, leaving her alone and shivering in the stern.

CHAPTER 7

RUNAWAYS ON THE RIVER

Charlotte made her way up the stairs to the pilothouse. Pa shoved his spyglass into her hands. "Stay topside and keep watch on the river. If you see any runaway barges, come get me. I have to fire up the boiler."

"But, Pa, you don't have a crew. Just Robbie and me."

"You'll do." Pa turned to Robbie. "Come on, buster, think you can watch the steam gauge and shovel in a little coal?"

"Sure, Pa." Robbie grinned. "And Charlie, look, in the bend of the river. Look with the glass." He pointed to the far northern bank of the Mon. "A pile of metal."

Pa clattered down the steps, with Robbie following right behind. Charlotte let herself sink into Pa's captain's chair. She heard thumps below as Pa opened the firebox and started to shovel in coal.

She scanned the river with the glass. No sign of barges,

just bits of trash carried by the rushing water. After a spell of rain like this, the banks always got littered. She turned the glass to where Robbie had pointed. Sure enough, a bigger-than-usual pile of junk covered a steep part of the bank. But who cared? Within minutes the *Rose* would be fired up and rolling with no real crew.

"Down here, Lottie," Pa shouted. "I need you on deck."

She tightened her oilskin and stepped down to join Pa. Rain spattered her face. The deck felt greasy underfoot.

He pointed to one of the coiled mooring lines—a heavy rope with a loop at the end. "Stand here, at the front. The minute we spot a runaway barge, I'll steer up close. You drop this line around the barge's mooring pin, then haul her up tight, and we'll tow her back to the docks, slick as a whistle."

"But, Pa . . ." There was no railing around the flat nose of the tug. Only a few feet of deck and then—river. A single slip and . . .

"Easy as catching a fish, sweetheart," Pa said. He pinched her cheek with wet, cold fingers.

"Pa, coal barges aren't fish, they're whales. I can't—"

"'Course you can. I'll keep my window open so we can shout to each other. Hold tight now, and cast off when I get her humming."

Inside the heavy gloves, Charlotte's hands felt clammy and sore. Rain pounded the deck. Through the soles of her feet she could feel the engines begin to pump.

Pa signaled and she cast off, loosening the heavy ropes that bound the tug to the dock pilings. Then she crept to the middle of the tug's front. There at least she was farthest from the roiling brown water. She watched the banks as Pa brought the *Rose* around and headed her upstream. The engines hummed as the *Rose* bit into the current.

From port to starboard, she checked the river. If only it weren't Sunday, there'd be plenty of other boats to help. But today only the big working boats would be hauling, and they could be miles away. So it was up to her and Pa. *Darn rain. Why did barges always break free?* It happened every spring with high water—a cable would snap and barges would get loose. Why didn't somebody tie them down tighter? Or could it be they tied them too tight?

"Lottie, look ahead, starboard bank," Pa shouted.

She peered through the rain. A dark shape hovered on the horizon, hulking and huge. Pa steered the *Rose* toward starboard. As they chugged closer, Charlotte could see more clearly. It wasn't one barge, it was two, and both of them piled high with coal.

She clenched her fingers and turned toward the pilot-house. "Pa, what do we do?"

He motioned her toward the starboard mooring lines. "Grab your line and get ready to throw it. I'll bring her as close as I can."

"But, Pa, two barges . . ." Roped together side by side,

they were bigger than a football field, at least sixty feet
wide and three times that long.

Pa waved her on.

She inched out, looked upriver, and blinked hard.
Hundreds of tons of coal were headed straight toward
them. Sure, Pa could steer the *Rose,* but those barges were
runaways. Charlotte knew that full barges could float any
which way. They had no rudders, no controls at all. Her
stomach clenched. What if they rammed into the *Rose?*
She could nearly taste the water.

"They're loaded, Pa!"

"Better full than empty," he called back. "Empties flop
around more."

Pa steered closer. Rain soaked Charlotte's hair and
her gloves. She uncoiled the heavy line and held the loop
in both hands, watching. Fifty feet, then twenty-five. Her
breath came in fast, short bursts that burned her lungs.

She squinted through the heavy rain until she could
see the mooring pins on the nearest barge. Darn, they
were small. They looked like coffee cans at this distance.
How close would Pa dare get? How far could she throw
the line? She looked down at the rushing brown river.
Mistake. Her stomach heaved.

Pa eased the *Rose* closer. She could see a spill of coal along
the near edge of the barge. Water surged in the gap between
tug and barge, like the river was angry at being trapped.

"Now!" Pa shouted.

She flung the line out. The loop end snaked out like a lasso, then splashed into the river. She hauled it in again, colder and wetter than before. She'd missed the first pin.

"Lottie, go closer."

She took a deep breath and half a step forward. She tossed the rope toward the second mooring pin as Pa steered parallel to the huge barge. Her line thumped the side, then splashed again. The angry river slapped at the side of the tug and pulled the rope under.

Her feet could feel the *Rose*'s engine slowing as Pa kept her alongside the barge. The third mooring pin was coming. If she missed this one, they'd have to pull away and start over. She took another half step forward. There was nothing to hold onto but a cold, slippery rope. Churning water gushed between the tug and the barge. They were edging so close a person would be squished if she went overboard.

She held her breath, then threw the line as hard and as straight as she could. The loop snagged the pin, flopped, then held.

She yanked the line tight and forced the heavy rope into a hitching loop, and then another and another, until the first barge was secure against the nose of the tug.

"Good work, Lottie," Pa called. She sidestepped away from the edge, feeling the shift of weight as the tug's engine began to haul at the corner of the barge. Charlotte knew what Pa was doing. The two barges were still dangerous, floating alongside the tug and hitched in only one place. Pa had to line up the *Rose* square behind the barges, so he could push them.

He steered the tug around slowly. The engine rumbled in protest. "Get ready to secure another line, Lottie. Port side, so we can balance these babies," Pa shouted.

"I can't," she whispered. But she knew she didn't have a choice. An inch at a time, she made her way across the slippery deck to the port-side mooring line.

When Pa finally got the *Rose* lined up behind the barges, Charlotte dropped the port line over the second barge's closest mooring pin. As she hauled in the line to secure it, the palms of her hands stung.

Pa called her up to the pilothouse to join him. "That was some job, sailor," he said, pulling her into his arms and hugging her tight. "How are your hands?"

"Sore." She stepped back and peeled off her wet gloves. Red lines cut into the palms of her hands. "Oh, Pa, I'm no sailor. I was so scared."

"Scared or not, you came through." He hugged her again. Then he turned to his rudder sticks and began to steer. The *Rose*'s engines thrummed and groaned. Slowly the pair of barges nosed out into the middle of the muddy Mon.

Back at the dock, Pa pulled three short blasts on the whistle to let Ma know they were coming home soon. He tied up the tug and both barges until the barge owners could come the next day to collect their coal. Then he went below to shut down the engines.

Robbie bounded up to the deck with Pa. "Wow! Charlie, Pa says you're a hero! You roped two barges. Me too! I kept the steam coming. Wow, look at those barges." He grabbed Charlotte's hand and tugged her closer to the starboard side.

She held back.

"What's the matter? How come you're shaking?"

She closed her eyes. "I'm just cold," she said. "Freezing. I was on deck in the rain while you were warm and dry in the engine room."

As they walked home, Robbie talked nonstop about the barges and the pile of metal he'd seen and how, once he got his stitches out, he'd start collecting again. "I'm gonna keep helping with the war," he bragged.

"You already have," Pa told him. "You and your sister both." He pointed upriver toward the railroad bridge as a train whistled in the distance. "If we hadn't caught the barges . . ." His voice quit.

Charlotte turned toward him. "What, Pa, what if we hadn't?"

"River's up and running," he said, pointing. "At the speed they were traveling, those loads could have knocked out the bridge. You know how important bridges are, especially that railroad bridge."

Charlotte looked where Pa pointed. As she stared,

a train rounded into sight. The last time she'd looked at that bridge there'd been a train on it too. Jim's train, full of soldiers and sailors.

＆

Sunday Night, May 17, 1942

Dear Jim,

I haven't written for a while. First, nothing much was going on. Then we got real busy and it was hard to find time. Now I'd better write. So much has happened, if I don't write soon, I'll forget parts.

This all started about three weeks ago. The President got on the radio and talked about the home front and everybody pitching in to help win the war. Even us kids. Well, you'll be proud to know I figured out a way—we started a scrap metal drive at school. It was going swell, too.

Then, guess what? Some low-down sneak stole all the metal. We have lots of suspects and we're watching them close. We'll have to work fast, for school will be out soon. Next letter I hope to tell you the wicked thief is in jail.

I think Ma was about ready to throw ME in jail last Thursday. Robbie's been helping us look for junk, and he's good at it. This will be no surprise to you since he's raided your room for marbles and stuff to use in his boats plenty of times.

Anyway, on Thursday we went to a dump at the end of Second Avenue. He and another kid found an old car door. We were all hauling it out of the dump, but we dropped it and Robbie sliced up his hand on some broken glass in the car window. He got five stitches and a tetanus shot. Ma says no more scrapping for us.

Now here's the biggest surprise of all. Remember how every spring a few barges pop loose at high water? It happened again today while Pa had Robbie and me helping on the Rose. Guess who lassoed not one but two coal barges? Give up? Me, that's who! Was I scared? You bet. Can you read my writing? I'm still shaking and it's been hours.

Pa was pretty tickled, and I guess it felt okay to help out. But don't worry. I'm not planning to join the Navy and come pester you on your ship. Robbie's the one who's planning to do that. And I'm not sure I want to join up for factory work either. A person gets real tired and dirty. Did Ma write and tell you? She's working at the mill. So you see, we're all helping out, one way or another.

Take care of yourself, Jim, and come home as quick as you can. We love you. We miss you.

Your sister,
Charlotte

Charlotte stretched her fingers. It felt good to write to Jim, even if her hands got tired. Red marks from that rope still crisscrossed the palms of her hands. And she hadn't lied to Jim—it was nearly midnight and her insides still felt wobbly.

Jim might not even think it was worth writing about. He probably did worse things, harder and scarier things, every single day in the Navy. Rough water on the Mon, how did that compare to an ocean?

Charlotte closed her eyes and tried to imagine what kind of ship Jim served on. She'd seen plenty of them on the newsreels at the movies—every time a new ship was finished, some movie star in an evening gown broke a bottle over the bow. Just a few miles down the Ohio River, in Ambridge, they were building battleships. Maybe using some of Ma's steel plate. The Navy had even taken over some fancy ocean liners to use for troop ships. Imagine if Jim got to work on one of those. They were so huge, a person wouldn't even feel like she was on the ocean. Wouldn't have to look at the water.

Charlotte felt a shameful heat rush into her cheeks. Here she was sitting at home, safe, and not able to sleep because she was scared of the river. Somewhere, in a huge ocean, her brother braved storms and enemy planes, rough water and torpedoes. Why was she such a coward?

She sighed and looked back over the letter she'd written, checking it. She'd been careful. She hadn't put in anything the censors might snip out, like their town, or the name of the mill, or what Ma was working on. No defense secrets at all.

Then she frowned. She herself had been a censor. She'd left out something important. It wasn't something they would cut out of her letter with their tiny, sharp scissors. But it wasn't a thing Charlotte could admit, even to her brother. Yes, what she'd written was true. She missed him and wanted him to come home safe. But her reasons—they weren't all so good. She scratched a few words on the back of an old arithmetic paper.

Come home, Jim. We miss you. I miss you. I want you back here where you belong so Ma gets that gray look out of her eyes and remembers how to smile again. I miss the old Ma. And it sure would make Pa happy to have you working on the Rose like you used to. And then I wouldn't have to.

Charlotte blinked back tears. How could a person say such a selfish thing? Or even think it? She balled up the paper and threw it into the trash.

CHAPTER 8

DOWN BY THE TRACKS

The next morning, Charlotte had to take Robbie to get his stitches out before school. She had a late-note for Robbie's teacher and one for Mrs. Alexander too. It must have been a morning for notes, for when she reached into her desk for her history book, she found a folded scrap of paper with her name written in careful letters. She opened it quickly.

Meet me at recess! The mystery is solved! Sophie.

Was that possible? Had something happened this morning while she was getting Robbie to the doctor? Charlotte glanced at Betsy and motioned toward Sophie's desk. Betsy shrugged, then turned back to her book.

The morning seemed to go on forever. Finally lunchtime arrived, and after lunch, recess. In the school yard, Charlotte spotted Sophie partly hidden in the shadows of the building, talking to her older sister.

Sophie looked like she was asking for something.

Her sister Helen was shaking her head. Sophie turned and pointed toward Charlotte and Betsy. Helen kept on shaking her head. Finally Sophie snatched something from Helen's pocket and hurried over to where the girls stood.

She pulled on Charlotte's arm. "Come on. Over there in the corner. Where nobody will see." She held something in her hand.

"What is it, Sophie?"

"Charlotte?" Mrs. Alexander's voice came up behind her.

Sophie spun around and quickly stuck her hand into her jacket pocket.

"Charlotte, dear, I came over to ask about your brother's injury, but I seem to have interrupted something. Sophie, what's that in your pocket?"

"Nothing."

Mrs. Alexander held out her hand. "Sophie Jaworski . . ."

Sophie reached into her pocket and pulled out two small squares of stiff paper. She gave them to the teacher, then looked down at her shoes.

"Why . . . whatever is going on? The three of you, follow me."

Next thing Charlotte knew, the girls were upstairs sitting on stools in Mr. Costa's science room. He and Mrs. Alexander were shaking their heads. What had Sophie gotten them into?

"Charlotte Campbell, what's going on?"

"I don't know, ma'am. You got there just when I did."

Her voice quavered. Charlotte wasn't a tattletale, but even if she were, this time she had no idea what Sophie was up to.

"Betsy?"

"Me neither. I don't know what Sophie had."

"What she had is quite clear," Mrs. Alexander said. "Mr. Costa's draft card. And a club membership card. How and why is not clear. Sophie Jaworski, did you take these?"

Sophie shook her head slowly. "No, ma'am. I didn't take anything."

Mr. Costa frowned at them. "Jaworski. You have a sister? Helen? In the eighth grade?"

Sophie nodded, looking more miserable every second.

"Shall we get Helen, or do you want to tell us what happened?" Mrs. Alexander's eyes had turned so dark they looked black.

"I think I know what's going on," the science teacher said. He sighed, then sat behind his desk. "Midmorning sometime, I discovered my wallet lying on the floor next to the windows. I checked it and no money was missing, so I thought I'd somehow dropped it. I hadn't dropped it, though, had I, Sophie?"

She didn't speak, just shook her head and looked sick.

"I don't understand," Mrs. Alexander said.

By now, Charlotte was beginning to. Apparently, so was Mr. Costa. "Your sister and her friends," he began. "They've had their suspicions, haven't they?" He turned to

Mrs. Alexander. "Ever since the metal was taken, the eighth grade has been buzzing like a hive of yellowjackets. Evidently, I'm one of their suspects."

"But why?" Mrs. Alexander looked shocked. "Sophie . . ."

"That—that draft card," Sophie stammered. "Helen says if you have one, it means you're supposed to be in the Army. And you're not. That other card, it says 'Sons of Italy.' Helen says it means you're on the wrong side in the war. With that Mussolini . . ."

Mr. Costa turned toward Sophie, and Charlotte could see how young he was. "Oh, Sophie. I'd hoped I wouldn't have to go into all this. But clearly, there's been some confusion. A draft card simply means a man has registered for the draft. It doesn't mean he can join up."

Mrs. Alexander shot such a ferocious glare at Sophie, it made Charlotte feel the tiniest bit sorry for the girl.

Mr. Costa took a tired breath and went on. "I tried to enlist, you see. I argued and argued with Mr. Butler down at the draft board, but it didn't do any good. They classified me 4-F—unfit for combat." He pointed to a spot on the card. "I had rheumatic fever as a child. It damaged my heart." He put the draft card in his pocket.

"As you now may understand, I can't serve in the Army, much as I'd like to. I'm not a coward or a slacker, just not strong enough. I hope my draft status is clear now, although it would have been much easier just to ask me, wouldn't it?" He lifted the other card and looked at it before he put it in his pocket. "The Sons of Italy is a lodge, sort of like the Elks or the Moose lodges. I joined because my father asked me to. Not because of Mussolini."

"What should we do next?" Mrs. Alexander asked.

"These girls aren't to blame," he said in a quiet voice. "I'll deal with the eighth graders."

Charlotte let out her breath as they walked down the hall. Poor Mr. Costa. He'd been innocent all along. "Sophie Jaworski, I'm never believing another thing you say. You got us into big trouble."

"We're not in trouble, not yet," Betsy said. Her blue eyes had dark circles underneath and she was frowning. "But we will be."

"Why? What's the matter?"

"This morning before school, while you were taking Robbie to the doctor . . ." Betsy hugged herself.

"What?"

"I'll tell you what," Sophie interrupted. "Zalenchak and Merkow came back to school today."

"And?" Charlotte really didn't want to know, but she had a feeling she couldn't escape this one.

"They've challenged Pete and his friends to a fight today, that's what," Betsy said. "Down by the tracks. After school."

Charlotte's stomach turned. A fight wouldn't solve anything. It would just make things worse. For a moment, Charlotte imagined she had some of Pa's heavy line in her

hands. Wished she could swing a rope around those mean
eighth graders and stop the fight.

But Zalenchak and Merkow weren't like barges. They
had minds of their own and they'd steer where they wanted.
She couldn't do anything to stop them.

ᝋ

There was an empty place, down near the river and
the railroad tracks, where the houses stopped and before
the factories started. Once a long row of houses had
stood there, with families and kids and dogs filling the
street with noise. But years back, one of the houses had
caught a spark from the mill and the whole row had
burned. Now, only crumbling stone foundations marked
where the houses had stood. Nobody wanted to rebuild
there, on the chance that another spark might find a roof.
So the street was clear for the whole length of a block,
and a person could see a fair distance in both directions.

When anybody said a fight *down by the tracks,* they
meant that spot. Charlotte knew about it; every kid in
school knew, even the little ones. But she hadn't ever gone
there and watched before. Sure, she'd walked by, but only
when it was empty, a weedy patch with old cracked cement,
tumbling-down stones, and a broken bottle or two.

She held tight to her schoolbooks and hurried along,
wishing she didn't have to go. She glanced sideways at

Betsy, whose face was pale and stiff-looking. "You sure you want to see this?"

"I don't want to. I have to. Pete's my cousin. He got into this trouble because of me. You don't have to come, Charlotte."

"Of course I do. If I hadn't gotten this dumb idea of collecting scrap, and if we hadn't been so darn good at it, nobody would have stolen anything. So it's my fault too."

"Charlotte—"

"It's true, Bets. People are all fighting and snooping and suspecting each other. I wish we'd never started the drive."

"Too late for that," Betsy said. "Come on. We can stand over there, near the alley. So we won't be in the middle of things."

Other kids were gathering in the alley, and some had climbed onto old foundation stones for a better view. At least half the school had shown up for the fight. A familiar shape brushed past. Charlotte reached out and grabbed Robbie. "What are you doing here, buster?"

"Watching."

"Nope. You get home."

"Will not."

"Come on, Robbie. You could get hurt."

"So could you."

"I don't think they'll punch any girls. But you—"

"They won't mess with little kids either. So, is it true? Is Betsy's cousin going to plaster them?"

Betsy nodded. "That's what Pete says. He's got five of his pals to back him up. Look." She pointed.

Pete Schmidt and five other seventh-grade boys marched down the street and across the tracks. From the other direction, Zalenchak and Merkow and their friends swaggered up.

Betsy grabbed Charlotte's arm. "It's really going to happen."

"There are so many people, I can't see from here." Robbie grumbled and tried to pull loose.

Charlotte held him tight by his belt. "You're sticking with us, buster. I got in enough trouble when you cut your hand. What do you think Ma would do to me if I let some kid crack you in the head? Now be quiet and stop squirming."

Near the tracks, the two lines of boys stepped closer to each other. The onlookers bunched together in tight little knots and stopped whispering. Pete's chin jutted out and his cheeks burned bright red.

Frankie Zalenchak had on the meanest scowl Charlotte had ever seen. And he was bigger than Pete. "Filthy Kraut! Nazi scum!" Frankie yelled.

Pete stepped closer. "Dirty stinking Hunky," he shouted. "Go back to Hungary or wherever you came from. You don't belong here."

"Who's gonna make me leave, huh?" Frankie stuck his chin out. "*You*, pip-squeak?"

Pete hauled back and socked Frankie in the stomach.

Frankie popped him one in the jaw.

After that, it was all grunts and punches and kicks. The other fellas made a circle around the fighters with their hands bunched into fists at their sides. How long until the whole lot of them started pounding on each other? A smell rose in the air, dust and sweat. Charlotte's stomach jumped around.

"Get him, Pete, get him," Robbie yelled.

Charlotte clapped her hand over his mouth. "You hush. You want them coming over here and smacking you?"

He shook his head and she let go, putting her arm around Betsy's waist. She could feel her friend shaking. Or maybe Charlotte was the one shaking.

A car engine sounded from the avenue. One of the boys in the circle turned, then shouted, "Hey, Frankie Z. Hold up, Frank, somebody's coming."

Boys from the circle stepped in and pulled Pete and Frankie apart. But they didn't seem to be looking at the dirty faces and bloody noses. They all turned and stared toward the avenue. Even Frankie and Pete. It was so quiet you could hear the spin of tires on pavement.

Charlotte turned, and what she saw made her breath catch. The brown car from the government. The car every family dreaded.

Frozen in place like the rest, she could only watch and mumble prayers. "Please, please, not my house. Don't stop at my house. Please."

The brown car crossed the tracks and turned onto Talbott Avenue. She hugged Betsy tighter and felt Robbie pull close on her other side.

"No. No. No," she whispered.

One of the boys in the circle crossed himself.

"Keep going. Keep going."

The only thing that moved was the brown car. It rolled slowly down Talbott Avenue, stopping at the cross streets and then starting up again.

Charlotte could tell when the car had passed a boy's street, when his shoulders let down and he could breathe again. But *she* couldn't. Not yet.

"Jim?" Robbie whispered.

"Hush. Don't say it. Don't say anything." She gripped his arm.

She stared down the avenue, and at last the brown car passed by her house and Betsy's and turned up a side street. It parked there, still in sight.

She felt her breath come out, and she drew in fresh, sweet air. She stretched her shoulders, but still she couldn't take her eyes off the street, off the man who was climbing out of the brown car. Now he was shutting the car door, and now, walking around the front and up the steps to the second house in from the corner.

"No! Not Tony. Oh, Ma . . ."

A cry rose from the knot of boys, and they separated. One kid stood alone for a moment rubbing his eyes. Then he dug his heels into the pavement and ran down the avenue, pumping his arms and legs so hard Charlotte could feel sweat rise on her own body.

Every kid watched him run, sorry as could be, except for that one part, the selfish part that was saying thank you. *Thank you for not letting it stop in front of my house.*

Slowly, one at a time, the kids drifted down the avenue. Charlotte held tight to Betsy and Robbie as her feet began to move.

Nobody said anything. Nobody had to. Everybody knew that by tomorrow, Frankie Zalenchak's ma would have a gold star hanging in her front window instead of a blue one.

CHAPTER 9
A ROCKY COVE

When they reached home, Robbie ran for the third floor. Charlotte went to her room and sat on the bed, trying to make her legs stop trembling. She searched among her schoolbooks and papers for her history book, then flipped through until she found her list of suspects. As she read the names, all she could feel was shame. Who was she to accuse these people of stealing?

And what a list she'd made — Paul Rossi, who had brothers fighting; Mr. Costa, who wanted to enlist and couldn't; the school janitor, who'd only been nice to everybody for his whole life; some poor little kid in Robbie's class with a busted lunch pail. And there at the bottom, Zalenchak and Merkow. Seeing Frankie Zalenchak's name on her list was the worst. She tore up the paper and flushed the little pieces down the toilet.

She gathered her books and wandered downstairs to

the kitchen, wishing hard that today of all days Ma could be home. But she wasn't. She'd made a noodle casserole for supper, and Charlotte was supposed to put it in to heat. She did that, then settled at the kitchen table to do her homework. But no matter how many times she stared at the fractions in her arithmetic book, all she could see was the brown car. All she could hear was Frankie Zalenchak's voice crying out, "No! Not Tony."

She stood and paced around the house, then stopped by the front window to touch the points of Jim's blue star. *Could have been me,* she thought. *Could have been Robbie and me, or Betsy or anybody. We've all got brothers.*

Ma had heard about Frankie's brother at the mill. When she walked in the door, grimy as she was, she grabbed onto Charlotte and hugged her so hard it hurt. "You heard?"

Charlotte nodded. "We saw the brown car come. I was afraid—"

"Oh, honey, this is so hard." Ma buried her face in Charlotte's hair.

"I hate it, Ma. I want it all to just go away. I want to close my eyes, and when I open them again, it will all be over—the war and the fighting and the ships going down and that brown car . . ."

"I know, honey, I know. We all want that. But . . ."

They stood holding on to each other for a long time, then Ma seemed to straighten herself. "I'm going to take my bath. Will you set the table? Your pa should be home soon."

Pa came home wearing a stern face, but carrying two bundles. He set one at Robbie's place and one at Charlotte's. "I bought these this morning to celebrate my brave crew of yesterday," he began. "Maybe after supper . . ."

When they sat to eat, nobody seemed very hungry. Robbie's eyes were puffy and red, and so were Ma's. Charlotte couldn't tell if she'd scorched the casserole or if the odd taste in her mouth came from seeing the brown car. Somehow they managed to eat part of the meal, and after a while, they began to talk, about ordinary things.

"I've got a long haul coming," Pa said. "One of the big tugs is down for repair, and they need me to tow coal in from a mine down in Fayette County. I'll be gone most of the week. Will you be all right?"

Ma shook her head. "Seems like everything goes wrong at once. Somebody's sick at the mill and they asked me to cover the swing shift for the rest of the week. Charlotte, can you manage here alone from four until midnight? I could get somebody to stay, but . . ."

"She won't be alone," Robbie said. "I'll be here too. We aren't babies."

"We'll be fine, Ma," Charlotte said. "Betsy's right next door. Her ma will help if we need anything."

Ma patted Charlotte's hand. "Thanks, honey. In spite of everything, we do have to keep going."

Then Pa pointed to the packages. "I know this is a bad night. With a war on, we'll have some bad nights, no hiding from that. We've all got to hang on to each other to make it through the rough spots. But yesterday was a good day. I was very proud of both of you. So today I stopped by the store and . . . well, open them up."

Robbie smiled a little as he lifted the box lid. He held up a white shirt with a square collar and a tie in the front. A boy-size Navy shirt. "Neat, Pa. It's like Jim's. Can I put it on right now?"

"Let Charlotte open hers first," Ma said.

Charlotte slipped her box open. Inside, she saw tan cloth—a jacket with wide lapels and buttons. Underneath, she found a matching skirt. "Oh, Pa. It's a WAC suit? Really?" It was like a woman's Army uniform, but in her size. The Cussick twins had worn suits just like this to school last week, and Sophie Jaworski had bragged that her ma was buying one too. Last week Charlotte would have loved the suit, loved the chance to wear it before Sophie got one. But now it just made the war seem closer.

"Thanks, Pa," she whispered. "It's really swell."

Pa nodded. "I'll understand if you want to wait a few days . . ."

After supper was finally over and the kitchen clean, Charlotte sat in her room to study for a history test. The WAC uniform hung on the doorknob, sturdy and serious. A knock came at the door.

"Charlie, can I come in? It's important."

"Sure, Robbie." She set her book aside.

He stepped into her room, wearing his sailor shirt. He'd tied a square knot in the front, but it was crooked.

"You want me to fix that?"

"I guess." He stood and fidgeted while she straightened the knot.

"There. You look like a real sailor," she said.

He frowned at her, then took a deep breath. "I didn't really come about shirts or knots, Charlie. We have to go get more scrap, right away. I got my stitches out now."

"Ma doesn't want us collecting scrap," Charlotte warned.

"Ma doesn't have to know. Come on, Charlie. It's important. If we keep on collecting metal, maybe they can make a ship or a plane with it. So we can beat the Japs and the Germans. So Jim doesn't . . . you know." He wouldn't look at her.

"The brown car?"

He nodded and sat next to her on the bed. He swung his legs. "We gotta do something, Charlie. We can't just sit around. If you won't help, I'll do it by myself."

"You'll do what by yourself?"

"Promise not to tell."

"I won't."

"Okay. You know that pile of metal we saw from the *Rose?* I want to get it and take it to school."

Charlotte's stomach tightened. "It was steep there. We'll never find that junk from the riverbank."

"So what? We'll find it from the water then. Unless

you're too scared. Unless you're such a chicken you'd rather sit home than help win this war."

Charlotte winced. Was she a chicken? She didn't like the river, that wasn't news. But she had helped Pa rope in those barges. So maybe she could at least try to find the metal. "How about looking from the bank first? After school tomorrow? We'll ask Betsy to come along."

"And your friend Paul. I like that guy," Robbie said. "He knows about stitches and shots. Besides, he carried me—imagine how much junk he can lift."

"I guess," Charlotte said. "With Ma working the swing shift and Pa on a long haul, we could spend a while there. But don't wear your new shirt unless you want Ma to figure out what we're up to."

Robbie saluted. "Aye, aye. Top secret. No uniforms." He raced from her room and she heard his footsteps thumping up to the third floor.

As she stood to close her door, she ran her hand along the shoulder of the WAC uniform. In her mind, she heard again the voice of the President, calling for sacrifice on the home front.

"It is for them. It is for us. It is for victory."

But how much will victory cost, she wondered. How many more brown cars?

❧

"We can't go down there. It's too steep," Charlotte said
the next day after school. They'd trudged along the railroad tracks into North Braddock—upriver, past the mill,
past the railroad bridge. Here the banks narrowed, with
weeds and small trees clinging to the slope, a tumble of
pale spring greens and golds. Instead of flats with houses,
massive piles of limestone boulders guarded the water's
edge. On the other side, a rocky hill seemed to climb
straight out of the muddy Mon. She peered down through
overgrown bushes toward the river, holding tight to a
small tree so she wouldn't slip.

"But, Charlie, there's so much good stuff down there.
And it's ours, if we just climb down and—"

"And what, buster? Get your other hand torn up?
What do you want, a matched set? We aren't going down."

Betsy gave Charlotte a hand and pulled her up higher
where the bank flattened out. "Can't we do anything? There
is a lot of metal down there. You can see it shine in the sun."

Robbie grinned at Betsy, like she'd taken his side.
"Yeah, Charlie. Can't we? Not everybody is a scaredy-cat.
How about it, Paul?"

Paul Rossi had been standing to the side, studying
the rocky wall that dropped down toward the river. He
looked up when Robbie mentioned his name. "Your sister's right. We can't climb down this, and even if we could,
we'd never be able to carry the stuff out. It's too steep."

"So it's a dead end?" Charlotte sighed. Partly she was

relieved, but there *was* a lot of scrap down there, metal
for bombs or bullets.

Paul shook his head. "I didn't say it was a dead end.
I just said we couldn't climb down. No reason we can't get
in there with a boat."

"If we had a boat," Betsy said. "Charlotte's father has
a tug, but he's away all week."

"We don't need a tug," Paul said. "I got a rowboat at
home. Belongs to my brothers, but they'd let me use it.
Especially for this."

"But—" Charlotte began.

"Great! I knew we could do it!" Robbie shouted. "Let's
go right now."

"Wait a minute," Charlotte said.

"Come on. Nobody's home. We won't get in trouble.
I'm going with Paul, even if you aren't. So there."

"I can't go," Betsy said. "I promised my mother I'd get
home in time to help with supper. I've got to hurry now
or she'll holler."

"Fine," Robbie snapped. "You dumb girls just go home
then. Me and Paul can—"

"Watch it, Robbie," Paul said. "Betsy can't help it if her
ma's expecting her home." He looked at Charlotte, and
she saw a challenge in his eyes.

"I'll come," she said.

After Betsy left for home, Charlotte and Robbie followed Paul to his house. From a shed back in the alley, he hauled out a rowboat on a small wheeled trailer. Then he tossed in a pair of fishing poles.

"We're not going fishing," Robbie said. "How come you're taking poles?"

Charlotte wondered the same thing, but she was glad Robbie'd been the one to ask.

"Never hurts to have fishing stuff along," Paul said. He tugged on the trailer and pulled the boat toward the water. "Gives us a good excuse to be on the river. Before they went off to the war, my brothers used to row up and down near the banks and watch for girls. But they kept their fishing gear out so nobody would know what they were up to."

"Girls? That's dumb," Robbie said. "I'd rather catch fish. Even catfish are better than girls."

Charlotte grinned. She pushed the rowboat from behind as they neared the tracks. The sun behind her sat low in the sky. The Rankin Bridge cast long, rippling shadows on the water, but it was still light enough that she could see to ease the rowboat into the river without slipping.

Paul held a rope by the bow. "Go ahead, climb in. I'll steady the boat."

"Where are the life jackets?" Charlotte asked.

"Life jackets? To go rowing on the Monongahela? We'll stay close to the banks, I promise. Come on."

Charlotte climbed in and the little boat rocked from
side to side. When Robbie stepped in, she leaned hard to
balance his weight. Little boats were so tippy. Compared
to this tub, the *Rose* was an ocean liner.

Paul stepped aboard smoothly and took up the oars.
He rowed close to shore as he'd promised, and soon they
were making good time against the current. "Get out your
fishing poles," he said. "And try to look like you know
what you're doing."

A large working boat passed them in the middle of the
channel, sending out a hefty wake. The rowboat rocked
and Charlotte's stomach rocked right along with it. She
dropped a line in the water. She knew how to fish, but she
was used to a bigger boat.

As they headed upriver, the sun sank lower, turning
the sky and the water around them pale pink. Paul pulled
closer to the shoreline, into a small cove. "About here,
don't you think?"

Robbie shifted so he could see the bank, and then
leaned out, nearly sending Charlotte overboard. "Yeah.
I see the stuff. There's a whole pile there. Boy oh boy!
I'm gonna—"

"You're gonna sit tight, buster," Charlotte growled.
"Otherwise you'll get us all wet. Wait till Paul pulls the
boat in before you start jumping around."

Paul shoved on the oars and the boat scraped along
the river bottom. Robbie hopped out with a splash and

yanked on the rope, pulling the nose of the boat onto shore. Charlotte climbed out carefully, glad for solid ground underfoot. When Paul climbed out, he beached the boat and looped the rope around a low-hanging tree.

Robbie ran ahead toward the stash of metal. "Oh, wow! Look at this. So much stuff!"

By the time Charlotte caught up to him, he was climbing over the junk. "Watch out," she ordered. "If you're not careful, you'll get cut again or twist an ankle, and it's a lot harder to get to the doctor's office from here."

"But, Charlie—"

"Listen to your sister," Paul said. "You don't want another shot, do you?"

"No, but look. Right up here. I collected this baby buggy once before. Look, Charlie, it's the exact same one."

"Come on, Robbie. You're nuts."

"It *is* the same. Look." He yanked hard and some of the metal came loose from the pile.

"What's he talking about, Charlotte?" Paul asked.

"We cleaned out an old lady's backyard and cellar for the scrap drive. He thinks he recognizes junk from her place."

"Is it possible? If it's the same baby buggy . . . that means . . ."

Charlotte's breath caught. "It means we've found the thief's hiding place," she whispered. "That's halfway to catching him. Let me see that buggy, Robbie."

She climbed up to where she could reach the old buggy. With Robbie and Charlotte each holding up one end, they picked their way down the pile of junk and set the frame on flat, damp ground.

"Look, it's gray cloth, just like the one we found in Mrs. Dubner's cellar." Robbie shoved the frame. Like before, three wheels worked, but one stuck. The left rear one.

"Is it the same?" Paul asked.

"You bet," Robbie said.

"Charlotte?"

"I . . . I think so. The color matches, and the stuck wheel. The one we found had a rough, rusty place under the handle, on the right side."

Paul studied the handle. "Right here? Like this?"

Charlotte ran her fingers along the bar. On the right side something snagged her fingertips. She looked underneath and found a circular patch of rust. "We found it, then. The thief's hiding place."

"What should we do next, Charlotte? What do you think?" Paul had a serious look on his face.

She scanned the bank on both sides of the junk pile. Then she rubbed her arms to chase away a sudden chill. "I think we should get out of here. Right away, before he comes back."

CHAPTER 10
NIGHT FISHING

I say we go back after supper tonight and watch for the thief," Paul began. "We know to be careful now. With three of us, we'll be all right." He'd beached his rowboat near his house and was tipping it on one side to dump out any water.

"I don't know," Charlotte said. "What if there are three of *them*? Or five? There's so much metal there, you'd need an army to carry it all."

"You're just being chicken again," Robbie said. "If Jim were home, he'd come."

"Make sense, Robbie. If Jim were home, there wouldn't be a war on and we wouldn't be collecting all this junk in the first place." She sighed.

"What do *you* think we should do, Charlotte?" Paul asked.

"How about telling the police? Wouldn't they be better at catching the thief? We could tell them where to look."

"Yeah," Robbie said. "They could set up a trap, like in the movies."

Paul shook his head. "Do you think they'd bother with a pile of junk? They don't have enough men for their regular work these days. They'd call this kid stuff. They'd laugh."

"Maybe." Charlotte frowned. If Paul was right, then the three of them had to catch the thief. Or thieves. "Okay, *if* we go back and keep watch, I'd like to figure things out better first. So we know what we're looking for."

Robbie rolled his eyes at her. "Come on, Charlie, we're looking for a thief. You know that."

"Okay, Mr. Smarty-Pants." Charlotte shook her head. "What I'd like to know is *why* the thief took the stuff. And how he knew about it in the first place. That might tell us what kind of thief we're trying to catch. If it's some robber gang with knives or guns, I'm not going near the place."

"But, Charlie—"

Paul tipped his head to one side. "Your sister's right," he said. "If we think things through, try to put ourselves in the criminal's mind . . ."

A shiver went up Charlotte's back. She couldn't help remembering all those newspaper articles Paul brought to school. "You can think like a criminal if you want, but I'm not going to."

"I bet you already have, without knowing it," he said. "Good cops do it all the time. I know, 'cause I'm going to be a cop one of these days."

"Really? Is that why you're always collecting crime stories?" Charlotte began.

Paul shook his head at her. "That's my business. Right now, we've got a thief to catch. I bet you've already figured out how he knew about the metal. Haven't you?"

Charlotte looked at him, puzzled.

"It just makes sense that he's connected to the school," Paul said. "He must go there, or work there, or something. He knows about the metal because he's there. And if he's not a stranger, nobody gets suspicious."

Charlotte thought about Paul's words. She *had* known that, maybe not in words, but inside. Most of the people on her old suspects list were connected to the school. A shadow flitted across her mind. Mr. Willis. No, absolutely not. She wouldn't think that about a nice old man who was kind to everybody. "Okay, but why? Why take all that junk?"

"He's mean, that's why," Robbie said. He picked up a stick and smacked it against the rowboat. "I want to catch him and pop him one, right in the kisser."

"I don't think that's the reason," Paul said. "I've been trying to figure it out all along. There's only one reason a person would take the stuff. He's planning to sell it. He needs the money."

Charlotte shook her head. "Swell—that helps a lot. Who wouldn't like a pile of free money? Last time I looked, Braddock wasn't exactly swimming in millionaires."

Paul looked at her like she was Robbie's age. "There's a difference between wanting money and needing it. Sure, most people would like extra moolah. Who wouldn't like to find a ten-spot on the sidewalk?"

"Think of all the candy bars you could buy." Robbie patted his stomach and grinned.

"Shh. Go on, Paul."

"It's simple. With the war on, most people are working hard. Bringing in good money. So they're doing okay. If a family has boys in the service, they get an allotment every month too. My ma does."

"So?" Where was he going with all this?

"Taking that metal is like stealing from the war. A person would have to be pretty desperate. Flat-out broke, if you ask me."

Charlotte rubbed her forehead. "If you're right, that's all the more reason we should tell the police and stay away. If the thief's a desperate person—"

"Aaack!" Robbie grabbed his own neck with his hands and made nasty, choking sounds.

"Desperate poor, not desperate mean," Paul said. He scowled at Robbie. "There's a difference, believe me."

The way he said it gave Charlotte a creepy feeling, like Paul might know what it was like to be that poor. She needed to change the subject right away.

"I still don't want to sit there in a little rowboat and watch for the crook," she began. "But maybe I'd do it if there were some way to hide. If we could watch without being spotted . . ."

"We can do that," Robbie said. "Easy as pie. All we've got to do is row up there at night. Once it's dark, nobody will see us. Of course, we'll have to wear dark clothes and sneak around and not talk, but we can do that."

"Ridiculous," Charlotte began.

"Swell," Paul said at the same moment. "We'll take along the fishing gear, just in case."

Robbie grinned. Paul punched his shoulder. And Charlotte's stomach began to tie itself in knots.

On the river? In a rowboat? At night? She'd never survive it.

 ❧

The sky had turned a deep bluish gray by the time Charlotte and Robbie rejoined Paul beside the river. Full darkness would come in a half hour, and they'd need that time to get themselves into position.

Charlotte carried a bag of supplies—some cheese and crackers, a jar of water, a flashlight, a sweater. In the other hand she held Jim's baseball bat, and slung over her shoulder, a life jacket. "I can't believe I let you two talk me into this," she grumbled. She'd tried to get Betsy to come along, but with no success.

"Come on, Charlie, get in the boat," Robbie said.

"I can't wait to get started. It's a real spy mission."

"Real spies are quiet," Paul reminded him. "Get all your gabbing done before we reach that cove."

"Roger, capt'n."

Paul reached out and messed Robbie's hair, just like Jim always did. Charlotte had to bite down on her bottom lip to keep from crying. *Don't think of him now,* she scolded herself. But wait—Jim was the exact person she ought to think about. He was a sailor. He was good with boats. And he was brave. So maybe if she thought about him, some of his courage might rub off. And besides, this hunt for the thief, the scrap drive, all of it—if it wasn't for Jim, who was it for?

Paul settled into the rowboat and dipped his oars. Charlotte felt the current surge and push against them. It seemed stronger somehow than it had in the afternoon. Along the bank, trees and bushes became shadow creatures with long arms and sharp claws.

Robbie leaned forward in the boat and pointed upstream. "Look, Charlie, the sky. It's like the Fourth of July."

In the distance, she could see the mill chimneys—skinny, shadowy pipes that blasted the darkening sky with red and orange flame. On flat land beside the chimneys, slag heaps burned like yellow-gold mountains. As Charlotte stared, a huge ladle poured a stream of liquid fire from furnace to mold. Steel, running like water but so hot that just the fumes could scorch a person's lungs. Ma was in there, in that mill, working a crane near those furnaces. It was nearly as scary as being on the river.

"Shh. We're getting close. I'll row upstream a ways and let her drift back so we can watch the whole cove. But we'll stay away from the bank so if he comes, he won't see us."

"Right, Paul," Charlotte said. "And so we can escape if there are a bunch of them."

"Chicken," Robbie whispered.

"Shh."

That was the last talking anybody did. Paul had the boat pointed upstream, and every once in a while he'd row a few strokes beyond the bend in the river and then let the current carry them back.

Charlotte focused her eyes on the dark riverbank. When she'd looked at the mill chimneys, the flaming sky had taken away some of her night sight. So she kept her eyes down—down where she had to look at the black water rippling past, carrying them backward. The water reminded her of black velvet, except that velvet was soft and warm and comforting. The Mon was harsh and cold and threatening, even on a May night. A train whistle blew, and downstream a tug's whistle answered. She pulled her sweater from her bag and slipped it on.

As she was buttoning it, she heard a voice—no, two voices, raised in an argument. She reached out to touch Robbie's hand. In the dark, she could see his face nodding. He'd heard it too. She strained to listen. It sounded like a man and a child.

"I don't want to," the child said.

"What you want don't matter. You'll do as I say."

"But—"

"No buts," the man's voice said.

Charlotte fisted her hands and felt her fingernails bite into her palms. Were these their thieves? She ran a finger along the handle of Jim's baseball bat. Would she dare swing it?

"Please don't make me," the child's voice continued. Charlotte heard sniffs; the poor kid was crying. And then a slap and the rough sound of a person hauling somebody where he didn't want to go.

She turned and caught Paul's eye. He shook his head. He was staring at the riverbank just like she'd been. Neither of them had seen a thing.

The boat rocked slightly, and Charlotte felt Robbie creep back from the bow to sit close beside her. Noiselessly, she slid over to make room. Little brother or not, he was a comfort. His hand reached out for hers, and it was cold and shaking. Were those voices coming toward them?

Except for the regular lapping of the river against the rowboat, she hadn't heard any water sounds. So if the crooks were coming, it had to be by land. But even as Paul drew the boat closer to shore, nothing moved, nothing showed in the bend of the river but the shine of water, the bare branches of trees, and the misshapen shadows that outlined the scrap pile.

Minutes went by—fifteen, maybe twenty—and still nothing happened. Paul kept rowing upstream to keep the cove in view, but except for that, nothing moved.

Then a splash. And another, coming toward them from the middle of the river. Whatever it was, it sounded big. Charlotte grabbed her flashlight in one hand, the bat in the other. She waited, counting her breaths. The splashing got closer.

From behind, Paul nudged her. She shoved the flashlight into Robbie's hands and gripped the bat with both of hers. She elbowed Robbie's side and he switched on the light, pointing it toward the sounds.

"Oh, geez. A dumb mutt." Paul's voice came out shaky.

Charlotte released the bat and stared where the light pointed. A shaggy, good-sized dog was swimming across the water toward them. He looked almost like he was trying to wag his tail.

"If we don't watch out, that dog will try to climb in this rowboat and dump us all out," she said. "Let's go home. I've had enough excitement for one night."

Robbie's voice chimed in, "Me too. I'm kinda cold."

Then she heard herself saying, "Well, smarten up, buster. Tomorrow night wear a sweater."

Had she really done that? Had she somehow agreed to come out here again? She looked out on the river and shivered. Where had those voices come from?

Chapter 11
Voices in the Fog

The next morning, Charlotte awoke to a gray and rainy sky. Thank heavens, they wouldn't have to go out on the river today. Only a crazy person would do that. As she dressed for school, she peered out the window. A steady rain, the kind that could go on all day. *Good for the garden,* she thought. *And good for me.*

She needed a gentle day and evening. After last night's hours on the river, she'd stayed awake a long time, afraid to let herself drift off to sleep. And when she finally did sleep, the dream came again—Jim and the water and the ship, but this time with ghostly voices floating in the mist.

It took the whole walk to school to fill Betsy in on the night's adventures. At school, the rain clouds had cast shadows on everyone. Nobody could remember how to smile. Of course, it didn't help that Frankie Zalenchak came back to school after his brother's funeral. Everywhere

Frankie walked, silence followed. Even when he wasn't nearby, Charlotte didn't dare laugh, because what if he happened to turn the corner and she was laughing? If you had a dead brother, could you ever stand the sound of kids laughing?

By lunchtime, Charlotte felt as stretched and thin as a rubber band on a package. If anybody did or said one more bad thing . . .

"Hey, Charlotte, guess what?" Sophie Jaworski stood with her arms folded across her chest and grinned.

Charlotte had the feeling Sophie might just say that one bad thing. "Not right now, Sophie. I've got to go check with Betsy about something."

"I'll come too," Sophie offered. "That way I can tell you both at the same time." She tagged along like a stray puppy, reminding Charlotte of the dog they'd seen in the river. She shivered at the thought.

When they reached Betsy, Sophie began to talk right away. "We know who the thief is," she began.

"Oh, come on." Charlotte snapped her mouth shut before she said any more, but inside, questions pushed so hard she had to clench her jaw to keep from spitting them out. *What do you know, and how? Did you find the thief's hiding place? No. Did you lurk in the shadows in a puny little rowboat to watch for him? No. Can you do anything at all, besides flap your tongue?*

"Who is it?" Betsy asked.

"Wagon Willie. We know for sure."

Charlotte felt her lungs swell. She took in a huge breath, then another. Her cheeks burned and she made her hands into fists. "That's the dumbest thing I've ever heard, Sophie Jaworski. Take it back."

"I will not. It's true."

"How do you know?"

"He's got keys to the school. By the second time the thief came, there was a lock on the cellar door, remember? So the room was locked up tight. But the thief didn't break the lock to get in. Which means he must have had keys. Wagon Willie has keys. So he's got to be the thief."

"I don't know, Sophie," Betsy began. "Mr. Willis doesn't seem like a bad man."

"Betsy, you should be glad it's him. That way, kids will stop blaming you. You should help prove he did it, don't you see?"

"No." The word came out so hard it nearly burned Charlotte's tongue. "What if somebody else has keys? What if somebody swiped his keys? What if he forgot to lock up that night? What if he put the lock in wrong and it didn't work? What if—"

"Why do you care, Charlotte?" Sophie interrupted. "He's just a crazy old man. My sister says they shouldn't let people like that work in schools. He could scare kids."

"Your sister also said Mr. Costa was an Italian spy," Charlotte said. "When it comes to meanness, your sister's a hundred times more scary than Mr. Willis. And so are you." She grabbed Betsy's arm and marched away from Sophie, who for once had nothing more to say.

They held recess in the gym because of the rain. Charlotte grabbed a jump rope and spun it, jumping as fast as she could. She didn't even count the jumps, her mind was so stirred up. Rumors, suspicion, finger-pointing— it was rotten to think about poor Mr. Willis like that. It made Charlotte furious.

But by the end of recess, his name was a hum, spreading around the room under the sound of jumps and bounces and yells.

Charlotte wanted to stick her fingers in her ears. "What are we going to do, Betsy? Poor Mr. Willis."

"Are you sure he didn't do it?" Betsy replied. "I mean, he could have taken the scrap upriver as easy as anybody else, couldn't he?"

"Not you too!" Charlotte turned away and bumped into Paul Rossi, who was charging toward her with a frown on his face.

"You hear what they're saying? About Wagon Willie?"

"Yeah." Charlotte nodded.

"So what are we going to do about it, Charlotte? Unless you think, like the rest of these bozos, that Mr. Willis has a criminal mind just because he can't talk real smooth."

"I don't think that! But what can we do?"

"Catch the real thief."

Charlotte shook her head. "You don't mean . . . Not tonight . . . Not in the rain . . ."

"Why not? It's a perfect night for a thief. He can come and haul his loot away and nobody will see. Who else would be out?" He grinned at her.

Charlotte swallowed hard. She turned. "Betsy? Can you come?" Betsy understood how she felt about the river. With Betsy in the boat, she might make it through another night on the water. "Please."

"I'd help if I could, Charlotte. You know that. But my ma is so strict."

"But the rain . . ." Charlotte protested, turning back to Paul.

"Come on, Charlotte, your pa's a river man. You've got old oilskins around the house. If not, we've got extras from my brothers. Besides, it's May. A little spring rain never hurt anyone."

Right, Charlotte thought. Spring rain was soft and gentle. Spring rain fed the flowers. But it also fed creeks and rivers. It turned into river water and popped huge barges from their moorings and set them adrift.

"Decide, Charlotte. We have to catch the real thief, or Wagon Willie could be in a lot of trouble. He could lose his job. Unless that doesn't matter to you."

"Of course it matters, but—"

"Great," he said, smacking her shoulder. "Meet me by the boat then. Same time as last night."

"Come on, Charlie. Hurry up. It's getting dark." Robbie stood by the back door, wrapped in one of Pa's old jackets. He kicked at the bottom of the door.

Charlotte buttoned her sweater. "Don't hurry me, buster. I don't want to go at all, so don't push."

"Fine. Me and Paul will do better without you." He reached for the doorknob.

She knocked his hand away. "Let me finish getting dressed. Are you sure you're wrapped up enough?"

"Stop fussing, Charlie. You're worse than Ma."

"Yeah, and how am I supposed to explain to Ma if your clothes get soaked? Should I tell her you took a bath with your pants on?"

"We've been over this already. If anything gets wet, we hide it in Jim's closet. Come on. Paul will leave without us."

Charlotte tightened Jim's spare oilskin around herself. She checked her bag from the night before and picked up the baseball bat. "Okay. I'm ready."

What a lie that was. She'd take ten spelling tests, twenty arithmetic tests, if it meant she didn't have to go out on the water tonight with all that rain. But when she thought about poor Mr. Willis, what choice did she have? She'd spent the afternoon trying to think of a better way to catch the thief and she'd come up empty. Even if they showed the police the stash of metal, somebody could still say Mr. Willis had taken it and hidden it by the river.

She stood on the back porch and locked the door, wishing that somehow Betsy could sneak out and join them.

Robbie bounced down the steps. "Hurry up. I think tonight's the night. I got a feeling about it." He splashed through a puddle and onto the street.

She hurried to catch up. "So do I, buster. A bad feeling."

Her worry didn't lighten when they reached the river. Even in the near-darkness, she could see how angry and muddy it looked. When she stepped into the rowboat, the current rocked her. "Water's high, Paul."

"I know. We'll have to be extra careful. You too, Robbie."

"Aye, aye. Let's go get the crooks."

Paul rowed. The beat of rain on the water hid their slight splashes as the boat nosed into the river. When he pulled his oars out between strokes, the current shoved the boat backward. Staying even with the cove would be hard work tonight. Charlotte might have to take a turn at the oars.

She peered forward into the gloom. If she were rowing, she wouldn't have to look out at the water rushing past. She'd be working too hard to hear it slap against the sides of the boat. She closed her eyes. They hadn't reached the cove yet. She didn't have to look at all. But not seeing was worse, for she could imagine . . .

"Paul. When we get there tonight, could we tie up somewhere? I don't like the feel of the river."

"Maybe. But it would make a getaway harder. I'm not sure which is worse."

Charlotte sighed and huddled on the seat. Already rain was leaking in around her collar and at the tops of her boots. She hugged herself and tried not to shiver. "Maybe we should just wait till Pa comes home and haul the metal to the scrap yard on his tug. Forget about the thief."

"If we don't catch him before your pa comes home, maybe. But tonight we've got to keep watch for the thief. It's a perfect night."

"Perfectly awful," Charlotte grumbled.

"What if they have a motor?" Robbie asked. "We'll never catch them if they have a motor."

"With gas shortages? Not likely," Paul said.

"They could too have a motor," Robbie argued. "If they could steal our metal, they could steal somebody's gas. So there."

"Come on, buster. We've got to be quiet, remember?"

As they neared the small cove, the night grew darker, and fog began to drift along the river, mixing with the rain. Upstream somewhere a train whistle blew, long and loud and so lonesome Charlotte wanted to cry. "We should go home," she said softly. "It's nuts to be out here tonight."

"Shh," Paul warned. "Watch the bank now. I'm going in closer."

Closer meant shallower water. That made Charlotte feel a little better, but in a cove the currents sometimes acted funny. And with fog coming down, a boat could get lost just a few feet from shore.

"Do you see anything, Charlie?" Robbie whispered. "I don't."

"I can barely see the bank. Paul, we really should go home. We won't catch anybody if we can't see."

"I'll tie up then," he said. "We'll use our ears."

As he finished speaking, a low wail blasted the air around them. A tug in midriver. The sound came three times. Charlotte braced herself for the wake. It hit them broadside, knocking the rowboat sideways toward the bank and sloshing water in over their feet.

When the river calmed, Paul rowed toward an overhanging tree. "We'll tie up here. If we can't see the crook, he can't see us. So we'll be fine."

"I'm not sitting in this boat," Charlotte said. "I want solid ground under my feet."

"Come on, Charlie. Don't turn chicken again. The banks are all mud anyway."

"I'll find a rock to sit on." She climbed out, carrying the bat and her bag of supplies.

"Shh," Paul warned again. "Sounds can carry a long way on the water."

Like last night, Charlotte thought. Were that man and child going to come back? Were they mixed up in the stealing? She squinted, trying to spot a protected place to sit. There didn't seem to be any flat rocks nearby, but she found a beached log that was better than mud. She sat, wishing for a thick umbrella of pine branches overhead. But no big trees grew this close to the river, so the rain trickled down her neck.

Minutes crept by, then a half hour. Another train blew. The chuffing of wheels grew loud, then soft, finally disappearing into the fog. "How long?" she whispered. "It's really bad out here."

"Another hour?" Paul said.

"Half? Please?"

"Okay, half."

"Aw, Charlie—"

"Shh. I hear something," Paul whispered.

Charlotte held her breath. Footsteps? The splash of water against a boat? She listened hard over the river noise and the rain.

"It's too hard. I can't bear it, Johnny." A woman's voice.

"I know. I know. But I got no choice." A man.

Robbie slipped out of the boat and crawled next to her on the log. She threw her arm around him. These people didn't sound like thieves, but they sure sounded spooky. They had to be mighty desperate to be out on such a night. And where were they? On the river? On the bank? Charlotte listened for boat sounds but didn't hear any. Just sad voices.

"Do you have to? If you love me . . ."

"I have to. Because I love you. What kind of man would I be if I didn't?"

Charlotte pulled Robbie closer. She heard no more talking, but there was a sound, soft crying, like a kitten would make. They weren't supposed to be hearing this. Nobody was. It felt all wrong.

"Paul. I want to go home. Now." She opened her bag and pulled out the flashlight. Turning sideways to keep any stray light from reaching the river, she flicked on the flashlight, checked her watch quickly, then switched off the light. "We've been out here for more than an hour. The next dry night I'll come back, I promise."

"Shh." His warning came as a soft hiss, barely reaching her ears.

What had he heard or imagined this time? Charlotte held her breath and listened, so hard she could hear her own heart beating and Robbie's soft breathing next to her. Then she heard it too, upstream. The scrape of wood against rock. A splash and the gentle thwack of a rope being tossed to shore.

CHAPTER 12
AT WHISPER BEND

Charlotte froze. She felt Robbie's hand inch over onto her arm, and he dug his nails in, like a kitten will when it's scared. His fingers crept down until they reached her right hand. He tugged on the flashlight she still held. His motion thawed her muscles.

She passed him the flashlight with her right thumb covering the switch, protecting it. With her left palm she covered the end with the lightbulb, then shook her head as if to say, *Don't turn it on yet.* She prayed he understood.

He nodded and she released it into his hands. Bending slowly, she reached for the baseball bat and wrapped both her hands around it.

Upstream, a thump and footsteps.

She peered into the darkness, trying to see Paul's face, but he was too far away, a pale blur in the rainy night.

The footsteps came closer. Was it just one person?

Robbie poked her side with his elbow.

She shook her head. Not yet, not until the thief was close enough to catch. She lifted the bat from the ground and set it on her right shoulder. She glanced toward Paul again and saw motion. She wasn't sure what he was up to.

A twig snapped, so close she could almost feel the bark splinter. She tightened her grip on the bat and prepared to stand. She nudged Robbie.

He flicked on the light.

"Stop right there!" she shouted.

Paul leapt from the rowboat with an oar, ready to swing it.

The light wobbled, then Robbie caught a face in its beam. A boy, or a young man. Dark clothes. A cap. His mouth open, his eyes wide. Then a deep voice. "Oh, geez. No!"

"Don't you move," Robbie warned.

Paul slipped behind the guy. "Not unless you want a taste of this," he shouted, slapping his oar against the water.

Charlotte stood and stepped closer. He was a boy, but older. Jim's age maybe, his size. She could see shadows of a beard on his jaw. Dark hair and dark eyes.

"Joey? Joey, what's happening?" A voice from upstream, from the darkness. A kid's voice.

"Hush. Stay in the boat." He turned to Charlotte and let out a sigh. "It's me you want, not them. They did-n't do anything."

"Did you steal our metal?" Robbie demanded.

"Joey, I'm coming to help," the kid called again.

"No! Stay back!"

Noises from upstream, splashes and voices. Then running feet. Two kids burst from the bushes and grabbed Paul's legs from behind.

The thief turned and tugged on them, freeing Paul. "I said not to," he began.

Robbie shined his flashlight on the kids. "I told you, Charlie. I told you it was Tommy Stankowski."

The boy in the light blinked, scowled, and stuck out his jaw. The other kid, a little girl, started to cry.

"Give me that light," Charlotte said. She set down her bat in Paul's boat and took the flashlight from Robbie. She fumbled, then flicked off the switch. "What do we do now?" she asked Paul.

"Take them to the cops," Robbie said.

"Please. I can explain. Just hear me out," the guy said. He threw an arm around each of the kids.

Paul stepped closer and Charlotte watched him study the three thieves. "I think we should hear what he has to say. We can always take him to the cops after. Go on."

"It could take a while," Joey said. "But the little fella is right. I'm Joseph Stankowski. This here's my brother Tommy and my sister Tessa. They didn't do none of this." He pointed to the metal.

"But, Charlie—" Robbie began.

A voice from the bank cut him off. "N-nobody move!"

A powerful glare hit Charlotte in the eyes, blinding her. She raised her hand as a shield. "Who is it?" Was there another thief?

Nobody moved. Charlotte heard scrambling sounds, branches breaking, boots hitting rocks with loud thuds. And then she found herself looking right into a familiar face. "Mr. Willis? What are you doing here?"

"M-m-missy. Shame." He shook his head at her, angry.

She touched her chest. "Me? You think I'm the thief? Not me. We found the metal. We've been watching for two nights from the river."

He nodded, as though maybe he believed her.

"How about you, Mr. Willis?" Paul asked. "How come you're here?"

"G-garden," the man said.

"Garden? You can't grow nothing on the riverbank," Robbie said. "It's all muck."

Mr. Willis shook his head. "G-garden," he repeated.

Charlotte frowned, trying to understand. "Were you *guarding*? Keeping watch on the metal? Did you see it and decide to wait for the thief too? That's what we were doing."

Mr. Willis nodded. "Guarding. W-waiting for the thief. Th-three nights."

"Well, you caught me," Joseph Stankowski said.

His voice sounded so tired, so sad, it made Charlotte want to cry. What was it Paul had said a while back? That their thief was desperate. And not *mean* desperate, but poor. Flat-out broke.

Charlotte's cheeks were wet, even if she hadn't let go and cried. They were still standing out in the rain, and she was shivering. "Come on. Let's go to our house. We'll untangle this mess where it's dry."

Robbie stood with his feet planted. He crossed his arms and glared. "I don't want them coming to our house."

"Hush, Robbie," Charlotte said. She gathered her belongings and stepped closer to the rowboat. "We don't know the whole story yet."

"We know they took the metal. That means they're crooks. We don't need crooks at our house."

"Robert Michael Campbell, you hush. You're talking about a little girl. A boy you go to school with—" Charlotte's words got stuck in her throat. She saw Paul Rossi staring at her through the rain and she knew she had to say more.

She lifted her head and met Paul's eyes. "I . . . I did that too, Robbie. I accused somebody without knowing enough. I did it and I was wrong and I'm sorry. I know better now."

Paul ducked his head, then gave her a small smile.

"I heard what he said," Tommy Stankowski interrupted. "And I won't set foot in his darn house."

"You will if I tell you to," Joseph said. He hadn't raised his voice, but Charlotte heard steel in the quiet words.

"Would you come with us, Mr. Willis? We could use your help," Paul said.

"I-I c-can row." He stepped toward Joseph.

"You'll row my boat for me?" Joseph glanced down at his brother and sister. "All right, let's get us out of the rain."

Paul helped Charlotte and Robbie into his boat.

"You watch them good, Mr. Willis," Robbie shouted as he climbed aboard.

"Yep," Mr. Willis called. He followed the Stankowski kids along the bank to where they'd tied up their boat.

Paul gave his rowboat a shove and clambered in, then slid the loose oar into its oarlock.

"You're the one who needs watching," Charlotte told her brother. "No more nasty talk. At least not until we've heard what Joseph has to say."

Paul rowed across the current to the middle of the river and steered the boat so it was heading downstream. He held the oars out, steadying the boat against the current. "Thought we better row both boats down together. Is that all right?"

"Sure," Charlotte said. She could feel the current pushing against the bottom of the boat. "So they find the house."

"So they don't escape," Robbie said.

Charlotte knew that if she shined her flashlight on Robbie's face he'd be glaring. Well, tough. She watched upstream, and the Stankowskis' boat appeared. Mr. Willis was rowing. Joseph sat on a bench with the little girl. She was so small, six or seven at the most. Tommy perched in the bow, looking as stiff and stubborn as Robbie.

The river kept shoving them, the current strong and insistent. Paul pulled on the oars to steer and let the Mon carry them downstream toward home.

"Turn on the flashlight, Charlie," Robbie said.

"Good idea. Then they can see to follow us." She fumbled for the light.

"Give it to me," Robbie demanded, reaching across her lap. "I'm going to shine it on them, so they don't try to pull nothin'."

"You are the most mule-headed boy on the Monongahela." Charlotte tightened her grip on the flashlight.

Robbie grabbed an end of it and tugged hard.

"Hey, you two, quit rocking the boat," Paul warned.

Robbie didn't listen. He gave another hard yank and the boat lurched. Robbie tumbled over the side and into the fast-moving river.

CHAPTER 13
ALL WET

R obbie!" Charlotte screamed. Her thoughts raced every which way. It was just like the dream, her brother falling overboard. No. She shook her head. It couldn't be the dream. The wrong brother had fallen in the water.

"Charlotte!"

Paul's shout cleared her mind in an instant. This was no dream. She had one very real brother thrashing around in the deepest part of the Monongahela River.

"Go after him," Paul urged. "I'll keep the boat right with you."

"Me? In the river? How can I?" She didn't know if she'd spoken aloud. But of course she had to go after him. She kicked off her boots and wrestled free of the oilskin.

"Slide in. Don't jump or I'll capsize," Paul warned. "Go easy now."

Easy? Charlotte slipped her legs over the side. Icy water

sucked on her feet. Robbie was wearing shoes and a thick oilskin. He'd never be able to swim with all that on. She let herself slide in and cold smacked her in the chest. The river drew her head under and she got a mouthful. That familiar taste—mud and oil. Her clothes felt as heavy as pig iron. She struggled to the surface, shook her head and spit.

Paul had somehow reached the flashlight and was shining it on the river, dancing lights on muddy blackness. "There," he called. "Behind us. Toward the middle." He shined the light on a frothy, splashing place.

Fighting the current and the dead weight of her clothes, Charlotte churned upstream. A clumsy stroke, then another and another. The river pushed and she pushed back, swimming in a ragged line toward Robbie.

At last she reached him and grabbed an arm. "Robbie?"

He coughed and twisted, towing her under the surface.

She fought her way upward and pulled him along, spitting and coughing out water. Then there were arms reaching for them. Boats on either side, oars to grab. A grunt, and someone released the burden of Robbie's weight from her arms. Then a strong arm hoisted her upward, shoved her into Paul's boat.

Sprawled on the bottom, she heard voices. Coughing. "Are you all right?"

"Charlie?" More coughs.

She pulled up into a sitting position in the bottom of the boat, leaned against the seat. She was breathing hard, and so cold. She tried to wipe the water from her face, but more streamed down from her hair.

The boat rocked. Under the bottom boards, she could feel the water, angry and roiling. Someone threw a heavy covering over her shoulders, and the boat turned, catching the current.

"Charlotte. Are you all right?" Paul's voice.

"I—I think so. Where's Robbie?"

"Other boat. He's okay. I'll get you home as fast as I can."

"Yes. Thanks." She let her eyes drift shut. Let the boat and Paul and the river do what they would. All she could think about was Robbie. He was safe.

That dream. She'd gotten it all wrong. She started to explain to Paul but her voice came out crooked and she was crying. More water, as if she needed more on a night like this.

By the time they climbed out of the rowboat, she'd caught her breath and stopped crying, but she couldn't seem to stop shivering. Paul took an arm to hold her steady as they made their way to her house. She glanced over her shoulder. Mr. Willis was half-carrying Robbie. Joseph marched at the end of their bedraggled parade, towing his brother and sister.

At the back door, Charlotte had to untangle herself enough to reach for her key, still hanging on a soggy string around her neck. At least that hadn't fallen off. But even if it had, they would have been fine—didn't they have a family of thieves coming home with them? She bit back a giddy laugh.

After a quick scrub of her hands and face, and a whole new set of clothes, Charlotte headed downstairs to the kitchen, toweling her hair. She was the last to arrive. Robbie had also changed, wrapping himself into his warmest sweater. The rest had peeled off wet outer clothing. Damp towels and gear lay piled on the counter. Everybody had gathered around the kitchen table.

Robbie and Mr. Willis were handing out plates of scrambled eggs. "Missy?" he asked. "Y-you hurt?"

"No. Just cold."

Paul was passing out cups of hot chocolate. She couldn't wait to wrap her hands around one.

Nothing had ever smelled quite so warm or wonderful. She sipped, and it tasted sweet. And Mr. Willis had made the best eggs. The table was silent as people ate and drank. She wasn't the only cold and hungry person tonight. Just the wettest. Her thick hair wouldn't dry till morning.

Somehow, she found her voice. "Thank you, whoever pulled us out. Are you okay, Robbie? You didn't hurt yourself, did you?"

"Nah, I'm okay. That Joseph, he hauled me in." Robbie

had the grace to look apologetic. He turned. "Thanks."

"Hey. I got a brother. And a sister." He looked at Charlotte. "Are you really all right, or should we leave and come back tomorrow? You look like you could use a good night's sleep."

Charlotte shot a warning look toward Robbie. If he said another word about them running away, she'd pound him. But he didn't. "I'm fine. Just wet. Besides, I'll never sleep if you go home now. What's going on, Joseph? Are you a thief? How come you took our scrap?"

Joseph sat straight, with his hands flat against the kitchen table. "Like I said, I got a brother and a sister—"

"I helped," Tommy interrupted.

"Hush now, Tom," Joseph said.

Tommy didn't listen. "I did too help. I stuck gum in that lock so we could bust it open the second time. If you're sending him to jail, you gotta send me too." He folded his arms across his chest and tried to look ferocious.

To Charlotte's eye, he looked closer to tears. "Nobody's talking about jail just yet," she said. "Let your brother finish talking."

Joseph ducked his head as if to say thanks. "I ain't saying what we did was right or nothin'. But I had to do something. Kids got to eat." Joseph's cheeks were red, but his eyes had dark shadows underneath that made him look like he was sick with a fever.

"How'd you carry all that stuff?" Robbie demanded.

"Why'd you dump it by the river?"

"I boosted a truck," Joseph said. "But I didn't want to use up too much gas and make somebody suspicious. So I dumped the scrap upriver, and figured I'd collect it at night in my boat."

"Wow, he stole a truck too," Robbie said.

"Borrowed, not stole." Tommy said. "He put the truck back."

Joseph threw an arm around Tommy. "I'll do the talking now."

Charlotte couldn't help staring at Joseph. He was a medium-sized guy, and bony. His cheeks and jaw looked hard. In the light of the kitchen, she could see that his hair wasn't black, just a dark brown.

"How about your folks? Can't they take care of things?" Paul asked.

"They're gone."

The little girl sniffed. Joseph threw his other arm around her. "It's all right, Tessa. I promised Ma, remember?"

She nodded and curled into his side. Tommy looked at his lap.

"It's a long story," Joseph continued. "Our pa left back in the thirties. Tessa was still a baby. He went to find work. Never came back. We don't even know if he's alive."

"And your ma?" Charlotte asked.

"She died. She'd been real sick, and we was keeping care of her. But her lungs just gave out. It was cold and damp where we was staying. But even if she'd been in the hospital, she was so sick . . ."

Charlotte squeezed her eyes shut. If Pa left, or if something happened to Ma, what would she and Robbie do?

"You ain't the only one whose pa left." Paul spoke so softly Charlotte wasn't sure she'd heard the words right. "Mine went for work too, but he never found it. Found the wrong end of somebody's knife instead. At least my ma don't have to worry. She knows the truth."

"I didn't know . . ." Charlotte began. Poor Paul. No wonder he wanted to be a cop.

Paul shook his head. He turned back to Joseph. "With your folks gone, then, you've been taking care of these two?"

"Yep."

A thousand questions leapt into Charlotte's mind. How could he manage? How long had he been doing that? Did he have a job? Where did they live? Did anybody know? How did they get clothes? Food?

Paul's voice cut into her thoughts. "It's what my brothers would do."

"It's what our Jim would do too." Robbie's voice sounded like an echo.

Jim. That's who Charlotte had thought of when she'd first seen this Joseph Stankowski. And Robbie was right.

Jim would do whatever he could to keep them safe. So this man—this boy—in their kitchen wasn't mostly a thief. He was mostly a brother.

"When . . . when did your mother die?" she asked. "How long have you been taking care of everything?"

"About six months ago Ma got too sick to work anymore. We had to move then. Couldn't pay rent. I found us a shack down near the Rankin Bridge. Ain't much, but it keeps the worst of the weather out. She died a few weeks back. End of April."

"What did you do then?" Paul asked.

"Kept going, best we could. I fish some. The sisters at the convent help out with used clothes for the kids. They been doing that for a long while. I chop wood to keep a fire going. Work odd jobs when I can."

Paul shook his head. "No. I mean, what did you do about your mother? When she died?"

Charlotte rubbed at a scratch on the kitchen table. She didn't want to hear any more about dead mothers.

"We took her to church," Joseph said. He pulled his brother and sister closer to him. "Once we knew she was gone, we said our good-byes. Prayed over her. Then I tucked a blanket around her and wrapped her rosary around her hand. So they'd know she was a good Catholic. And we took her down to the Polish church in Pittsburgh."

"The woman on the church steps," Paul whispered. "St. Stanislas. Wow."

"Why?" The questions popped out before Charlotte could stop them. "Why didn't you tell the sisters at the convent and have the funeral here? We've got plenty of churches."

Joseph shook his head at her. "Don't you see? I couldn't tell the sisters. If I told, they'd take Tommy and Tessa away. Put them in an orphanage. Split up the family."

Tommy spoke again. He sat straight and stared right at Robbie. "Joey didn't tell nobody. And you can't neither. Me and Tessa, we ain't going to no orphanage."

"I—I wouldn't tell," Robbie said. "I promise. Cross my heart. But I do have a question. How come you didn't get the scrap last night? We heard you on the river."

"We weren't on the river last night," Joseph said. "Tessa had a stomachache."

"But I heard you," Robbie insisted. "There was a guy and he was yelling at a kid. Sounded just like you and Tommy. Tell him, Charlotte. You heard it too."

"We did," Charlotte said. "And we heard other people tonight, before you came. They sounded so close, but we didn't see any boats. It was spooky."

Joseph nodded. "Whisper Bend."

"What?" Paul asked.

"Whisper Bend. That's the name the river people give to the place where I stashed the scrap. There's something special about the limestone cliffs and the hill across the way. Makes sounds carry a long distance. When I was little,

my pa had a pal stand way back on the top of the hill and
sing old country songs in a real soft voice. Then Pa took
me out in his boat. At Whisper Bend we could hear every
word the guy sang. We could even hear when he stopped
to cough and clear his throat."

"Whisper Bend," Charlotte repeated. She wondered
if her pa knew about it. Wouldn't he be surprised if she
could tell him something new about the river?

While Joseph talked, Mr. Willis had been leaning back
next to the stove, watching. Now he stepped closer to the
table and pointed to Tessa.

"L-little missy. Going to s-sleep."

He was right. She'd nodded off.

"Put her on the sofa in the living room, Joseph,"
Charlotte said. "I'll get a blanket."

It felt so good to move away from the table, away from
the ugly facts Joseph had told. Charlotte climbed the steps
to her room and pulled a quilt off her bed. Bending, she
picked up a small soft doll and carried them both downstairs.

Joseph tucked his sister in, careful as any mother,
and kissed her forehead. He was a good brother all right.
He was Tessa's Jim. Charlotte glanced toward the front
window, to Jim's star. She took a few steps and reached
out to touch the points and whisper his name.

As she did, familiar footsteps sounded on the sidewalk.
It was only ten-thirty, not nearly time for the shift change
at the mill, but Ma was home. Charlotte heard more

footsteps, then the kitchen door opening and shutting. She turned.

Ma strode into the living room, sooty and smudged. "Charlotte! Robbie! Who are these people? What in thunderation is going on?"

CHAPTER 14
EXTREME HARDSHIP

 Nobody spoke at first. Charlotte and Robbie knew better. Ma didn't use strong language much, so when she came out with a *thunderation,* a person needed to watch out.

"Mrs. Campbell," Paul began. "We've been out on the river. We found the stolen metal and—"

Everyone else joined in, and even Charlotte couldn't make sense of the noise.

Ma held up her hands. "Quiet! First I just want to know, is anybody hurt? In danger?"

"No. We're just trying to figure out what happened," Charlotte said. "How come you're home so early, Ma?"

"I'll answer your questions after you've answered mine, thank you. But first, I'm going to get out of these filthy overalls. Don't anybody go anywhere." She marched upstairs.

Nobody else moved.

"She'll skin us alive," Robbie said. "I wish Pa were home."

"Don't worry," Charlotte grumbled. "We'll have to go through it all over again when he gets here."

"I'm sorry. It's my fault. We shouldn't have come back here," Paul said. "But my house—"

Charlotte shook her head at him. "Ma's mad now. Imagine if she'd come home and found nobody here. That would be a hundred times worse."

When Ma arrived with a clean face and wearing fresh clothes, they all marched back into the kitchen. Charlotte introduced everybody, then started to explain what had happened. People interrupted to tell their parts, and Ma had a bunch of questions. By the time Joseph had told about his mother dying, Charlotte knew Ma was finished being mad. Her eyes had filled up.

"You poor children," Ma said. "Whatever are you going to do?"

Tommy stuck out his chin again. "We ain't going to no orphanage. We'll run off to California first."

Tommy made Charlotte want to smile. He and Robbie were so much alike.

"Hush, Tommy," Joseph said. "I've been trying to figure that out, ma'am. I ain't afraid of work. And Tommy, he's all set to help at the grocery store, stacking food on the shelves this summer. That and what I can pick up doing odd jobs—"

"Odd jobs?" Ma asked. "I don't understand. There are jobs going begging all up and down the river. Why not get a real job with good pay?"

You had to give it to Ma, Charlotte thought. Her temper might get steamed up, but she could untangle troubles like nobody else.

Joseph shook his head. "I would if I could. But I turned eighteen back in the winter, when Ma was real sick. I had to kinda hide out, or Uncle Sam would come after me."

"The draft board." Ma's eyes narrowed. "Did you register?"

Joseph stared down at his feet. "No, ma'am. I know this is going to sound like I'm a slacker. And I know you've got a boy over there. Saw the blue star in your window. I'd go and do my bit if I could. Shoot, I wanted to enlist. But with Ma sick and the little ones . . ."

"Oh, what a mess." Ma ran her hand through her dark hair. "If you get a job, the draft board finds you. But if you don't work, how will you take care of your family?"

This was getting worse by the minute. What would Charlotte do in such a terrible situation? Or Jim, for that matter? What could anybody do?

"Yes, ma'am. That's why I took . . . stole the metal. There's a junk man down in Hazelwood. He don't ask too many questions. Pays in cash. I was planning to take the scrap down to him in my boat."

"M-m-mister. B-b-butler," Wagon Willie said. Every-one turned to look at him. It was the first he'd spoken since Ma had come home.

"Pardon me, Mr. Willis? What did you say?" Ma looked at him kindly.

"D-d-draft board."

Charlotte frowned. What was he talking about?

Ma shook her head. "I don't understand."

Mr. Willis took a deep breath. "H-h-hardship."

"Do you mean Mr. David Butler?" Ma's head snapped up and her eyes went wide. "He's head of the draft board, isn't he? Oh, Mr. Willis." Ma stood and reached out to shake Mr. Willis's hand. "I think you may have saved this poor boy."

"What?" "Who?" "How?" The table came alive with questions. Charlotte didn't know all the answers yet, but she recognized the look on Ma's face. It was the one she got when she was about to turn the whole house upside down for spring cleaning, and anybody who got in her way had better look out.

"Mrs. Campbell?" Joseph looked at her with serious brown eyes.

"What I think Mr. Willis is trying to tell us is this," Ma said. "We need to speak to Mr. Butler. The draft board has choices in situations like this one. There's a classification—extreme hardship, I believe it's called. Is that what you meant, Mr. Willis?"

The man nodded and smiled at Ma. "B-butler. I-I cut his g-grass."

She returned his smile. "You know Mr. Butler? Would you be willing to go with me and see Mr. Butler on this boy's behalf?"

Mr. Willis nodded again.

"But what would you say?" Joseph asked. "I ain't the kids' pa, I'm just their brother."

Charlotte shook her head. "You're the only pa they've got. And the Army isn't drafting fathers for the war. Won't that count for something?"

"Indeed it will," Ma said. "That's what I meant when I said it was a hardship case."

"And if they don't draft you, you can get a real job." Charlotte smiled. This could work. She went on. "If you had a real job, you'd make money, and they wouldn't have to send your brother and sister to an orphanage."

"But, Charlie, what about the metal?" Robbie said.

"We won't tell who took the metal. We'll just say we found it. Then we can haul it to the scrap yard," Charlotte said. "The whole town doesn't need to know the rest. We found it, so we can decide. But I would like to tell Mrs. Alexander and the principal. And Betsy."

She looked around the table. Robbie was nodding. So were Ma and Mr. Willis. Joseph and his brother Tommy had soft looks on their faces, like maybe they had a chance.

Paul was the only one not smiling. "I'm still worried.

What if the draft board is strict? What if they want to punish Joseph for not registering right away? If he goes to the draft board without enough strong arguments, they might say no."

"But it *is* a hardship case," Ma said. "Surely the draft board will see that."

Charlotte sighed. "If he already had a job and a house, he'd look like more of a real pa."

"You don't ask for much, do you, Charlotte," Paul said.

"I don't know. Charlotte's right." Joseph sounded worried. "If I don't go in strong to the draft board, I'd better not go in at all."

Charlotte jumped up. "If he could get a *war* job, the draft board would excuse him from the Army, wouldn't they? What's that called, Ma?"

"It's called a deferment. Men get them for working at defense jobs in vital industries. Of course—I could recommend you at the mill! We're shorthanded. We had a breakdown on the line tonight, and they've had to shut down production until it gets fixed. With not enough people, maintenance is tough. And they're building a new furnace, so they're looking for strong young men. They'd take you on in a minute."

Charlotte felt a huge weight lift off her shoulders. If the draft board treated Joseph like a father to his brother and sister, *and* he had a war job . . . She smiled at him, but he'd turned pale.

"In the mill?" He took a deep breath. "Sure, I'll give it a try . . ." His Adam's apple bobbed as he swallowed a couple of times.

"What?" Charlotte asked. "What's the matter?"

Joseph looked ashamed. "I'll do it. I'll do whatever it takes. But I'm a river rat. They got a concrete fence around the mill and barbed wire, like a prison. And all that fire— when I look at the mill at night, I think that's what the priest must be talking about when he warns about the fires of hell." Joseph shuddered.

Charlotte understood exactly how he felt. She felt like that every time Pa made her help on the boat. The boat! "You're a river rat. How about working on a tug? Pa's short-handed. And it's defense work."

"Would he hire me?"

"I'm sure he would," Ma said.

Charlotte knew from the look on Ma's face that if Pa had his doubts, Ma would convince him. But Pa wouldn't need much convincing. Hadn't he said they all needed to hold on to each other to get through the hard times? If this wasn't a hard time, what was?

Even Paul was beginning to look happier. "Now all we have to do is find him a place to live. Shoot, it's too late . . ." He paused. "See, my ma rents our top floor to some girls who came up from West Virginia to work in the mill. That's why we couldn't go there tonight—I'm not supposed to make a racket or bother them. If only

Ma could kick them out. But she can't."

"Maybe the job will be enough for the draft board," Joseph said. "If you mean it."

"Of course we do," Ma said. "If there were just a place for you to stay, and someone to care for the children while you're working. But so many women are working full shifts in the factories and mills . . ."

"I know!" Robbie said. He pounded the table and grinned. "I got it. It's perfect. You can stay with Mrs. Dubner."

Charlotte's mouth fell open. "Robbie, you're nuts! Mrs. Dubner's crazy. And all those cats."

"Only three," he said.

"You mean three hundred," she laughed.

Robbie sighed. "She feeds all the strays, but only three live there. Two gray ones and a stripey kitten. And she's not crazy, Charlie. She's just lonely."

Ma turned to him, a serious look on her face. "What do you mean, Robbie?"

He shrugged. "Well, with her boys gone, she hasn't had anybody. And she's real nice. Bakes good ginger cookies."

Charlotte could not believe her brother had been spending time with old Mrs. Dubner. Was he turning crazy too?

Ma looked stern. "Robert Michael Campbell, how do you know all this?"

"Aw, Ma, I didn't have anything to do after I hurt my

hand—you wouldn't let me collect scrap. So I went to see her. She gave me cookies and let me pet her cats. She's got lots of room with just her living there."

"Wait a minute," Charlotte interrupted, as the rest of Robbie's words finally hit her. "What boys? Does she really have kids?"

"Not anymore." Robbie shook his head and sighed again. "They both died. Long time ago. They got gassed in what she calls the Great War. But she's got beds and stuff. It's lots better than a shack. And I bet if you gave her some money, she'd cook for you too."

Ma looked around the table. "I don't know about the rest of you, but it sounds to me like things may work out." Ma checked her watch. "It's awfully late. I'd say we have plenty to keep us busy tomorrow. Joseph, will you and your family stay here tonight? We've got a room free on the third floor."

"Yes, ma'am. And thank you. Thank you all. Getting caught might have been the best thing that's happened to us in a while." With that he stood and picked up Tessa to carry her upstairs.

Ma shook hands with Mr. Willis. "Thank you so much. Shall we meet with the principal tomorrow and then arrange things with Mr. Butler?"

Mr. Willis nodded and smiled. Paul stepped toward the door and grinned at Charlotte. He stuck out his hand. "Shake?"

"Shake. We did a great job. Wait till we tell Betsy tomorrow. Wait till she finds out all she missed."

He waved and followed Mr. Willis back out into the rainy night.

Ma turned to Charlotte. "Now, young lady, will you tell me why I found two sets of soggy clothes in the bathtub? And why your hair looks like a rat's nest? You seem to have left out that part."

In all the excitement, Charlotte had actually forgotten. "I . . . Robbie . . . We . . . Well, he fell in the river, and I went in after him."

"*You?* You went in the water?"

"I had to, Ma. Paul was steering the boat. I guess I'm part river rat too."

Ma pulled Charlotte into her arms and held her tight. "I should scold you for being out there in the first place, but somehow, I haven't the heart. That was a brave thing to do, sweetheart. Your pa and I—I can't tell you . . . With Jim gone, if you or Robbie—"

"It's okay, Ma. Really. Robbie and I are swell. And there's something else." Charlotte took Ma's hand and tugged her toward the front window. She reached up and touched the points of Jim's star. "Jim's going to come home safe. I just know he is."

"Because?"

"Because he's as bad as Robbie. Worse maybe."

"What are you talking about, Charlotte?"

"Jim's nosy. He can't stand it if somebody knows something that he doesn't." Charlotte's fingers itched for paper and a pencil. "I've got a plan, Ma. I'll write a letter and tell him a little about tonight. But I'll leave out all the good parts. I'll pretend it's because of the censors. But then Jim will *have* to come home so he can find out what we've been up to. I'm sure of it."

"Ah, Charlotte," Ma said. She hugged her again. "What will you cook up next, girl?"

"Please, Ma, don't!" Robbie raced in. "Don't let her cook any more potatoes. She always burns them." He made a face.

"Oh you, buster. You'll eat what I cook and you'll like it." Charlotte messed up his damp hair with both her hands.

Brothers, she thought. Brothers.

A Peek into
the Past

LOOKING BACK: 1942

In the spring of 1942, the world was at war. German troops had taken over nearly all of Europe, and Japan had conquered most of Asia. But wartime was still new to Americans. The United States had entered the war only a few months earlier. Many families, like Charlotte's, had sent sons or brothers to fight.

On April 28, 1942, the day Charlotte's story opens, President Franklin D. Roosevelt spoke to the nation in one of his frequent radio talks, called "fireside chats." He admitted the war was going badly for the United States, and he asked ordinary Americans at home to sacrifice for victory, just as their fighting men were doing overseas. Like Charlotte, adults and children everywhere quickly found new ways to pitch in and help their country win the war.

President Roosevelt's radio speeches inspired the nation during World War II.

The president's message had special meaning in steel-producing towns. To win the war, America needed ships and weapons—which required steel, and lots of it. During the war, western Pennsylvania river towns blazed night and day. Smoke and soot from tall chimneys filled the skies, slag heaps smoldered, tugs and barges clogged the rivers. Mills like the Edgar Thomson added new furnaces so they could pour endless tons of steel. In fact, the Pittsburgh area, including Braddock, poured nearly 30 percent of all the steel used by America and her allies during World War II. This amazing effort earned the area a new name—*Victory Valley*.

All over the country, schools, scout troops, and church groups held scrap drives, collecting metal to be recycled. They gathered items made of aluminum, tin, copper, iron, and steel, sorted them, and sent them to factories to be melted down. Eventually, so much metal was turned into war supplies that there wasn't even enough to make diaper pins! People also collected and

Above: A steel mill at night.
At right: A proud scrapper

Standing on a scrap pile, these schoolchildren are all making the "V for Victory" sign.

recycled paper, rubber, and even lard, which was used in making artillery shells and grenades.

Americans pitched in to be sure their soldiers and allies also got the tons of food, clothing, and other supplies they needed. Families planted backyard "Victory gardens" so more farm products could go to soldiers. Schools in farm areas closed in spring and fall so students could help plant and harvest crops. And everyone saved money to buy war bonds and stamps to help the government pay for all the needed supplies.

The United States shipped so many goods overseas that serious shortages occurred at home. Sugar, fruit, meat, rubber, metal, paper, clothing, leather, and gasoline all grew scarce. The government began *rationing*, or limiting, how much of these products each family could buy. Imagine having to make one pair of shoes last a whole year, or saving sugar coupons for weeks to bake holiday cookies!

With so many men overseas, workers were in short supply, too. Women like Charlotte's mother, who had worked at home caring for their families, took

The government issued ration coupons to each household. People couldn't buy scarce products like sugar or gas without them.

factory jobs. They traded dresses for overalls and made steel, ships, bombs, bullets, and thousands of airplanes. Their work was vital to America's war effort. And 350,000 women joined the military, handling non-combat jobs such as nursing, office work, packing parachutes, and testing new airplanes, so that men could fight.

Millions of women took jobs making war supplies.

As Americans at home did their part for the war, a sense of unity and shared purpose took hold across the country. People grew strong and deter-mined. But they were often afraid, too. Air-raid drills frightened many children. As sirens blared, people in homes and schools dark-ened their windows and

Many families made a special shelter in the basement, where they hid during air-raid drills.

hid in basements, practicing what to do if warplanes attacked. Children in industrial areas knew that their towns were likely bombing targets if German warplanes crossed the Atlantic.

Radios and newspapers reported battles lost, islands over-run, and ships sunk. Movie theaters ran vivid newsreels before every featured film. Up on the movie screen, children saw battle scenes, German soldiers, and Japanese warplanes. Such images were especially chilling to people with loved ones fighting in the war.

Theaters showed newsreels about the war, including scenes of battles and sinking ships.

When America first entered the war, only young single men, like Charlotte's brother Jim, were called into service. Soldiers agreed to serve as long as the war lasted, plus six months. Young men like Jim ended up serving four or five long years—from 1941 until the war ended in 1945, or even longer.

Mothers hung a blue star in the window for each son in service, as Charlotte's mother did. If a son was killed, a gold star replaced the blue one. Some families had more than one gold star before the war was over.

Eventually, married men and fathers also had to serve in the military. Only men with medical problems, extreme family hard-ships, or jobs vital to the war—like the work Charlotte's father did—were *deferred*, or excused, from service.

Lonely soldiers cherished letters from home.

When a man served in the war, his family did not know where he was or how much danger he was facing. The government *censored* all letters to and from servicemen, cutting out words that might tell enemy spies about troop movements or war production. Letters between soldiers and their families show the heartbreak and sadness these separations caused, and also the bravery of women at home, who wrote strong, encouraging letters to their men overseas. One such woman signed each letter "all my love, all my life."

Millions of American men and women served in the war. Many did not return—400,000 Americans died in World War II, and nearly 17 million people died across the world.

In the steel towns of Pennsylvania, as in the rest of the country, World War II required patriotism and sacrifice. Americans turned all their efforts to victory, believing with President Roosevelt that freedom must be preserved, whatever the cost.

GEOGRAPHICAL NOTE

There really is a Whisper Bend on the Monongahela River, but for purposes of this story, the cove has been moved several miles downstream to the town of Braddock, and a lock and dam have been moved upstream.

ABOUT THE AUTHOR

Katherine Ayres loved hearing stories and making them up even before she could read and write. She did part of her growing up near the beach in Long Island, New York, where she enjoyed the water all year round and especially in summer. Now that she lives in Pittsburgh, many trips take her near one of the city's three rivers, where she can watch tugboats pushing heavy barges. As she prepared to write this book she spent a day on a tug and observed the muddy Monongahela up close. Studying history and learning about interesting places is one of the best parts of writing books, says Ms. Ayres. She's also written two books that take place in Ohio (where she was born), *Family Tree* and *North by Night*.

Free Catalogue!
It's great to be an American girl.

Something to stand up and shout about. Something to celebrate!
Discover a catalogue packed with things you love:

- ★ good books
- ★ beautiful dolls
- ★ doll accessories
- ★ doll furniture
- ★ comfy clothes
- ★ lots more!

Send for your **FREE** catalogue, and you'll see that it's true.
It's full of fun things for American girls like you!

Send me a catalogue:

My name

My address

City   State   Zip   12948

My birth date: ___ / ___ / ___
month   day   year

Parent's signature

Send my friend a catalogue:

My friend's name

Address

City   State   Zip   12955

If you liked this book, you'll love *American Girl*® magazine!

Order your subscription today! For just $19.95, we'll send you 6 big bimonthly issues
of *American Girl.* You'll get even more games, giggles, crafts, projects, and helpful
advice. Plus, every issue is jam-packed with great stories about girls just like you!

Yes! I want to order a subscription.

Send bill to: (please print)

Adult's name

Address

City   State   Zip

Send magazine to: (please print)

Girl's name

Address

City   State   Zip

Girl's birth date: ___ / ___ / ___
month   day   year

Parent's signature

☐ Bill me   ☐ Payment enclosed

Guarantee: You may cancel anytime for a full refund.
Allow 4–6 weeks for first issue. Canadian subscription $24 U.S.
© 1998 Pleasant Company

K91L1

Grayslake Area Public Library District
Grayslake, Illinois

1. A fine will be charged on each book which is not returned when it is due.

2. All injuries to books beyond reasonable wear and all losses shall be made good to the satisfaction of the Librarian.

3. Each borrower is held responsible for all books drawn on his card and for all fines accruing on the same.

DEMCO

King Lear

SCOTT P. RICHERT

INTRODUCTION BY JOSEPH SOBRAN

mc Marshall Cavendish
Benchmark
New York

Other Marshall Cavendish Offices:
Marshall Cavendish International (Asia) Private Limited, 1 New Industrial Road, Singapore 536196 • Marshall Cavendish International (Thailand) Co Ltd. 253 Asoke, 12th Flr, Sukhumvit 21 Road, Klongtoey Nua, Wattana, Bangkok 10110, Thailand • Marshall Cavendish (Malaysia) Sdn Bhd, Times Subang, Lot 46, Subang Hi-Tech Industrial Park, Batu Tiga, 40000 Shah Alam, Selangor Darul Ehsan, Malaysia

Marshall Cavendish is a trademark of Times Publishing Limited
All websites were available and accurate when this book was sent to press.

Library of Congress Cataloging-in-Publication Data
Richert, Scott P.
King Lear / by Scott P. Richert.
p. cm. — (Shakespeare explained)
Includes bibliographical references and index.
Summary: "A literary analysis of the play "King Lear." Includes information on the history and culture of Elizabethan England"—Provided by publisher.
ISBN 978-1-60870-016-5
1. Shakespeare, William, 1564-1616. King Lear—Juvenile literature. 2. England—Civilization—16th century—Juvenile literature. I. Title.
PR2819.R48 2010
822.3'3—dc22
2010007060

Photo research by: Linda Sykes
The photographs in this book are used by permission and through the courtesy of: ©Copyright Utah Shakespeare Festival. Photo by Karl Hugh: front cover; iStockphoto.com: 1; Mikhali/Shutterstock: 2–3; Neven Mendrila/Shutterstock: 3; Raciro/istockphoto: 4, 40, 44, 96, back cover; Art Parts RF: 6, 8, 13, 26, 27, 34; ©Nik Wheeler/Corbis: 11; Portraitgalerie, Schloss Ambras, Innsbruck, Austria/Erich Lessing/Art Resource, NY: 20; Travelshots.com/Alamy: 22; ©Hideo Kurihara/Alamy: 24; Corbis/Sygma: 29; Andrew Fox/Corbis: 32; ©WGBH The Everett Collection: 39; PBS and The Royal Shakespeare Company: 43; ©Nigel Norrington/ArenaPAL/Topfoto/ The Image Works: 46, 66, 99; ©Copyright Utah Shakespeare Festival. Photo by Karl Hugh: 59, 90, 111. Photo by Liz Lauren: 84; The Everett Collection: 95.

Editor: Megan Comerford
Publisher: Michelle Bisson
Art Director: Anahid Hamparian
Series Design: Kay Petronio

Printed in Malaysia (T)
135642

Contents

Shakespeare and His World

WILLIAM SHAKESPEARE, OFTEN NICKNAMED "THE BARD," IS, BEYOND ANY COMPARISON, THE MOST TOWERING NAME IN ENGLISH LITERATURE. MANY CONSIDER HIS PLAYS THE GREATEST EVER WRITTEN. HE STANDS OUT EVEN AMONG GENIUSES.

Yet the Bard is also closer to our hearts than lesser writers, and his tremendous reputation should neither intimidate us nor prevent us from enjoying the simple delights he offers in such abundance. It is as if he had written for each of us personally. As he himself put it, "One touch of nature makes the whole world kin."

Such tragedies as *Hamlet*, *Romeo and Juliet*, and *Macbeth* are world famous, still performed onstage and in films. These and other plays have also been adapted for radio, television, opera, ballet, pantomime, novels, comic books, and other media. Two of the best ways to become familiar with them are to watch some of the many fine movies that have been made of them and to listen to recordings of them by some of the world's great actors.

Even Shakespeare's individual characters have lives of their own, like real historical figures. Hamlet is still regarded as the most challenging role ever written for an actor. Roughly as many whole books have been written about Hamlet, an imaginary character, as about actual historical figures such as Abraham Lincoln and Napoleon Bonaparte.

Shakespeare created an amazing variety of vivid characters. One of Shakespeare's most peculiar traits was that he loved his characters so much—even some of his villains and secondary or comic characters—that at times he let them run away with the play, stealing attention from his heroes and heroines.

So in *A Midsummer Night's Dream* audiences remember the absurd and lovable fool Bottom the Weaver better than the lovers who are the main characters. Romeo's friend Mercutio is more fiery and witty than Romeo himself; legend claims that Shakespeare said he had to kill Mercutio or Mercutio would have killed the play.

Shakespeare also wrote dozens of comedies and historical plays, as well as nondramatic poems. Although his tragedies are now regarded as his greatest works, he freely mixed them with comedy and history. And his sonnets are among the supreme love poems in the English language.

It is Shakespeare's mastery of the English language that keeps his words familiar to us today. Every literate person knows dramatic lines such as "Wherefore art thou Romeo?"; "My kingdom for a horse!"; "To be or not to be: that is the question"; "Friends, Romans, countrymen, lend me your ears"; and "What fools these mortals be!" Shakespeare's sonnets are noted for their sweetness: "Shall I compare thee to a summer's day?"

COME NOT BETWEEN THE DRAGON AND HIS WRATH.

SHAKESPEARE'S LANGUAGE

WITHOUT A DOUBT, SHAKESPEARE WAS THE GREATEST MASTER OF THE ENGLISH LANGUAGE WHO EVER LIVED. BUT JUST WHAT DOES THAT MEAN?

Shakespeare's vocabulary was huge, full of references to the Bible as well as Greek and Roman mythology. Yet his most brilliant phrases often combine very simple and familiar words:

"WHAT'S IN A NAME? THAT WHICH WE CALL A ROSE BY ANY OTHER NAME WOULD SMELL AS SWEET."

He has delighted countless millions of readers. And we know him only through his language. He has shaped modern English far more than any other writer.

Or, to put it in more personal terms, you probably quote his words several times every day without realizing it, even if you have never suspected that Shakespeare could be a source of pleasure to you.

So why do so many English-speaking readers find his language so difficult? It is our language, too, but it has changed so much that it is no longer quite the same language—nor a completely different one, either.

Shakespeare's English and ours overlap without being identical. He would have some difficulty understanding us, too! Many of our everyday words and phrases would baffle him.

Shakespeare, for example, would not know what we meant by a *car,* a *radio,* a *movie,* a *television,* a *computer,* or a *sitcom,* since these things did not even exist in his time. Our old-fashioned term *railroad train* would be unimaginable to him, far in the distant future. We would have to explain to him (if we could) what *nuclear weapons, electricity,* and *democracy* are. He would also be a little puzzled by common expressions such as *high-tech, feel the heat, approval ratings, war criminal, judgmental,* and *whoopee cushion.*

So how can we call him "the greatest master of the English language"? It might seem as if he barely spoke English at all! (He would, however, recognize much of our dirty slang, even if he pronounced it slightly differently. His plays also contain many racial insults to Jews, Africans, Italians, Irish, and others. Today he would be called "insensitive.")

Many of the words of Shakespeare's time have become archaic. Words like *thou, thee, thy, thyself,* and *thine,* which were among the most common words in the language in Shakespeare's day, have all but disappeared today. We simply say *you* for both singular and plural, formal and familiar. Most other modern languages have kept their *thou.*

Sometimes the same words now have different meanings. We are apt to be misled by such simple, familiar words as *kind, wonderful, waste, just,* and *dear,* which he often uses in ways that differ from our usage.

Shakespeare also doesn't always use the words we expect to hear, the words that we ourselves would naturally use. When we might automatically say, "I beg your pardon" or just "Sorry," he might say, "I cry you mercy."

Often a glossary and footnotes will solve all three of these problems for us. But it is most important to bear in mind that Shakespeare was often hard for his first audiences to understand. Even in his own time his rich language was challenging. And this was deliberate. Shakespeare was inventing his own kind of English. It remains unique today.

A child doesn't learn to talk by using a dictionary. Children learn first by sheer immersion. We teach babies by pointing at things and saying their names. Yet the toddler always learns faster than we can teach! Even as babies we are geniuses. Dictionaries can help us later, when we already speak and read the language well (and learn more slowly).

So the best way to learn Shakespeare is not to depend on the footnotes and glossary too much, but instead to be like a baby: just get into the flow of the language. Go to performances of the plays or watch movies of them.

THE LANGUAGE HAS A MAGICAL WAY OF TEACHING ITSELF, IF WE LET IT. THERE IS NO REASON TO FEEL STUPID OR FRUSTRATED WHEN IT DOESN'T COME EASILY.

Hundreds of phrases have entered the English language from *Hamlet* alone, including "to hold, as 'twere, the mirror up to nature"; "murder most foul"; "the thousand natural shocks that flesh is heir to"; "flaming youth"; "a countenance more in sorrow than in anger"; "the play's the thing"; "neither a borrower nor a lender be"; "in my mind's eye"; "something is rotten in the state of Denmark"; "alas, poor Yorick"; and "the lady doth protest too much, methinks."

From other plays we get the phrases "star-crossed lovers"; "what's in a name?"; "we have scotched the snake, not killed it"; "one fell swoop"; "it was Greek to me"; "I come to bury Caesar, not to praise him"; and "the most unkindest cut of all"—all these are among our household words. In fact, Shakespeare even gave us the expression "household words." No wonder his contemporaries marveled at his "fine filed phrase" and swooned at the "mellifluous and honey-tongued Shakespeare."

Shakespeare's words seem to combine music, magic, wisdom, and humor:

"THE COURSE OF TRUE LOVE NEVER DID RUN SMOOTH."

"HE JESTS AT SCARS THAT NEVER FELT A WOUND."

"THE FAULT, DEAR BRUTUS, IS NOT IN OUR STARS, BUT IN OURSELVES, THAT WE ARE UNDERLINGS."

"COWARDS DIE MANY TIMES BEFORE THEIR DEATHS; THE VALIANT NEVER TASTE OF DEATH BUT ONCE."

"NOT THAT I LOVED CAESAR LESS, BUT THAT I LOVED ROME MORE."

"THERE ARE MORE THINGS IN HEAVEN AND EARTH, HORATIO, THAN ARE DREAMT OF IN YOUR PHILOSOPHY."

"BREVITY IS THE SOUL OF WIT."

"THERE'S A DIVINITY THAT SHAPES OUR ENDS, ROUGH-HEW THEM HOW WE WILL."

Four centuries after Shakespeare lived, to speak English is to quote him. His huge vocabulary and linguistic fertility are still astonishing. He has had a powerful effect on all of us, whether we realize it or not. We may wonder how it is even possible for a single human being to say so many memorable things.

Only the King James translation of the Bible, perhaps, has had a more profound and pervasive influence on the English language than Shakespeare. And, of course, the Bible was written by many authors over many centuries, and the King James translation, published in 1611, was the combined effort of many scholars.

EARLY LIFE

So who, exactly, was Shakespeare? Mystery surrounds his life, largely because few records were kept during his time. Some people have even doubted his identity, arguing that the real author of Shakespeare's plays must have been a man of superior formal education and wide experience. In a sense such doubts are a natural and understandable reaction to his rare, almost miraculous powers of expression, but some people feel that the doubts themselves show a lack of respect for the supremely human poet.

Most scholars agree that Shakespeare was born in the town of Stratford-upon-Avon in the county of Warwickshire, England, in April 1564. He was baptized, according to local church records, Gulielmus (William) Shakspere (the name was spelled in several different ways) on April 26 of that year. He was one of several children, most of whom died young.

His father, John Shakespeare (or Shakspere), was a glove maker and, at times, a town official. He was often in debt or being fined for unknown delinquencies, perhaps failure to attend church regularly. It is suspected that John was a recusant (secret and illegal) Catholic, but there is no proof. Many

SHAKESPEARE'S CHILDHOOD HOME IS CARED FOR BY AN INDEPENDENT CHARITY, THE SHAKESPEARE BIRTHPLACE TRUST, IN STRATFORD-UPON-AVON, WARWICKSHIRE, ENGLAND.

scholars have found Catholic tendencies in Shakespeare's plays, but whether Shakespeare was Catholic or not we can only guess.

At the time of Shakespeare's birth, England was torn by religious controversy and persecution. The country had left the Roman Catholic Church during the reign of King Henry VIII, who had died in 1547. Two of Henry's children, Edward and Mary, ruled after his death. When his daughter Elizabeth I became queen in 1558, she upheld his claim that the monarch of England was also head of the English Church.

Did William attend the local grammar school? He was probably entitled to, given his father's prominence in Stratford, but again, we face a frustrating absence of proof, and many people of the time learned to read very well without schooling. If he went to the town school, he would also have learned the rudiments of Latin.

We know very little about the first half of William's life. In 1582, when he was eighteen, he married Anne Hathaway, eight years his senior. Their first daughter, Susanna, was born six months later. The following year they had twins, Hamnet and Judith.

At this point William disappears from the records again. By the early 1590s we find "William Shakespeare" in London, a member of the city's leading acting company, called the Lord Chamberlain's Men. Many of Shakespeare's greatest roles, we are told, were first performed by the company's star, Richard Burbage.

Curiously, the first work published under (and identified with) Shakespeare's name was not a play but a long erotic poem, *Venus and Adonis*, in 1593. It was dedicated to the young Earl of Southampton, Henry Wriothesley.

Venus and Adonis was a spectacular success, and Shakespeare was immediately hailed as a major poet. In 1594 he dedicated a longer, more serious poem to Southampton, *The Rape of Lucrece*. It was another hit, and for many years, these two poems were considered Shakespeare's greatest works, despite the popularity of his plays.

O, LET ME NOT BE MAD, NOT MAD, SWEET HEAVEN!

SHAKESPEARE ON FILM: A SAMPLER

TODAY MOVIES, NOT LIVE PLAYS, ARE THE MORE POPULAR ART FORM. FORTUNATELY MOST OF SHAKESPEARE'S PLAYS HAVE BEEN FILMED, AND THE BEST OF THESE MOVIES OFFER AN EXCELLENT WAY TO MAKE THE BARD'S ACQUAINTANCE. RECENTLY, KENNETH BRANAGH HAS BECOME A RESPECTED CONVERTER OF SHAKESPEARE'S PLAYS INTO FILM.

As You Like It

One of the earliest screen versions of *As You Like It* is the 1936 film starring Laurence Olivier as Orlando and Elisabeth Bergner as Rosalind. The *New York Times*, in a movie review, praised both the directorial interpretation and the actors' portrayals. British actress Helen Mirren starred in a 1978 BBC production that was filmed entirely outdoors. The most recent film version, directed by renowned Shakespearean actor Kenneth Branagh, aired in 2006 on HBO. Set in nineteenth-century Japan, it is visually stunning and a decent interpretation of the play. It also boasts an impressive supporting cast, including Kevin Kline as Jaques, Alfred Molina as Touchstone, and Romola Garai as Celia.

Hamlet

Hamlet, Shakespeare's most famous play, has been well filmed several times. In 1948 Laurence Olivier won three Academy

Awards—for best picture, best actor, and best director—for his version of the play. The film allowed him to show some of the magnetism that made him famous on the stage. Nobody spoke Shakespeare's lines more thrillingly.

The young Derek Jacobi played Hamlet in a 1980 BBC production of the play, with Patrick Stewart (now best known for *Star Trek: The Next Generation*) as the guilty king. Jacobi, like Olivier, has a gift for speaking the lines freshly; he never seems to be merely reciting the famous and familiar words. But whereas Olivier has animal passion, Jacobi is more intellectual. It is fascinating to compare the ways these two outstanding actors play Shakespeare's most complex character.

Franco Zeffirelli's 1990 *Hamlet*, starring Mel Gibson, is fascinating in a different way. Gibson, of course, is best known as an action hero, and he is not well suited to this supremely witty and introspective role, but Zeffirelli cuts the text drastically, and the result turns *Hamlet* into something that few people would have expected: a short, swiftly moving action movie. Several of the other characters are brilliantly played.

Henry IV, Part One

The 1979 BBC Shakespeare series production does a commendable job in this straightforward approach to the play. Battle scenes are effective despite obvious restrictions in an indoor studio setting. Anthony Quayle gives jovial Falstaff a darker edge, and Tim Pigott-Smith's Hotspur is buoyed by some humor. Jon Finch plays King Henry IV with noble authority, and David Gwillim gives Hal a surprisingly successful transformation from boy prince to heir apparent.

Julius Caesar

No really good movie of *Julius Caesar* exists, but the 1953 film, with Marlon Brando as Mark Antony, will do. James Mason is a thoughtful Brutus, and John Gielgud, then ranked with Laurence Olivier among the greatest Shakespearean actors, plays the villainous Cassius. The film is rather dull, and Brando is out of place in a Roman toga, but it is still worth viewing.

King Lear

In the past century, *King Lear* has been adapted for film approximately fifteen times. Peter Brook directed a bleak 1971 version starring British actor Paul Scofield as Lear. One of the best film versions of *King Lear*, not surprisingly, features Laurence Olivier in the title role. The 1983 British TV version, directed by Michael Elliott, provides a straightforward interpretation of the play, though the visual quality may seem dated to the twenty-first—century viewer. Olivier won an Emmy for Outstanding Lead Actor for his role.

Macbeth

Roman Polanski is best known as a director of thrillers and horror films, so it may seem natural that he should have done his 1971 *The Tragedy of Macbeth* as an often-gruesome slasher flick. But this is also one of the most vigorous of all Shakespeare films. Macbeth and his wife are played by Jon Finch and Francesca Annis, neither known for playing Shakespeare, but they are young and attractive in roles that are usually given to older actors, which gives the story a fresh flavor.

The Merchant of Venice

Once again the matchless Sir Laurence Olivier delivers a great performance as Shylock with his wife Joan Plowright as Portia in the 1974 TV film, adapted from the 1970 National Theater (of Britain) production. A 1980 BBC offering features Warren Mitchell as Shylock and Gemma Jones as Portia, with John Rhys-Davies as Salerio. The most recent production, starring Al Pacino as Shylock, Jeremy Irons as Antonio, and Joseph Fiennes as Bassanio, was filmed in Venice and released in 2004.

A Midsummer Night's Dream

Because of the prestige of his tragedies, we tend to forget how many comedies Shakespeare wrote—nearly twice the number of tragedies. Of these perhaps the most popular has always been the enchanting, atmospheric, and very silly masterpiece *A Midsummer Night's Dream*.

Several films have been made of *A Midsummer Night's Dream*. Among the more notable have been Max Reinhardt's 1935 black-and-white version, with Mickey Rooney (then a child star) as Puck.

Of the several film versions, the one starring Kevin Kline as Bottom and Stanley Tucci as Puck, made in 1999 with nineteenth-century costumes and directed by Michael Hoffman, ranks among the finest, and is surely one of the most sumptuous to watch.

Othello

Orson Welles did a budget European version in 1952, now available as a restored DVD. Laurence Olivier's 1965 film performance is predictably remarkable, though it has been said that he would only approach the part by honoring, even emulating, Paul Robeson's definitive interpretation that ran on Broadway in 1943. (Robeson was the first black actor to play Othello, the Moor of Venice, and he did so to critical acclaim, though sadly his performance was never filmed.) Maggie Smith plays a formidable Desdemona opposite Olivier, and her youth and energy will surprise younger audiences who know her only from the *Harry Potter* films. Laurence Fishburne brilliantly portrayed Othello in the 1995 film, costarring with Kenneth Branagh as a surprisingly human Iago, though Irène Jacob's Desdemona was disappointingly weak.

Richard III

Many well-known actors have portrayed the villainous Richard III on film. Of course, Laurence Olivier stepped in to play the role of Richard in a 1955 version he also directed. Director Richard Loncraine chose to set his 1995 film version in Nazi Germany. The movie, which starred Ian McKellen as Richard, was nominated for two Oscars; McKellen was nominated for a Golden Globe for his performance. The World War II interpretation also featured Robert Downey Jr. as Rivers, Kristin Scott Thomas as Lady Anne, and Maggie Smith (from the *Harry Potter* movies) as the Duchess of York. A 2008 version, directed by and starring Scott Anderson, is set in modern-day Los Angeles. Prolific actor David Carradine portrays Buckingham.

Romeo and Juliet

This, the world's most famous love story, has been filmed many times, twice very successfully over the last generation. Franco Zeffirelli directed a hit version in 1968 with Leonard Whiting and the rapturously pretty Olivia Hussey, set in Renaissance Italy. Baz

Luhrmann made a much more contemporary version, with a loud rock score, starring Leonardo DiCaprio and Claire Danes, in 1996.

It seems safe to say that Shakespeare would have preferred Zeffirelli's movie, with its superior acting and rich, romantic, sun-drenched Italian scenery.

The Taming of the Shrew

Franco Zeffirelli's 1967 film version of *The Taming of the Shrew* starred Elizabeth Taylor as Kate and Richard Burton as Petruchio. Shakespeare's original lines were significantly cut and altered to accommodate both the film media and Taylor's inexperience as a Shakespearean actress.

Gil Junger's 1999 movie *10 Things I Hate About You* is loosely based on Shakespeare's play. Julia Stiles and Heath Ledger star in this interpretation set in a modern-day high school. In 2005 BBC aired a version of Shakespeare's play set in twenty-first-century England. Kate is a successful, driven politician who succumbs to cash-strapped Petruchio, played by Rufus Sewell.

The Tempest

A 1960 Hallmark Hall of Fame production featured Maurice Evans as Prospero, Lee Remick as Miranda, Roddy McDowall as Ariel, and Richard Burton as Caliban. The special effects are primitive and the costumes are ludicrous, but it moves along at a fast pace. Another TV version aired in 1998 and was nominated for a Golden Globe. Peter Fonda played Gideon Prosper, and Katherine Heigl played his daughter Miranda Prosper. Sci-fi fans may already know that the classic 1956 film *Forbidden Planet* is modeled on themes and characters from the play.

Twelfth Night

Trevor Nunn adapted the play for the 1996 film he also directed in a rapturous Edwardian setting, with big names like Helena Bonham Carter, Richard E. Grant, Imogen Stubbs, and Ben Kingsley as Feste. A 2003 film set in modern Britain provides an interesting multicultural experience; it features an Anglo-Indian cast with Parminder Nagra (*Bend It Like Beckham*) playing Viola. For the truly intrepid, a twelve-minute silent film made in 1910 does a fine job of capturing the play through visual gags and over-the-top gesturing.

THESE FILMS HAVE BEEN SELECTED FOR SEVERAL QUALITIES: APPEAL AND ACCESSIBILITY TO MODERN AUDIENCES, EXCELLENCE IN ACTING, PACING, VISUAL BEAUTY, AND, OF COURSE, FIDELITY TO SHAKESPEARE. THEY ARE THE MOTION PICTURES WE JUDGE MOST LIKELY TO HELP STUDENTS UNDERSTAND THE SOURCE OF THE BARD'S LASTING POWER.

SHAKESPEARE'S THEATER

Today we sometimes speak of "live entertainment." In Shakespeare's day, of course, all entertainment was live, because recordings, films, television, and radio did not yet exist. Even printed books were a novelty.

In fact, most communication in those days was difficult. Transportation was not only difficult but slow, chiefly by horse and boat. Most people were illiterate peasants who lived on farms that they seldom left; cities grew up along waterways and were subject to frequent plagues that could wipe out much of the population within weeks.

Money—in coin form, not paper—was scarce and hardly existed outside the cities. By today's standards, even the rich were poor. Life was precarious. Most children died young, and famine or disease might kill anyone at any time. Everyone was familiar with death. Starvation was not rare or remote, as it is to most of us today. Medical care was poor and might kill as many people as it healed.

This was the grim background of Shakespeare's theater during the reign of Queen Elizabeth I, who ruled from 1558 until her death in 1603. During that period England was also torn by religious conflict, often violent, among Roman Catholics who were

ELIZABETH I, A GREAT PATRON OF POETRY AND THE THEATER, WROTE SONNETS AND TRANSLATED CLASSIC WORKS.

loyal to the pope, adherents of the Church of England who were loyal to the queen, and the Puritans who would take over the country in the revolution of 1642.

Under these conditions, most forms of entertainment were luxuries that were out of most people's reach. The only way to hear music was to be in the actual physical presence of singers or musicians with their instruments, which were primitive by our standards.

One brutal form of entertainment, popular in London, was bearbaiting. A bear was blinded and chained to a stake, where fierce dogs called mastiffs were turned loose to tear him apart. The theaters had to compete with the bear gardens, as they were called, for spectators.

The Puritans, or radical Protestants, objected to bearbaiting and tried to ban it. Despite their modern reputation, the Puritans were anything but conservative. Conservative people, attached to old customs, hated the Puritans. They seemed to upset everything. (Many of America's first settlers, such as the Pilgrims who came over on the *Mayflower*, were dissidents who were fleeing the Church of England.)

Plays were extremely popular, but they were primitive, too. They had to be performed outdoors in the afternoon because of the lack of indoor lighting. Often the "theater" was only an enclosed courtyard. Probably the versions of Shakespeare's plays that we know today were not used in full, but shortened to about two hours for actual performance.

But eventually more regular theaters were built, featuring a raised stage extending into the audience. Poorer spectators (illiterate "groundlings") stood on the ground around it, at times exposed to rain and snow. Wealthier people sat in raised tiers above. Aside from some costumes, there were few props or special effects and almost no scenery. Much had to be imagined: Whole battles might be represented by a few actors with swords. Thunder might be simulated by rattling a sheet of tin offstage.

The plays were far from realistic and, under the conditions of the time, could hardly try to be. Above the rear of the main stage was a small balcony. (It was this balcony from which Juliet spoke to Romeo.) Ghosts and witches might appear by entering through a trapdoor in the stage floor.

Unlike the modern theater, Shakespeare's Globe Theater—he describes it as "this wooden O"—had no curtain separating the stage from the audience. This allowed intimacy between the players and the spectators.

THE RECONSTRUCTED GLOBE THEATER WAS COMPLETED IN 1997 AND IS LOCATED IN LONDON, JUST 200 YARDS (183 METERS) FROM THE SITE OF THE ORIGINAL.

"HOW FAR YOUR EYES MAY PIERCE I CANNOT TELL."

The spectators probably reacted rowdily to the play, not listening in reverent silence. After all, they had come to have fun! And few of them were scholars. Again, a play had to amuse people who could not read.

The lines of plays were written and spoken in prose or, more often, in a form of verse called iambic pentameter (ten syllables with five stresses per line). There was no attempt at modern realism. Only males were allowed on the stage, so some of the greatest women's roles ever written had to be played by boys or men. (The same is true, by the way, of the ancient Greek theater.)

Actors had to be versatile, skilled not only in acting, but also in fencing, singing, dancing, and acrobatics. Within its limitations, the theater offered a considerable variety of spectacles.

Plays were big business, not yet regarded as high art, sponsored by important and powerful people (the queen loved them as much as the groundlings did). The London acting companies also toured and performed in the provinces. When plagues struck London, the government might order the theaters to be closed to prevent the spread of disease among crowds. (They remained empty for nearly two years from 1593 to 1594.)

As the theater became more popular, the Puritans grew as hostile to it as they were to bearbaiting. Plays, like books, were censored by the government, and the Puritans fought to increase restrictions, eventually banning any mention of God and other sacred topics on the stage.

In 1642 the Puritans shut down all the theaters in London, and in 1644 they had the Globe demolished. The theaters remained closed until Charles's son, King Charles II, was restored to the throne in 1660 and the hated Puritans were finally vanquished.

But, by then, the tradition of Shakespeare's theater had been fatally interrupted. His plays remained popular, but they were often rewritten by inferior dramatists, and it was many years before they were performed (again) as he had originally written them.

THE ROYAL SHAKESPEARE THEATER, IN STRATFORD-UPON-AVON, WAS CLOSED IN 2007 TO BUILD A 1,000-SEAT AUDITORIUM.

Today, of course, the plays are performed both in theaters and in films, sometimes in costumes of the period (ancient Rome for *Julius Caesar*, medieval England for *Henry V*), sometimes in modern dress (*Richard III* has recently been reset in England in the 1930s).

PLAYS

In the England of Queen Elizabeth I, plays were enjoyed by all classes of people, but they were not yet respected as a serious form of art.

Shakespeare's plays began to appear in print in individual, or quarto, editions in 1594, but none of these bore his name until 1598. Although his tragedies are now ranked as his supreme achievements, his name was first associated with comedies and with plays about English history.

The dates of Shakespeare's plays are notoriously hard to determine. Few performances of them were documented; some were not printed until decades after they first appeared on the stage. Mainstream scholars generally place most of the comedies and histories in the 1590s, admitting that this time frame is no more than a widely accepted estimate.

The three parts of *King Henry VI*, culminating in a fourth part, *Richard III*, deal with the long and complex dynastic struggle or civil wars known as the Wars of the Roses (1455–1487), one of England's most turbulent periods. Today it is not easy to follow the plots of these plays.

It may seem strange to us that a young playwright should have written such demanding works early in his career, but they were evidently very popular with the Elizabethan public. Of the four, only *Richard III*, with its wonderfully villainous starring role, is still often performed.

Even today, one of Shakespeare's early comedies, *The Taming of the Shrew*, remains a crowd-pleaser. (It has enjoyed success in a 1999 film adaptation, *10 Things I Hate About You*, with Heath Ledger and Julia Stiles.) The story is simple: The enterprising Petruchio resolves to marry a rich

THE "REAL" SHAKESPEARE

AROUND 1850 DOUBTS STARTED TO SURFACE ABOUT WHO HAD ACTUALLY WRITTEN SHAKESPEARE'S PLAYS, CHIEFLY BECAUSE MANY OTHER AUTHORS, SUCH AS MARK TWAIN, THOUGHT THE PLAYS' AUTHOR WAS TOO WELL EDUCATED AND KNOWLEDGEABLE TO HAVE BEEN THE MODESTLY SCHOOLED MAN FROM STRATFORD.

Who, then, was the real author? Many answers have been given, but the three leading candidates are Francis Bacon, Christopher Marlowe, and Edward de Vere, Earl of Oxford.

Francis Bacon (1561-1626)

Bacon was a distinguished lawyer, scientist, philosopher, and essayist. Many considered him one of the great geniuses of his time, capable of any literary achievement, though he wrote little poetry and, as far as we know, no dramas. When people began to suspect that "Shakespeare" was only a pen name, he seemed like a natural candidate. But his writing style was vastly different from the style of the plays.

Christopher Marlowe (1564–1593)

Marlowe wrote several excellent tragedies in a style much like that of the Shakespearean tragedies, though without the comic blend. But he was reportedly killed in a mysterious incident in 1593, before most of the Bard's plays existed. Could his death have been faked? Is it possible that he lived on for decades in hiding, writing under a pen name? This is what his advocates contend.

Edward de Vere, Earl of Oxford (1550–1604)

Oxford is now the most popular and plausible alternative to the lad from Stratford. He had a high reputation as a poet and playwright in his day, but his life was full of scandal. That controversial life seems to match what the poet says about himself in the sonnets, as well as many events in the plays (especially *Hamlet*). However, he died in 1604, and most scholars believe this rules him out as the author of plays that were published after that date.

THE GREAT MAJORITY OF EXPERTS REJECT THESE AND ALL OTHER ALTERNATIVE CANDIDATES, STICKING WITH THE TRADITIONAL VIEW, AFFIRMED IN THE 1623 FIRST FOLIO OF THE PLAYS, THAT THE AUTHOR WAS THE MAN FROM STRATFORD. THAT REMAINS THE SAFEST POSITION TO TAKE, UNLESS STARTLING NEW EVIDENCE TURNS UP, WHICH, AT THIS LATE DATE, SEEMS HIGHLY UNLIKELY.

young woman, Katherina Minola, for her wealth, despite her reputation for having a bad temper. Nothing she does can discourage this dauntless suitor, and the play ends with Kate becoming a submissive wife. It is all the funnier for being unbelievable.

With *Romeo and Juliet* the Bard created his first enduring triumph. This tragedy of "star-crossed lovers" from feuding families is known around the world. Even people with only the vaguest knowledge of Shakespeare are often aware of this universally beloved story. It has inspired countless similar stories and adaptations, such as the hit musical *West Side Story*.

By the mid-1590s Shakespeare was successful and prosperous, a partner in the Lord Chamberlain's Men. He was rich enough to buy New Place, one of the largest houses in his hometown of Stratford.

Yet, at the peak of his good fortune came the worst sorrow of his life: Hamnet, his only son, died in August 1596 at the age of eleven, leaving nobody to carry on his family name, which was to die out with his two daughters.

Our only evidence of his son's death is a single line in the parish burial register. As far as we know, this crushing loss left no mark on Shakespeare's work. As far as his creative life shows, it was as if nothing had happened. His silence about his grief may be the greatest puzzle of his mysterious life, although, as we shall see, others remain.

During this period, according to traditional dating (even if it must be somewhat hypothetical), came the torrent of Shakespeare's mightiest works. Among these was another quartet of English history plays, this one centering on the legendary King Henry IV, including *Richard II* and the two parts of *Henry IV*.

Then came a series of wonderful romantic comedies: *Much Ado About Nothing*, *As You Like It*, and *Twelfth Night*.

In 1598 the clergyman Francis Meres, as part of a larger work, hailed

ACTOR JOSEPH FIENNES PORTRAYED THE
BARD IN THE 1998 FILM *SHAKESPEARE IN
LOVE,* DIRECTED BY JOHN MADDEN.

Shakespeare as the English Ovid, supreme in love poetry as well as drama.
"The Muses would speak with Shakespeare's fine filed phrase," Meres
wrote, "if they would speak English." He added praise of Shakespeare's
"sugared sonnets among his private friends." It is tantalizing; Meres
seems to know something of the poet's personal life, but he gives us no
hard information. No wonder biographers are frustrated.

Next the Bard returned gloriously to tragedy with *Julius Caesar.* In the
play Caesar has returned to Rome in great popularity after his military
triumphs. Brutus and several other leading senators, suspecting that Caesar
means to make himself king, plot to assassinate him. Midway through the

play, after the assassination, comes one of Shakespeare's most famous scenes. Brutus speaks at Caesar's funeral. But then Caesar's friend Mark Antony delivers a powerful attack on the conspirators, inciting the mob to fury. Brutus and the others, forced to flee Rome, die in the ensuing civil war. In the end the spirit of Caesar wins after all. If Shakespeare had written nothing after *Julius Caesar*, he would still have been remembered as one of the greatest playwrights of all time. But his supreme works were still to come.

Only Shakespeare could have surpassed *Julius Caesar*, and he did so with *Hamlet* (usually dated about 1600). King Hamlet of Denmark has died, apparently bitten by a poisonous snake. Claudius, his brother, has married the dead king's widow, Gertrude, and become the new king, to the disgust and horror of Prince Hamlet. The ghost of old Hamlet appears to young Hamlet, reveals that he was actually poisoned by Claudius, and demands revenge. Hamlet accepts this as his duty, but cannot bring himself to kill his hated uncle. What follows is Shakespeare's most brilliant and controversial plot.

The story of *Hamlet* is set against the religious controversies of the Bard's time. Is the ghost in hell or purgatory? Is Hamlet Catholic or Protestant? Can revenge ever be justified? We are never really given the answers to such questions. But the play reverberates with them.

THE KING'S MEN

In 1603 Queen Elizabeth I died, and King James VI of Scotland became King James I of England. He also became the patron of Shakespeare's acting company, so the Lord Chamberlain's Men became the King's Men. From this point on, we know less of Shakespeare's life in London than in Stratford, where he kept acquiring property.

In the later years of the sixteenth century Shakespeare had been a rather elusive figure in London, delinquent in paying taxes. From 1602 to 1604 he lived, according to his own later testimony, with a French immigrant family named Mountjoy. After 1604 there is no record of any London residence for Shakespeare, nor do we have any reliable recollection of him or his whereabouts by others. As always, the documents leave much to be desired.

Nearly as great as *Hamlet* is *Othello*, and many regard *King Lear*, the heartbreaking tragedy about an old king and his three daughters, as Shakespeare's supreme tragedy. Shakespeare's shortest tragedy, *Macbeth*, tells the story of a Scottish lord and his wife who plot to murder the king of Scotland to gain the throne for themselves. *Antony and Cleopatra*, a sequel to *Julius Caesar*, depicts the aging Mark Antony in love with the enchanting queen of Egypt. *Coriolanus*, another Roman tragedy, is the poet's least popular masterpiece.

SONNETS AND THE END

The year 1609 saw the publication of Shakespeare's Sonnets. Of these 154 puzzling love poems, the first 126 are addressed to a handsome young man, unnamed, but widely believed to be the Earl of Southampton; the rest concern a dark woman, also unidentified. These mysteries are still debated by scholars.

Near the end of his career Shakespeare turned to comedy again, but it was a comedy of a new and more serious kind. Magic plays a large role in these late plays. For example, in *The Tempest*, the exiled duke of Milan, Prospero, uses magic to defeat his enemies and bring about a final reconciliation.

According to the most commonly accepted view, Shakespeare, not yet fifty, retired to Stratford around 1610. He died prosperous in 1616 and left a will that divided his goods, with a famous provision leaving his wife "my second-best bed." He was buried in the chancel of the parish church, under a tombstone bearing a crude rhyme:

> GOOD FRIEND, FOR JESUS SAKE FORBEARE,
> TO DIG THE DUST ENCLOSED HERE.
> BLEST BE THE MAN THAT SPARES THESE STONES,
> AND CURSED BE HE THAT MOVES MY BONES.

This epitaph is another hotly debated mystery: did the great poet actually compose these lines himself?

SHAKESPEARE'S GRAVE IN HOLY TRINITY CHURCH, STRATFORD-UPON-AVON. HIS WIFE, ANNE HATHAWAY, IS BURIED BESIDE HIM.

THE FOLIO

In 1623 Shakespeare's colleagues of the King's Men produced a large volume of the plays (excluding the sonnets and other poems) titled *Mr. William Shakespeares Comedies, Histories, & Tragedies* with a woodcut portrait of the Bard. As a literary monument it is priceless, containing our only texts of half the plays; as a source of biographical information it is severely disappointing, giving not even the dates of Shakespeare's birth and death.

Ben Jonson, then England's poet laureate, supplied a long prefatory poem saluting Shakespeare as the equal of the great classical Greek tragedians Aeschylus, Sophocles, and Euripides, adding that "He was not of an age, but for all time."

Some would later denigrate Shakespeare. His reputation took more than a century to conquer Europe, where many regarded him as semi-barbarous. His works were not translated before 1740. Jonson himself, despite his personal affection, would deprecate "idolatry" of the Bard. For a time Jonson himself was considered more "correct" than Shakespeare, and possibly the superior artist.

But Jonson's generous verdict is now the whole world's. Shakespeare was not merely of his own age, "but for all time."

'TIS MOST IGNOBLY DONE TO PLUCK ME BY THE BEARD.

A GLOSSARY OF LITERARY TERMS

allegory—a story in which characters and events stand for general moral truths. Shakespeare never uses this form simply, but his plays are full of allegorical elements.

alliteration—repetition of one or more initial sounds, especially consonants, as in the saying "through thick and thin," or in Julius Caesar's statement, "veni, vidi, vici."

allusion—a reference, especially when the subject referred to is not actually named, but is unmistakably hinted at.

aside—a short speech in which a character speaks to the audience, unheard by other characters on the stage.

comedy—a story written to amuse, using devices such as witty dialogue (high comedy) or silly physical movement (low comedy). Most of Shakespeare's comedies were romantic comedies, incorporating lovers who endure separations, misunderstandings, and other obstacles but who are finally united in a happy resolution.

deus ex machina—an unexpected, artificial resolution to a play's convoluted plot. Literally, "god out of a machine."

dialogue—speech that takes place among two or more characters.

diction—choice of words for a given tone. A speech's diction may be dignified (as when a king formally addresses his court), comic (as when the ignorant grave diggers debate whether Ophelia deserves a religious funeral), vulgar, romantic, or whatever the dramatic occasion requires. Shakespeare was a master of diction.

Elizabethan—having to do with the reign of Queen Elizabeth I, from 1558 until her death in 1603. This is considered the most famous period in the history of England, chiefly because of Shakespeare and other noted authors (among them Sir Philip Sidney, Edmund Spenser, and Christopher Marlowe). It was also an era of military glory, especially the defeat of the huge Spanish Armada in 1588.

Globe—the Globe Theater housed Shakespeare's acting company, the Lord Chamberlain's Men (later known as the King's Men). Built in 1598, it caught fire and burned down during a performance of *Henry VIII* in 1613.

hyperbole—an excessively elaborate exaggeration used to create special emphasis or a comic effect, as in Montague's remark that his son Romeo's sighs are "adding to clouds more clouds" in *Romeo and Juliet*.

irony—a discrepancy between what a character says and what he or she truly believes, what is expected to happen and

what really happens, or what a character says
and what others understand.

metaphor—a figure of speech in which one thing is identified
with another, such as when Hamlet calls his father a "fair
mountain." (See also *simile*.)

monologue—a speech delivered by a single character.

motif—a recurrent theme or image, such as disease in *Hamlet*
or moonlight in *A Midsummer Night's Dream*.

oxymoron—a phrase that combines two contradictory terms, as
in the phrase "sounds of silence" or Hamlet's remark, "I must
be cruel only to be kind."

personification—imparting personality to something impersonal
("the sky wept"); giving human qualities to an idea or an
inanimate object, as in the saying "love is blind."

pun—a playful treatment of words that sound alike, or are
exactly the same, but have different meanings. In *Romeo and
Juliet* Mercutio says, after being fatally wounded, "Ask for
me tomorrow and you shall find me a grave man." *Grave* could
mean either "a place of burial" or "serious."

simile—a figure of speech in which one thing is compared to
another, usually using the word *like* or *as*. (See also *metaphor*.)

soliloquy—a speech delivered by a single character, addressed
to the audience. The most famous are those of Hamlet,
but Shakespeare uses this device frequently to tell us his
characters' inner thoughts.

symbol—a visible thing that stands for an invisible quality, as poison in *Hamlet* stands for evil and treachery.

syntax—sentence structure or grammar. Shakespeare displays amazing variety of syntax, from the sweet simplicity of his songs to the clotted fury of his great tragic heroes, who can be very difficult to understand at a first hearing. These effects are deliberate; if we are confused, it is because Shakespeare means to confuse us.

theme—the abstract subject or message of a work of art, such as revenge in *Hamlet* or overweening ambition in *Macbeth*.

tone—the style or approach of a work of art. The tone of *A Midsummer Night's Dream*, set by the lovers, Bottom's crew, and the fairies, is light and sweet. The tone of *Macbeth*, set by the witches, is dark and sinister.

tragedy—a story that traces a character's fall from power, sanity, or privilege. Shakespeare's well-known tragedies include *Hamlet, Macbeth,* and *Othello*.

tragicomedy—a story that combines elements of both tragedy and comedy, moving a heavy plot through twists and turns to a happy ending.

verisimilitude—having the appearance of being real or true.

understatement—a statement expressing less than intended, often with an ironic or comic intention; the opposite of hyperbole.

SHAKESPEARE AND
KING LEAR

British actor Ian Holm ▶
played King Lear in a 1998
film adaptation of *King Lear*
directed by Richard Eyre.

Chapter One

66929
66929
66929

Shakespeare and King Lear

CHAPTER ONE

MOST SCHOLARS HAVE SETTLED ON 1605 AS THE MOST LIKELY DATE OF **KING LEAR**'S COMPOSITION, WHICH WOULD PLACE IT BETWEEN **OTHELLO** AND **MACBETH**. ONE OF SHAKESPEARE'S MOST COMPLEX WORKS, BOTH IN STRUCTURE AND IN CONTENT, **KING LEAR** IS CONSIDERED ONE OF SHAKESPEARE'S GREATEST MASTERPIECES, RIVALED ONLY BY **HAMLET**.

The story of King Lear did not originate with Shakespeare. In the twelfth century, Geoffrey of Monmouth had placed Lear among the earliest kings of Britain—in the eighth century B.C.E.—in his *Historia Regum Britanniae* (*The History of the Kings of Britain*). Leir (as his name was spelled) was the longest ruling of all the British kings, having reigned in southwest England for sixty years before dividing his kingdom between his two oldest daughters.

Shakespeare likely derived most of his knowledge of Leir from Raphael Holinshed's *Chronicles of England, Scotlande, and Irelande*, which was first published in 1577. The account also appeared in Edmund Spenser's

The Faerie Queene and Sir Philip Sidney's *Arcadia*, both of which were published in 1590. *Arcadia* also contains a story about a blind king of Paphlagonia (a region of Anatolia on the Black Sea) who had two rival sons, one of whom saves his father from suicide.

Shakespeare's incorporation of this story as the Gloucester subplot in *King Lear* is only one of the changes he made to the traditional narrative that were significant enough to make it his own. Shakespeare's decision to end the play with the deaths of both Cordelia and Lear was long criticized for departing from the Monmouth and Holinshed versions, in which Leir returned triumphant to the throne, to be succeeded by Cordelia.

Shakespeare's decision to make Lear's insanity central to the plot may have had a contemporary historical parallel in the case of Sir Brian Annesley. Annesley's eldest daughter tried to take control of his estate in 1603 by having him declared insane, and she was supported by her younger sister. Annesley's youngest daughter, Cordell, interceded on behalf of her father.

Shakespeare's audience would have been familiar with the Annesley case, as well as with broader political themes that are reflected in the play. In 1603, as childless Queen Elizabeth I approached death, many in England feared that political divisions would destroy the country. Such fears were allayed when James VI of Scotland, next in line to the throne of England, succeeded Elizabeth upon her death and became James I of England.

James was a strong believer in the divine right of kings, a doctrine of royal absolutism based on the idea that political power is bestowed on the king by God. In the traditional story, Leir's decision to divide his kingdom is unusual but is not regarded as destructive in itself. However, the objections of Kent, Gloucester, and the Fool to the division of the kingdom in Shakespeare's *King Lear* would have resonated with an audience familiar with the idea that royal authority cannot be divided.

THE PLAY'S THE THING

- OVERVIEW AND ANALYSIS

- LIST OF CHARACTERS

- ANALYSIS OF MAJOR CHARACTERS

Ian McKellen received accolades ▶ for his performance as Lear in the Royal Shakespeare Company's 2007–2008 stage production that was filmed for television.

Richard Price, Chris Hunt and The Performance Co...

the 2007 stage-to-screen high definition presentation of the Royal Shakespeare

KING LEAR

BY WILLIAM SHAKESPEARE

Starring

Ian McKellen

with

Frances Barber
Monica Dolan
Romola Garai
William Gaunt
Jonathan Hyde
Sylvester McCoy
Ben Meyjes
Philip Winchester

"powerful...magnificent"
Daily Telegraph

★★★★★ "a superlative perf...
from Ian

"McKellen is arguably the finest l...
interpreter of Shakespeare" Arts Rev...

Directed by **Trevor Nun...**

66929

CHAPTER TWO

The Play's the Thing

ACT 1, SCENE 1

OVERVIEW

In the palace of Lear, king of Britain, the Earl of Kent and the Earl of Gloucester discuss Lear's plan to divide his kingdom and give up his throne. Kent and Gloucester, two of Lear's advisers, agree that in the past Lear had seemed to prefer the Duke of Albany to the Duke of Cornwall. Albany is the husband of Lear's eldest daughter, Goneril; Cornwall, the husband of Lear's second daughter, Regan. Now, however, it appears that Lear may divide his kingdom equally among his three daughters.

Kent asks Gloucester whether the third man in the scene, Edmund, is his son; Gloucester admits that Edmund is his "whoreson"—that is, a bastard, a child conceived and born out of wedlock. Although Gloucester has been reluctant to acknowledge Edmund in the past, he says he is now as pleased with Edmund as he is with his legitimate son, Edgar.

A trumpet announces the arrival of Lear, who is followed by Albany, Cornwall, and Lear's three daughters. Lear explains the purpose of his plan: by dividing Britain into three parts and giving up his crown while he is still alive, Lear hopes to avoid war between his daughters' husbands after his death. How Britain will be divided, however, depends on a contest that Lear has devised. Each daughter must explain why she loves him more than her sisters do.

Lear's eldest daughter, Goneril, declares that she loves Lear as much as a child has ever loved a father. While Lear announces Goneril's portion of the kingdom, his youngest daughter, Cordelia, tells the audience that she will remain quiet when it is her turn.

Lear's middle daughter, Regan, tells her father that she not only loves him as much as Goneril does, but more, because Regan is only happy when she is with Lear. In return, Lear grants Regan a portion of Britain equal to that which he gave to Goneril. In an aside, Cordelia tells the audience that her love for Lear is so great that she cannot put it into words.

Turning to his youngest daughter, Lear does not conceal that he favors Cordelia above her sisters. He offers Cordelia the best third of his kingdom if she will simply declare her love for him as her sisters did. Cordelia tells her father that she will say nothing. Lear, stunned, gives Cordelia a second and then a third chance to speak. Instead, Cordelia tells Lear that she simply loves him as a daughter should. Her answer enrages Lear, who swears by the gods that he disowns Cordelia.

Kent tries to convince Lear that he has misunderstood: Cordelia truly loves Lear. This only makes Lear angrier, and the king banishes Kent from Britain on pain of death. As Kent leaves, he asks the gods to protect Cordelia and urges Regan and Goneril to turn their words of love

LEAR (IAN MCKELLEN) SHOWS GONERIL (FRANCES BARBER) HER PORTION OF THE KINGDOM AS CORDELIA (ROMOLA GARAI) QUIETLY WATCHES.

toward Lear into action. Meanwhile, Lear divides Cordelia's third of the kingdom between Albany and Cornwall and divides his crown—his royal authority—between them. Lear makes only one condition: he will spend alternate months with Goneril and Regan, and the daughters will house and feed his one hundred knights.

Gloucester brings the King of France and the Duke of Burgundy—the two rivals for Cordelia's hand in marriage—into the hall. When Burgundy hears that he will not get a third of the kingdom, he loses interest in Cordelia. Lear tries to convince the King of France to cast Cordelia aside as well, but Cordelia explains her actions to the French king, who takes her as his queen. Saying good-bye to her sisters, Cordelia urges them to treat their father well and predicts that time will tell which of the three sisters loves Lear the most.

The scene ends with Goneril and Regan discussing Lear's impetuous actions toward both Cordelia and Kent, which they blame on the king's age as well as on his rashness. Goneril and Regan resolve to undermine what remains of Lear's authority.

ANALYSIS

In this opening scene, Shakespeare sets up the action, plot, and subplots of the play. Lear, through his division of his kingdom and his disavowal of Cordelia, places himself at the mercy of Goneril and Regan and their husbands. Hoping to avoid strife after his death, Lear has unwittingly created conditions that threaten to destroy Britain. Meanwhile, Gloucester, by drawing his illegitimate son, Edmund, to himself, sets in motion the events that will lead to the earl's own downfall.

Because of their loyalty to Lear, both Cordelia and Kent refuse to flatter Lear with words, but their lack of flattery leads to their banishment. Goneril and Regan are happy to flatter their father, but the end of the scene foreshadows their future treatment of him.

ACT I, SCENE 2

OVERVIEW

The action shifts to Gloucester's castle. In a short speech, Edmund contrasts custom, which has branded him illegitimate, with nature. He declares himself physically and mentally at least the equal of his half brother, Edgar,

Gloucester's legitimate son. Edmund has decided to turn the tables on his half brother by attempting to convince Gloucester to disown Edgar so that Edmund will inherit Gloucester's land.

As Gloucester enters, Edmund makes a show of hiding a letter. Gloucester notices and asks about it. Edmund pretends that he does not want to show the letter to Gloucester, which makes the earl all the more eager to see it. Edmund declares that the letter is from Edgar and pretends to find its contents disturbing. Feigning reluctance, Edmund hands the letter over to Gloucester. The letter suggests that Edmund should join Edgar in a plot against Gloucester: rather than grow old while waiting for their father to die, the two half brothers will dispose of Gloucester and divide his wealth between them.

Gloucester is upset that Edgar would betray him, and Edmund pretends to be surprised as well. Edmund says he cannot be certain that the letter is from Edgar, since it was supposedly placed in Edmund's study. Still, Edmund tells Gloucester that he has often heard Edgar say that fathers should hand over their wealth to sons when the sons come of age.

Gloucester declares that eclipses of the sun and moon are responsible for recent strange events: Lear's division of the kingdom, the banishment of Kent and Cordelia, Edgar's seeming betrayal. Yet after Gloucester leaves, Edmund denounces his father's view of fate, regarding it as an evasion of responsibility for one's actions. Edmund declares that he would be the same man if he had been conceived under completely different stars.

As Edgar enters, however, Edmund sighs "like Tom o' Bedlam" and speaks as Gloucester did, pretending to be worried about the effects of the eclipses. Edmund then changes the subject and asks Edgar when he last saw Gloucester. Edmund tells Edgar that Gloucester is upset with Edgar, either because Edgar offended him somehow, or someone has told the earl something untrue concerning Edgar.

Edmund urges Edgar to stay in his rooms until Gloucester calms down. Edmund also advises Edgar to carry a weapon if he must go out. As Edgar leaves, Edmund marvels at Gloucester's gullibility and Edgar's honesty, both of which will make Edmund's plan to usurp Edgar much easier.

ANALYSIS

Gloucester's acknowledgment of Edmund has given him what he needs to usurp Edgar and to gain control of Gloucester's wealth and lands. Edmund has cleverly constructed a plan to make it appear as if Edgar wishes to do what Edmund himself intends. Like Goneril and Regan do with Lear, Edmund flatters his father while acting against him.

The idea outlined in Edgar's supposed letter—that the young should control their fathers' wealth, and their fathers should be dependent on them—is essentially what Lear has put into place by dividing his kingdom and placing himself at the mercy of Goneril and Regan. The Gloucester-Edmund-Edgar subplot mirrors the main plot of the play.

Shakespeare has introduced a conflict between Gloucester's view of the gods, nature, and fate and Edmund's belief that men make their own destinies. Edmund mocks Gloucester's beliefs, but he is willing to use those beliefs to advance his own cause. Edmund also takes advantage of Edgar's honesty to convince his half brother that his lies are the truth.

Edmund uses "Tom o' Bedlam" to refer to his mimicking of Gloucester's behavior. In Shakespeare's day, "Tom o' Bedlam" was a generic name given to insane beggars who roamed the countryside. This term foreshadows Edgar's actions later in the play, when the young man disguises himself.

ACT I, SCENE 3

OVERVIEW

At Albany's palace, Goneril enters with her steward Oswald. Lear no longer has a place of his own, so he and his one hundred knights have been staying with Goneril. Oswald says that Lear has struck him for scolding his Fool. Goneril sees this as evidence that she and Regan were right: Lear is out of control. Moreover, Lear's knights are causing problems, which Goneril plans to resolve by refusing to speak to her father in the hope that he will decide to stay with Regan instead. Goneril orders Oswald to make sure that he and his fellow servants do not go out of their way to please Lear or his knights. Goneril will write a letter advising Regan to treat Lear the same way.

ANALYSIS

Lear has given up all his authority but has retained the title of king, and his one hundred knights are a symbol of that title. However, Goneril decides to treat Lear in a way that does not respect him either as the king or as her father: Goneril will ignore him and will urge Regan to do the same. As Cordelia predicted when she said good-bye to her sisters, the actions of Goneril and Regan are proving that their words of love to Lear were false.

ACT I, SCENE 4

OVERVIEW

After Goneril and Oswald leave, Kent enters Albany's palace. Although Lear banished him from Britain on pain of death, Kent still desires to serve him. To do so, however, Kent must appear in disguise.

With a flourish of horns, Lear returns from hunting. Noticing the disguised Kent, Lear asks who he is and what he wants. Kent answers that he is simply what Lear sees: a trustworthy man. Kent pledges to serve Lear, pretending not to know that Lear is the king of Britain and claiming it is Lear's air of authority that makes him want to serve the old man. Lear agrees to take the disguised Kent into his service, so long as he enjoys Kent's company over dinner.

Catching sight of Oswald, Lear asks where Goneril is. When the steward quickly exits without answering, Lear sends a knight to bring him back. The knight informs Lear that Oswald, who refuses to return, has said that Goneril is not well. Goneril, Albany, and all of their servants, the knight says, have not been treating Lear with the respect he deserves, and the king admits that he has noticed this, too.

Oswald returns, and Lear demands that the steward tell him who he—Lear—is. Oswald responds that Lear is Goneril's father, an answer that enrages the king, who strikes the steward. Kent trips Oswald. Pleased with Kent's action, Lear decides that he can stay in his service.

Hearing this as he enters, the Fool offers his coxcomb (his fool's cap) to Kent. One would have to be a fool to serve Lear, the Fool says, because Lear has fallen out of favor and has made mistakes concerning all three of his daughters. The Fool tells Lear that it was doubly foolish to give up his living—that is, his wealth—to Goneril and Regan. When Lear threatens to whip him, the Fool replies with a series of rhymes and riddles designed to illustrate the foolishness of Lear's actions. Lear, the Fool says, was born a fool. His authority lay in his crown, not in his intellect. Lear, the Fool points out, has "madest thy daughters thy mother"—that is, given Goneril and Regan authority over him.

The Fool notes that Goneril and Regan would have him whipped for speaking the truth, while Lear would have him whipped for lying. If he stays silent, the Fool says, he is sometimes also whipped. Thus, the Fool concludes, he would rather be anything other than a fool—yet he would not want to be Lear, because Lear is less than a fool.

As Goneril enters, Lear asks her why she is frowning. Goneril replies that the actions of his knights and attendants, and even of Lear himself, are the cause. Lear is astonished: Goneril's treatment of him shows a lack of respect. The Fool tells Lear why: Lear is but a shadow of his former self.

Goneril insists that Lear reduce the number of his knights. Lear replies by calling her a bastard and declaring his intention to stay with Regan instead. Albany arrives and tries to intervene, telling Lear that he knows nothing of Goneril's plan. Lear begins to regret his treatment of Cordelia now that Goneril's profession of love is not reflected in her actions.

Lear calls upon a nameless goddess and Nature to curse Goneril and make her unable to bear children. Should Goneril have a child, Lear asks that the child be to Goneril what she has been to Lear: a "thankless child" and a "torment."

Lear exits, but quickly returns, having learned the extent of the reduction in his entourage that Goneril wants him to make: one hundred to fifty within two weeks. Lear decides he will go stay with Regan. In Regan's household, Lear declares, he will recover his former authority.

After Lear, Kent, and Lear's attendants leave, Goneril reveals her fear to Albany: it was not safe to let Lear keep a hundred knights, because he would then be able to order her and Albany around. Albany tells Goneril that her fears may be unfounded. Goneril orders Oswald to deliver to Regan the letter explaining her plan and tells him to add reasons of his own to make the letter even more forceful. As Oswald leaves, Goneril chides Albany for his lack of wisdom, yet he tells his wife that she may have made matters worse.

ANALYSIS

Kent's loyalty to Lear is greater than his fear of death. While Kent has to deceive Lear in order to serve him, his deception is the opposite of Goneril's and Regan's: they pledged their love to Lear in words, but Kent shows his love in action.

The Fool is loyal to Lear in his own way. Even when Lear gets angry at the Fool for telling the truth, the Fool continues to point out that Lear is responsible for his own situation. Daughters should not have authority over their fathers, yet Lear has changed places with Goneril and Regan.

By demanding that Lear reduce his entourage, Goneril shows a lack of respect for Lear. The only condition Lear had placed on his division of the kingdom was that Goneril and Regan take turns entertaining him and his knights. Now Goneril refuses to honor that condition. In his anger Lear prays that Goneril be made barren. Having now renounced both Cordelia and Goneril, Lear is leaving himself at the mercy of his second daughter, Regan.

This scene also foreshadows Albany's later actions. Albany had interceded on Kent's behalf when Lear banished Kent; now Albany intercedes on Lear's behalf when Goneril reduces the number of knights. Albany's prediction that this will make things worse will soon be borne out.

ACT I, SCENE 5

OVERVIEW

Lear, Kent, and the Fool stand in front of Albany's palace, preparing to depart for Regan's residence. Lear gives a letter to Kent to deliver to Regan in advance of his arrival.

As Kent leaves, the Fool returns to the riddles that he had been asking Lear in the previous scene. The Fool tells Lear that Goneril and Regan may seem different on the surface, but that the two daughters are the same. While not mentioning Cordelia by name, Lear says that he "did her wrong." The Fool also says that Lear's mistake goes further: by dividing his kingdom between Goneril and Regan, Lear is like a snail who has given up his shell. The old, the Fool says, are supposed to be wise; but if Lear were his fool, the Fool would have Lear beaten for becoming old before he had gained wisdom. As he and the Fool depart, Lear fears that he is losing his sanity and begs heaven that this is not the case.

ANALYSIS

This scene is short but important. The Fool continues to speak the truth to

Lear: the king has gone against the natural order by dividing his kingdom. Goneril's actions are to be expected because she no longer has a reason to respect Lear. Regan, the Fool predicts correctly, will act the same way. While wisdom is supposed to come with age, Lear has not gained it. The destruction in the natural order that Lear has started will be reflected in the destruction of his own nature as he descends into madness.

ACT II, SCENE 1

OVERVIEW

The action shifts to Gloucester's castle, where a member of Gloucester's court tells Edmund that Cornwall and Regan will soon arrive. The courtier does not know the reason for Cornwall's visit, but he tells Edmund that there are rumors of a coming war between Cornwall and Albany. As the courtier leaves, Edmund realizes that he can use Cornwall's arrival to advance his own plan against Edgar.

Edmund calls Edgar onto the scene. Edmund urges his half brother to leave before Cornwall arrives, claiming there are rumors that Edgar has spoken out against Cornwall. Hearing Gloucester coming, Edmund draws his sword and convinces his half brother to do likewise. Edmund calls out to Gloucester and his servants as he sends Edgar away.

Before Gloucester arrives, Edmund cuts his own arm, drawing blood. Stalling for time to let Edgar get away, Edmund tells Gloucester that he found Edgar "conjuring the moon"—that is, casting spells to advance Edgar's supposed plot to murder Gloucester and inherit his land and wealth. Edmund also tells Gloucester that Edgar attacked him when he refused to take part in Edgar's plot.

Gloucester plans to convince Cornwall to close Britain's ports so that Edgar cannot leave the island. A reward will be offered for Edgar's capture, and anyone who hides him will be put to death.

Edmund tells Gloucester that Edgar had claimed that no one would believe Edmund because he is a bastard. Gloucester responds that he will do what it takes to make Edmund the legitimate heir to his land.

Cornwall and Regan arrive, and both allude to rumors of Edgar's plot against Gloucester. Regan notes that Edgar is Lear's godson and, having received Goneril's letter, suggests that Edgar may have come to the plot by associating with Lear's "riotous knights"—a suggestion Edmund quickly supports. Cornwall and Gloucester praise Edmund for his supposed attempt to capture Edgar, and Cornwall takes Edmund into his service. Regan announces that she has received letters from both Lear and Goneril, and she and Cornwall have come to Gloucester to seek his advice on how to proceed.

ANALYSIS

Just as Lear's subversion of the natural order has begun to have its effects, Edmund's attempt to usurp both Edgar and Gloucester is beginning to bear fruit. For now, Edmund needs to keep his father convinced that he is on Gloucester's side, so he manages to trick Edgar into drawing his sword. Edmund puts the words of his own plot into Edgar's mouth, knowing that he has turned Gloucester against Edgar already. The strategy pays off: Gloucester seals his own fate by disowning Edgar, who has been loyal, and embracing Edmund, whose words of loyalty cover the disloyalty of his action.

ACT II, SCENE 2

OVERVIEW

Kent and Oswald arrive in front of Gloucester's castle. While both men have come from Albany's palace, they have traveled separately, and Oswald does not immediately recognize Kent. When Oswald asks Kent where he can put his horse, Kent tells him to put the horse in the swamp.

The men begin to argue, and Kent calls Oswald every name in the Shakespearean book. When Oswald complains that Kent should not speak this way to a stranger, Kent reveals that he was the man who tripped Oswald after Lear struck him. Kent orders Oswald to draw his sword so that they can fight. When Oswald instead cries for help, Kent beats him with the flat of his sword.

Oswald's cries attract Edmund, Gloucester, Cornwall, and Regan. With sword drawn, Edmund separates Kent and Oswald. Gloucester and Cornwall demand an explanation for the fight, while Regan notes that Kent and Oswald were sent by Lear and Goneril, respectively. Oswald tells Cornwall that he cannot speak because he is out of breath, and Kent mocks the steward for his cowardice in refusing to draw his sword.

As Cornwall and Gloucester attempt to find out what caused the fight, Kent says that it was simply natural that he would grow angry at "such a knave" (a dishonest man) as Oswald. When Cornwall, frustrated by Kent's bluntness, says that he and his companions dislike Kent as much as Oswald does, Kent insults all of those assembled. Cornwall then asks Oswald how he offended Kent, and the steward tells the story of Lear striking him and Kent tripping him.

Cornwall orders that Kent be put in the stocks until noon, despite Kent's objection that placing him in the stocks would show little respect for Lear. Regan goes further, saying that Kent should be kept in the stocks all day and all night. Gloucester intervenes, noting that the stocks normally are only used for common criminals and that Lear will be upset that his messenger was treated in such a way. Cornwall and Regan are unmoved, and Kent is placed in the stocks.

After Edmund, Oswald, Cornwall, and Regan leave, Gloucester tells Kent that he is sorry for what has happened and predicts again that Lear will be angry when he finds him in the stocks. As Gloucester leaves, Kent reads a letter from Cordelia, who has learned of Lear's troubles and promises to come to her father's aid. Confined in the stocks, Kent falls asleep.

ANALYSIS

This scene at first seems confusing. Kent's anger at Oswald appears to be more than is necessary or useful; and, indeed, Kent's own actions result in him being placed in the stocks. In Act II, Scene 4, however, Shakespeare will reveal that there is more to the story.

Kent is punished for his bluntness, that same willingness to speak the truth that led Lear to banish him from Britain in Act I, Scene 1. Kent's bluntness is in defense of Lear. That was true in the earlier scene as well, but Lear did not realize it because he was used to being flattered.

While Cornwall and Regan have come to seek Gloucester's advice, Gloucester, who had doubted from the beginning the wisdom of Lear's plan to divide the kingdom, is disturbed by the treatment of Kent. Unlike Cornwall and Regan, Gloucester worries about what Lear will think, because Gloucester, like Kent, is still loyal to the king.

ACT II, SCENE 3

OVERVIEW

Edgar has eluded Gloucester's men thus far, but the ports are closed, and people everywhere are on the lookout for him. Edgar decides that the best way to keep from being captured is to take on a disguise: He will become a lunatic beggar, covering himself in dirt and wearing only a cloth about his waist. "Edgar I nothing am," he declares; he will go by the name of Tom.

ANALYSIS

In Act I, Scene 2, Edmund had sighed "like Tom o' Bedlam" when he lied to Edgar. Now Edgar, disguising himself in order to evade capture and possibly even death, becomes a "Bedlam beggar" named Tom. Like Kent, Edgar will bear his exile in disguise and be able to speak his mind because no one will recognize him.

ACT II, SCENE 4

OVERVIEW

Lear, the Fool, and a Gentleman arrive in front of Gloucester's castle. Lear finds it strange that Regan and Cornwall did not send Kent back to him after he delivered Lear's letter to them, especially since Regan and Cornwall have now traveled to Gloucester's castle. The Gentleman notes that Regan and Cornwall made the decision to travel only within the last day.

Kent, who has spent the night in the stocks, calls out to Lear. Lear demands to know who would show so little respect for his messenger. When Kent tells Lear that Cornwall and Regan have ordered him placed in the stocks, Lear cannot believe it. He insists that Kent must have done something to deserve the punishment, but Kent recounts the events, ending with his confrontation with Oswald.

The Fool has an explanation for Regan's desire to punish Lear's messenger: when fathers are wealthy and bestow goods on their children, their children are kind to their fathers; when fathers are poor, however, their children become "blind"—that is, ungrateful.

Telling the Fool and the Gentleman to stay with Kent, Lear enters the castle to find Regan. Meanwhile, in riddle and rhyme, the Fool answers Kent's question about why Lear's company has greatly decreased: now that Lear has fallen out of favor with his own daughters and cannot pay them, the knights have left him. The Fool, however, says that he will remain loyal.

Lear returns with Gloucester, furious that Regan and Cornwall have refused to speak with him. Briefly entertaining the idea that Cornwall may be sick, Lear looks at Kent and declares that the act of placing his messenger in the stocks proves that Regan and Cornwall are deliberately ignoring him.

Lear tells Gloucester that he himself will fetch Regan and Cornwall if they do not come to him. Gloucester goes to relay this message and shortly thereafter returns with Regan and Cornwall.

As Cornwall and Regan greet Lear, Kent is set free. Regan tells her father that she is glad to see him, to which Lear replies that if Regan were not glad, he would have to assume that she is not his daughter. As Lear relates Goneril's treatment of him, Regan rises to her sister's defense, saying that Goneril did the right thing in putting restrictions on Lear's knights.

Regan declares that Lear is in need of someone to rule him and suggests that he return to Goneril and ask her to forgive him. Lear says that such an action would make him no better than a beggar and vows never to return to

Goneril. Lear curses Goneril, and Regan replies that he will do the same to Regan when he is upset with her. Lear denies this, saying that Regan would never do the things that Goneril has done because Regan remembers her duty. As if immediately doubting his own words, Lear asks who put Kent in the stocks.

Lear has begun to suspect that Regan is more like Goneril than he had thought. Goneril arrives and Regan takes her sister's hand, confirming Lear's fears. Lear asks one last time who put Kent into the stocks, and Cornwall admits that the order was his.

Regan urges Lear to dismiss half of his knights and to return to Goneril for the rest of the month before coming to live with her, but Lear refuses. Lear says that he would sooner be homeless, or throw himself on the mercy of the King of France, or even be a slave to Oswald. Goneril tells Lear that the choice is his.

Lear resigns himself to Goneril's treatment of him. Goneril is still his daughter, Lear says, and one day she will come to her senses. In the meantime, he and his one hundred knights will stay with Regan. Not so fast, Regan replies. Lear can return to Goneril and keep fifty knights, but if Lear insists on coming to live with Regan, she will allow him to have only twenty-five. Lear decides that Goneril does not seem so bad after all; he will go with her and keep fifty of his knights. Goneril, however, has changed her mind. Both daughters now say that Lear needs no knights; their own servants should be enough for him. Lear replies that this is not a question of need; his knights are to him what a woman's clothes are to her. Lear blames the gods for the ingratitude of his daughters and asks them to grant him anger that will overwhelm his sympathy. He vows vengeance on Goneril and Regan and declares that he will go mad.

As a storm arises, Lear, Gloucester, Kent, and the Fool depart. Regan and Goneril renew their resolve not to take Lear in if he brings any knights.

Gloucester returns to tell them that Lear is exceedingly angry and has decided to leave. Gloucester is worried because the landscape is forbidding and the storm is coming on; however, Regan and Cornwall urge Gloucester to let Lear go and to shut the doors of the castle.

ANALYSIS

The puzzle of Kent's actions in Act II, Scene 2, is now explained. Kent's seemingly excessive anger at Oswald arose because the steward had delivered Goneril's letter to Regan, which undermined Lear's letter to his second daughter.

The full fruits of Lear's decision to divide his kingdom and give up his authority are on display. Goneril and Regan have no further use for their father. Rather than bidding for his affection by trying to trump each other by letting Lear keep more of his knights, they bid each other down until both say that Lear should have no knights or other servants. The knights, Lear admits, are not necessary. However, by taking the knights away, Goneril and Regan have deprived Lear of the last mark of his former authority—and the one that he had insisted he be allowed to keep after the division of his kingdom.

The storm is a reflection in nature of the disorder in the kingdom of Britain. Lear fears that he is losing his sanity, and his action confirms that fear: he decides to leave the safety of Gloucester's castle and to venture out into the storm. Goneril and Regan show their complete lack of affection for their father by telling Gloucester to shut the doors of the castle, leaving Lear stranded in the tempest.

ACT III, SCENE 1

OVERVIEW

As the storm rages, Kent encounters the Gentleman who had earlier accompanied Lear to Gloucester's castle. Both are looking for Lear on the heath, an area of open land with only small bushes and no shelter from the storm. The Gentleman tells Kent that Lear is alone with the Fool and seems to be losing his sanity, tearing at his hair and calling for the destruction of Britain.

Kent reveals to the Gentleman that Albany and Cornwall are plotting against each other. Through spies in the households of Albany and Cornwall, the King of France knows of this division and has decided to move on Britain. Kent sends the Gentleman to the port of Dover with instructions to let France know of Lear's plight. While Kent remains in disguise, he gives the Gentleman a ring and tells him that Cordelia will recognize it and thus know who sent him to her. As the Gentleman leaves, Kent resumes his search for Lear.

ANALYSIS

The storm reflects both the state of Lear's mind and the state of the kingdom of Britain. Lear is calling on nature to destroy the island, but his own actions have set into motion the events that are tearing Britain apart. Desiring to avoid division in the kingdom after his death, Lear has created division while he is still alive. While Kent knows that the King of France acts on behalf of Cordelia (and thus will act on behalf of Lear), France is still a foreign power whose victory would mean Britain's defeat.

ACT III, SCENE 2

OVERVIEW

Meanwhile, on another part of the heath, Lear and the Fool are caught in the storm. Lear is urging nature to destroy the world. The Fool suggests that Lear should return to Regan and Goneril and spend the night in safety. But Lear prefers the elements, because, unlike his daughters, they owe him nothing. Still, the wind and the rain, Lear says, have joined with Regan and Goneril in their attacks on him. In rhyme, the Fool replies that the man who turns things on their head must suffer the consequences.

Kent finds Lear and the Fool. Kent declares that the storm is the worst he has ever seen and that men cannot stand such weather either physically or mentally. Lear sees the storm as the work of the gods, who are uncovering the crimes of men; he says, however, that he is "More sinned against than sinning."

Kent notes that Lear's head is bare and directs him to a hovel—a small structure that will at least provide some protection against the elements. Kent will go seek help at a house nearby. As Lear and Kent leave the stage, the Fool offers a "prophecy" in rhyme: when men act as they should in England, the country will be a very different place.

ANALYSIS

The Fool, who has always spoken truth to Lear, knows that it is not good for Lear to be out in the storm. Even though the Fool sees through Goneril and Regan, he would rather have Lear return to them. But if Lear refuses, then the effects of the storm are simply the result of his foolish actions.

On one hand, Lear is right that he is "More sinned against than sinning." Goneril and Regan have not treated Lear with the respect that he is due as their father. On the other hand, as the Fool has repeatedly made clear, Lear's sufferings are of his own making. Lear's head is bare not only because it is exposed to the elements, but because he has given up his crown.

ACT III, SCENE 3

OVERVIEW

Back at Gloucester's castle, Gloucester tells Edmund that Lear is being treated unnaturally by Goneril, Regan, and their husbands. When Gloucester spoke on Lear's behalf, Regan and Goneril turned on him. But, Gloucester says, all will be made right soon. Albany and Cornwall are divided, and he himself has received a letter indicating that forces have already landed in Britain that will take Lear's side. Gloucester, too, will support Lear, even if it costs him his life, and he asks Edmund to speak with Cornwall so that Cornwall will not suspect Gloucester of favoring Lear.

When Gloucester leaves, Edmund tells the audience that he will find the letter, take it to Cornwall, and let him know that Gloucester supports Lear. Gloucester will lose his land and wealth, and Edmund, whom Cornwall has already taken into his service, will receive it all.

ANALYSIS

Gloucester's story has reached its turning point. He assumes that Edmund shares his loyalty to Lear—an assumption that will cost Gloucester greatly. Edmund is loyal only to himself; he will use Gloucester's loyalty to Lear to usurp his father, just as he earlier usurped his half brother, Edgar. "The younger rises when the old doth fall," Edmund says; as Goneril and Regan have risen above their father, Edmund will rise above his.

ACT III, SCENE 4

OVERVIEW

Back on the heath, Lear, Kent, and the Fool arrive at the hovel. Kent tries to convince Lear to enter, but he wants to stay out in the storm. The elements, Lear says, are a lesser ill than what he has suffered at the hands of Regan and Goneril. As Lear reflects on his daughters' ingratitude, he realizes once again that he is in danger of falling into madness. By enduring the weather, Lear thinks he can take his mind off Regan and Goneril.

As Lear sends the Fool into the hovel, he reflects that, as king, he thought little about his less-fortunate subjects who had no shelter against the weather on nights such as this. Lear's reflection is interrupted by a voice from within the hovel. It is Edgar, disguised as Tom o' Bedlam.

Kent orders Edgar to come out. Edgar pretends to be tormented by a demon, and Lear asks him whether he has been driven to madness by giving all that he owned to his own daughters. Only the ingratitude of daughters, Lear says, could bring a man to Edgar's condition.

As Edgar continues to rant, Lear asks, "Is man no more than this?" As Tom o' Bedlam, Edgar is man in his natural state. His condition is reflected in his clothing; he wears only a blanket around his waist. Lear begins to tear off his own clothes just as Gloucester arrives.

Edgar continues to rant in pretend madness, and his father, Gloucester, does not recognize him. Gloucester urges Lear to return with him. Lear, however, wishes to keep talking to Edgar, whom he calls a "philosopher." Lear, Kent tells Gloucester, is losing his sanity. That is only natural, Gloucester replies, since Lear's "daughters seek his death." Not realizing that he is talking to Kent in disguise, Gloucester praises the earl for his earlier prediction that Lear's banishment of Cordelia would end in tragedy.

Gloucester says that he can understand Lear's madness, because he himself has a son, Edgar, who wishes to kill him. Since Lear insists on speaking to the disguised Edgar as if Edgar were a wise man, Gloucester tells Lear to bring him along as the party finds shelter from the storm.

ANALYSIS

Lear's sorrow over his daughters' treatment of him is overwhelming his senses. It is not wise to stay out in the storm. Yet even now, Lear is beginning to understand that he neglected his duties to the poorest of his subjects, who have no choice but to endure such storms.

Edgar has decided to pretend not only to be insane but to be tormented by a demon, a decision that will play an important role in his later dealings with Gloucester.

Lear had told his daughters that his knights were to him what a woman's clothes are to her: a symbol of her status. Now Lear tears at his own clothes, which symbolize the difference between himself and the insane beggar,

LEAR LISTENS INTENTLY
AS EDGAR, DISGUISED AS
TOM O' BEDLAM, TALKS.

Tom. Lear is not only going insane, he welcomes insanity, because it will relieve him of his sorrow over Goneril and Regan.

ACT III, SCENE 5

OVERVIEW

Back at Gloucester's castle, Edmund has put the final touches on his plan. Cornwall announces that he will have revenge upon Gloucester. Edmund pretends to be torn between his natural bond to his father and his loyalty to Cornwall, but he declares that he will remain loyal to the latter.

Cornwall declares that Edmund is now the earl of Gloucester, explaining that Gloucester's concealment of the letter about France's forces proves Gloucester's treachery. Cornwall orders Edmund to find Gloucester. While Edmund has lost his natural father, Cornwall will become a "dearer father" through his trust in Edmund.

ANALYSIS

Edmund's treachery is complete; he has usurped both his half brother and his father. If he can find Gloucester in the company of Lear, Edmund can ensure that Cornwall will dismiss any final doubts he might have about Gloucester's treachery.

ACT III, SCENE 6

OVERVIEW

Gloucester, Lear, the Fool, and the disguised Kent and Edgar have found shelter in a farmhouse near Gloucester's castle. Gloucester leaves briefly to gather supplies at the castle, while Kent notes that Lear has completely lost his sanity.

Edgar continues to rant of demons, while Lear decides to put Goneril and Regan on trial. He appoints Edgar as the judge. Kent tries to convince Lear to rest, because he believes the king will regain his sanity if he simply sleeps. Edgar finds Lear's true insanity so heartbreaking that he tells the audience that he may not be able to keep up his own act.

As Kent convinces Lear to lie down, Gloucester returns with bad news. Lear's life is in jeopardy. Gloucester advises Kent to take Lear to Dover, where the King of France awaits. Kent fears that waking Lear will mean that he will never recover, but letting him sleep will cost him his life. As Kent and the Fool carry Lear away, Edgar realizes that his problems seem small compared with Lear's and decides to end his charade.

The plot is moving quickly now—too quickly, in fact, for Lear, whose only hope lies in rest. Having driven Lear mad, Goneril and Regan now wish him dead. Cordelia's prediction is unfolding; Lear's life will only be safe with the youngest of his daughters, whose love is proved through action rather than through words.

ACT III, SCENE 7

OVERVIEW

Back at Gloucester's castle, Cornwall, Regan, Goneril, and Edmund are discussing the letter Gloucester received. Cornwall tells Goneril to inform Albany that the army of France has landed. Cornwall declares Gloucester a traitor, Regan says that Gloucester should be hanged, and Goneril suggests that Gloucester's eyes be plucked out. Cornwall sends Edmund off with Goneril, telling him that he will not want to see what Cornwall intends to do to Gloucester.

Oswald arrives with the news that Lear is on his way to Dover. As Goneril, Edmund, and Oswald leave, Cornwall orders servants to find Gloucester. Cornwall admits that he does not have the authority to order Gloucester's death, but he will punish him nonetheless.

The servants return with Gloucester, who reminds Cornwall that he is a guest in Gloucester's castle. Bound to a chair, Gloucester is questioned by both Cornwall and Regan about the letter he received from France. Gloucester claims that the letter was sent by a neutral party, one not opposed to Cornwall, but he admits that he sent Lear to Dover to protect him from Goneril and Regan, who were crueler to their father than they would have been to wolves.

Gloucester tells Regan that he will see revenge visited upon her and Goneril, but Cornwall replies that he will see no such thing and destroys one of Gloucester's eyes. When one of Cornwall's servants begs him not to take the other eye, Cornwall draws his sword. As the two men fight, Regan takes a sword from a second servant and stabs the first one from behind, killing him. Cornwall, himself wounded, then destroys Gloucester's other eye.

When Gloucester calls out for Edmund to avenge him, Regan reveals Edmund's treachery. Recognizing his mistake, Gloucester calls on the gods to protect Edgar. At Regan's order, Gloucester is thrown outside the gates of his own castle. Regan leads the wounded Cornwall offstage. Two of Cornwall's servants, horrified at the actions of their master and his wife, decide to deliver Gloucester to Edgar.

ANALYSIS

The cruelty of Goneril and Regan toward Lear is matched by that of Edmund toward Gloucester. By law, Edmund, as Gloucester's illegitimate son, had deserved nothing; but Gloucester had first acknowledged him and then, believing that Edgar had betrayed him, made Edmund his heir. Edmund has responded not only by usurping Gloucester, but by allowing Cornwall to take Gloucester's eyesight. Cornwall will pay the price for his own cruelty with his life. Gloucester's condition now parallels Lear's. Gloucester is not insane, but he is blind, and his blindness will lead him to desperation.

ACT IV, SCENE 1

OVERVIEW

On the heath, Edgar has returned to hope, having seen that Lear is worse off than he. Yet at that very moment, Gloucester arrives, led by an Old Man. The Old Man wants to stay with him, but Gloucester insists that he leave. Gloucester replies that he is better off now that he is blind than he was when he was prosperous and had the use of his eyes; then, he stumbled, suspecting Edgar unjustly. Seeing Gloucester blinded, Edgar realizes that his earlier hope was misplaced: Gloucester's misfortune has made Edgar's own life worse.

The Old Man catches sight of Edgar and thinks him the insane beggar Tom. Gloucester recalls having seen Tom the night before and wonders why the beggar had reminded him of Edgar. Though Edgar wants to drop his disguise, he now thinks it best to keep it up.

Edgar greets Gloucester and the Old Man. Gloucester sends the Old Man away, though he asks him to bring Edgar some clothes. Gloucester asks Edgar if he knows the way to Dover. Edgar replies that he does and then speaks of demons, as he had the night before.

Gloucester gives Edgar his purse, which contains all the money that he has left. Gloucester asks Edgar to take him to a cliff in Dover, where he intends to jump into the sea.

ANALYSIS

Edgar had begun to rise above his own despair, but now he realizes that Gloucester's misfortunes are his own. Lear's and Gloucester's stories continue to intertwine. While Edmund's actions toward Gloucester parallel those of Goneril and Regan toward Lear, Edgar's feelings toward his father are similar to Cordelia's feelings toward hers. Both Gloucester and Lear are headed to Dover, where their loyal children will rescue them.

ACT IV, SCENE 2

OVERVIEW

Goneril and Edmund have arrived at Albany's palace. Oswald, who has gone on ahead, greets them with the news that Albany seems to welcome the King of France's attack on Britain. Moreover, Albany has seen through Edmund's plot. To protect Edmund, Goneril sends him back to Cornwall, telling him that she hopes she can dispose of Albany and take Edmund as her husband.

As Edmund rides off, Albany arrives. When he last appeared, Albany had doubts about Goneril's treatment of Lear; now he believes that his wife's unfaithfulness to her father might forecast unfaithfulness to her husband as well. Goneril's actions toward Lear, Albany predicts, will lead to ruin, through the vengeance of either heaven or man.

Goneril accuses Albany of being a coward. Villains such as Lear and Gloucester, she says, deserve their punishment, even if it has been delivered before they have done anything wrong. Goneril tells Albany that he should be raising his troops against the King of France rather than complaining about her actions. When he replies that Goneril's actions reveal her to be a demon in disguise, Goneril insults his manhood.

A Messenger arrives with the news that Cornwall has died from his wound and reveals that the duke had put out Gloucester's eyes. Albany sees Cornwall's death as divine vengeance for Cornwall's treatment of Gloucester. The Messenger gives Goneril a letter from Regan. Goneril fears that Regan might now pursue Edmund as her husband, but Goneril also sees this as an opportunity, because Edmund will now fill Cornwall's role.

Goneril leaves to answer Regan's letter, and Albany asks the Messenger where Edmund had been when Cornwall was putting out Gloucester's eyes. The Messenger reveals that Edmund had plotted against Gloucester and then had left his father at Cornwall's mercy. Albany recognizes Gloucester's service to Lear and vows to avenge the loss of his eyes.

ANALYSIS

Until now, Albany has been overshadowed by Goneril, but his character is coming out. Both Kent and Gloucester had suggested that Lear preferred Albany to Cornwall, and Albany now shows his loyalty to Lear. His loyalty rises above his marriage to Lear's daughter; in fact, Albany is loyal to the point of despising Goneril.

Albany's response to the news that Cornwall put out Gloucester's eyes shows that he believes in justice. Albany will have to defend Britain against the French invaders, but he will do so for the sake of Britain and Lear rather than for Goneril. Goneril, preferring Edmund to her husband, has made it clear that she is interested only in power, not in justice.

ACT IV, SCENE 3

OVERVIEW

Kent and Lear have arrived at Dover. Kent has left the king in the town and has gone to speak to the Gentleman with whom Kent had sent the letter for Cordelia. The Gentleman tells Kent that the King of France has had to return to his homeland but has left behind Cordelia and the Marshal of France to command his troops.

To Kent's questioning, the Gentleman replies that Cordelia had been moved to grief when she read Kent's letter. Kent sees in the Gentleman's description the proof of Cordelia's love. Kent declares that the stars must govern the lives of men, because there can be no other explanation for how different Cordelia is from Goneril and Regan. Lear, Kent says, occasionally recovers his wits, but refuses to see Cordelia—not because he is still angry with her, but because he is now ashamed of how he had treated the one daughter who truly loves him. Kent takes the Gentleman to Lear and promises him that he will be happy that he has assisted Kent, once Kent can remove his disguise.

ANALYSIS

Kent's remark about the stars governing the lives of men stands in contrast to Edmund's claim in Act I, Scene 2, that he would be the same man no matter which stars he was born under. Cordelia, confronted with Kent's description of her father's plight, still does not say much, but her love for Lear is apparent in her grief, and will soon be shown in action.

Lear's shame over his treatment of Cordelia parallels Gloucester's recognition that he had wronged Edgar by suspecting him of disloyalty.

ACT IV, SCENE 4

OVERVIEW

In the French camp, Cordelia speaks with a Doctor. Someone has seen Lear crowned with weeds and singing madly. Cordelia orders that her father be found and brought to her, though she fears that his sanity cannot be restored and that he might even take his own life. The Doctor holds out hope, though: all Lear needs is rest.

A messenger arrives with the news that British troops are descending on the French camp. The French, Cordelia says, are prepared. The French mission is not one of conquest but one of love: Cordelia wants to restore Lear to his rightful position.

ANALYSIS

Kent had suggested that Lear might recover his senses if he rested, and the Doctor echoes this. Nature can restore order if given the chance. Neither Cordelia nor Albany desires the battle that is coming. Both will fight it, however, for the same reason: out of loyalty to Lear, and in his defense.

ACT IV, SCENE 5

OVERVIEW

Back at Gloucester's castle, Oswald tells Regan that Albany is leading his army toward the French camp, though he seems reluctant to do so. Goneril, Oswald says, "is the better soldier."

Oswald has a letter from Goneril to Edmund, and Regan suspects that it has to do with Goneril's lack of love for Albany and her increasing affection for Edmund. But Regan tells Oswald that she has talked to

Edmund, and the two of them are considering marriage now that Cornwall is dead. This, Regan suggests, may be good for Oswald, who has always been close to Goneril.

Edmund, Regan believes, has gone in pursuit of Gloucester because Cornwall made a mistake in leaving Gloucester alive. Gloucester's blindness arouses pity among those he meets and turns them against Regan and Edmund.

Regan gives Oswald a note to take to Edmund, instructing the steward to kill Gloucester if he should meet him on the way. Oswald would be happy to do so, he says, to prove his loyalty.

ANALYSIS

Goneril and Regan, until now united against their father, are turning against each other. Both see in Edmund a kindred spirit, and Edmund's apparent willingness to kill his own father indicates that they are right.

ACT IV, SCENE 6

OVERVIEW

Gloucester and Edgar have arrived at Dover, where Gloucester intends to end his life by jumping off a cliff. Edgar is now dressed as a peasant in the clothes that the Old Man had promised to bring him. Gloucester notes that Edgar's speech, too, has changed, but Edgar denies it.

Edgar tells Gloucester that they have arrived at the edge of the cliff and describes the scene below. Edgar can look no longer, he tells Gloucester, for fear of losing his own balance and falling. Gloucester is convinced and asks Edgar to place him at the very edge. He gives Edgar a purse with a valuable jewel in it, then sends him away. In an aside, Edgar gives the audience the first indication that things are not what they seem; he is playing a trick on Gloucester, he says, in order to cure his despair. Gloucester kneels and tells the gods that he can no longer fight their will.

"If Edgar live, O bless him!" Gloucester prays and then throws himself forward, fainting as he falls.

The trick is revealed: Edgar and Gloucester are not on a cliff. Edgar fears, though, that his deception may still have resulted in Gloucester's death. Convinced that he was throwing himself off the cliff, Gloucester may have died of fear. Edgar approaches his father, pretending to be a man who, standing at the bottom of the cliff, watched him fall.

Edgar tells Gloucester that he has been saved by a miracle. Edgar asks Gloucester about the "thing" that led him to the edge of the "cliff." When Gloucester tells Edgar that it was a beggar, Edgar describes the "thing" as a "fiend" (a demon). That, he says, must be why the gods preserved Gloucester. Gloucester, recalling the continual remarks about demons made by Tom o' Bedlam, is convinced. He vows to bear his afflictions until the natural end of his life.

Lear enters, crowned with weeds as Cordelia had described. The sight, Edgar says, is heartbreaking. Though alone, Lear gives orders as if he were still the king at court. Turning to Edgar, Lear asks for a password. When Edgar replies, "Sweet marjoram," Lear accepts the password.

Gloucester says that he knows Lear's voice, and Lear, seeing Gloucester, compares him with Goneril. In his insanity, Lear sees clearly now that his daughters and the members of his court had flattered him for years. Goneril, Regan, and the courtiers had told Lear that he was wise; they said "ay" when Lear wanted them to say "ay" and "no" when he wanted them to say "no." Yet Lear's two elder daughters and the courtiers had not meant any of it.

Gloucester says that he knows the voice is that of the king, and Lear replies by pardoning an imaginary subject for the crime of adultery— the very crime that Gloucester had committed. Not knowing what Gloucester now knows, Lear says that the illegitimate Edmund has been kinder to his father than Regan and Goneril, Lear's legitimate daughters, have been to himself.

Overcome with emotion, Gloucester asks to kiss Lear's hand, but Lear says that his hand smells of death. When Gloucester asks Lear if he knows him, the king makes cruel jokes about Gloucester's eyes. But then Lear tells Gloucester that it is possible to understand the world without seeing it. The mighty and the greatest sinners get away with things that the poor and lowly would never do. Edgar says that Lear's words are "Reason in madness." Lear recognizes Gloucester and urges Gloucester to be patient—he will have revenge upon Albany and Cornwall (who Lear does not realize is dead).

The Gentleman that Cordelia sent to find Lear arrives with some attendants, and he orders them to grab hold of Lear. The king thinks that he has been taken prisoner, but the Gentleman tries to reassure him. When Lear declares that he is a king, the Gentleman tells him that he and the attendants obey Lear. That, Lear says, means there is hope. Lear then runs away, pursued by the attendants. The Gentleman tells Edgar that Albany's army will arrive within the hour. France's army has gone to meet Albany's, but Cordelia remains behind.

Gloucester asks the gods to take his life before he is tempted to commit suicide again. Edgar, still concealing his true identity, offers to lead his father to a place where he can stay. Just then, Oswald arrives and declares his intention to kill Gloucester. Gloucester is prepared to accept death, but Edgar intervenes. Adopting a strange accent, Edgar tells Oswald that if he does not leave Gloucester alone he will have to fight Edgar. Oswald attacks, and Edgar delivers him a mortal blow. Before he dies, however, Oswald begs Edgar to take the letters that he has been carrying and deliver them to Edmund, who is with Albany's army.

Reading the letter from Goneril to Edmund, Edgar discovers that she is urging his half brother to take advantage of the coming battle to kill Albany.

If Edmund succeeds, Goneril will marry him; if he fails, she will have to remain married to Albany. Edgar plans to take the letter to Albany.

Gloucester laments that he is not mad like Lear, because then he would not suffer. As a drum heralds the arrival of the British army, Edgar leads Gloucester to safety.

ANALYSIS

This scene, which marks the redemption of Gloucester, is built around a trick. The audience, watching Edgar lead his father to the edge of the "cliff," is as blind to what is about to happen as Gloucester is. Edgar gives a slight clue to his plan, but it is only after Gloucester has "fallen" from the "cliff" that the audience realizes that Edgar deceived his father in order to save his life. Like Kent with Lear, Edgar shows his loyalty to Gloucester through his actions.

The many references to demons Edgar made while in the guise of Tom o' Bedlam allow him to carry off his ruse. Since Gloucester believes in the gods and fate, he can see his survival as a miracle.

As Gloucester's story and Lear's come together again, both men are redeemed through the love of their faithful children. When Edgar gives the password "sweet marjoram" and Lear accepts it, he shows that he still suffers from madness: marjoram is an herb related to oregano that, in Shakespeare's time, was thought to cure insanity. Cordelia will soon restore Lear to his true nature, as Edgar has restored Gloucester.

ACT IV, SCENE 7

OVERVIEW

In a tent in the French camp, Cordelia thanks Kent for his service to Lear and tells him that he should drop his disguise. Kent, however, asks Cordelia to let him keep it up for a while longer, and Cordelia agrees. She prays to the gods that Lear's insanity may be cured, and the Doctor decides that it is time to wake him up. Lear is brought in, carried in a chair. The Doctor asks Cordelia to draw close to her father as they wake him. Cordelia kisses Lear and then reflects on the cruelties of her sisters.

As Lear awakes, Cordelia asks him how he is and whether he knows her. Lear is confused by his clothing and surroundings, and Cordelia thinks that he is still insane. However, as he comes to his senses, Lear replies that he thinks her to be his daughter Cordelia.

In sorrow, Lear tells Cordelia that he would drink poison if she wished. Cordelia cannot love him, Lear says, because of what he had done to her. She replies that she has no cause to hate him. The Doctor declares that Lear is recovering but needs more rest. As Cordelia escorts her father from the tent, he begs her forgiveness.

The final battle is about to begin. Kent, having been banished from Britain by Lear, knows that the battle will decide his own destiny as well.

ANALYSIS

As Kent had suspected, rest was all Lear needed to restore him to his true nature. As Lear comes to his senses, Cordelia asks him for his blessing, but he kneels before her instead. Cordelia tells him that he "must not kneel" because it is not fitting for a king to kneel even before his daughter. Lear's kneeling, however, is a sign that, in recovering his sanity, he has become better than he was before. Lear once enjoyed being flattered; now he wants to acknowledge his errors.

ACT V, SCENE 1

OVERVIEW

At the British camp, Edmund asks an officer to find out whether Albany intends to fight the French. Albany, Edmund says, has been changing his mind constantly; now it is time for him to make a final decision.

After the officer leaves, Regan once again declares her intention to marry Edmund, but she asks him whether his love for Goneril ever became physical. Edmund swears that it has not and never will.

As Albany and Goneril arrive, Goneril tells the audience that she would rather have Britain lose the battle than have Regan end up with Edmund. Albany explains the reason for his indecision: while the King of France is supporting Lear, the French are still an invading army. Goneril urges Regan and Edmund to forget the earlier division between Albany and Cornwall and to join forces with her husband.

Edgar enters, still in disguise, and asks to speak to Albany. As the rest leave to consult with the commanders of the British army, Edgar gives Albany the letter Goneril had written to Edmund, which Edgar had found on Oswald's body. Edgar urges Albany to read it before going into battle. He tells Albany that he will return when the duke has a herald blow a trumpet.

As Edgar leaves, Edmund enters. Edmund gives Albany an estimate of the size of the French army, which is now within sight. While Albany goes off to prepare, Edmund mulls over his situation. He has pledged his love to both Goneril and Regan, but he cannot have either "if both remain alive." Goneril will be angry if he marries Regan; but he cannot marry Goneril unless Albany is dead.

Edmund decides to accept Albany's help in the battle with the French, after which Goneril can devise some way to bring about her husband's death. Albany, Edmund fears, would show mercy to Lear and Cordelia, but with the duke dead, Edmund could protect his hard-won position by preventing their pardon.

ANALYSIS

Albany is loyal to both his king and his country, and thus the decision to enter into battle with the King of France, who is supporting Lear, has been a hard one. As the final scene will reveal, Albany thinks that he has figured out how to protect both Britain and Lear.

The division between Edmund and Edgar is reaching its climax, and it is mirrored in the increasing division between Goneril and Regan. Even though it would mean offending Goneril, Edmund could marry Regan and have half of the kingdom, but he is constantly fearful that someone will overturn his fortune. Edmund cannot bear to leave anything to chance, and that will prove his downfall.

ACT V, SCENE 2

OVERVIEW

The battle has begun. On the field between the two camps, the army of France rushes forward, along with Cordelia and Lear. As all move out of sight, Edgar and Gloucester enter. Edgar tells his father to sit under a tree and pray for the success of the French forces. Edgar then follows the French army, only to return quickly. The battle has been lost; Lear and Cordelia have been taken prisoner. Edgar urges Gloucester to come with him, but the earl says that he will stay and die. Edgar reminds Gloucester that he has vowed to let the gods determine his time of death, and Gloucester relents and leaves with his son.

ANALYSIS

This short scene sets up the climax of the play and gives Gloucester one last chance to reaffirm his faith in the gods and fortune—a faith that is not mere fate, since the earl reaffirms it by agreeing to leave and thus save his life.

ACT V, SCENE 3

OVERVIEW

In the British camp, Edmund holds Lear and Cordelia prisoner. Cordelia asks whether she and Lear will see Goneril and Regan, and Lear replies that he would rather spend the rest of his days in prison in the company of Cordelia. They would replay the scene of their reunification: Cordelia will ask for Lear's blessing, and Lear will kneel before her and ask for her forgiveness. Only death, Lear says, can part them.

Edmund orders Lear and Cordelia taken away and then calls a Captain and hands him a note. Edmund has written instructions for how Lear and Cordelia are to be treated, and he promises to reward the officer if the instructions are carried out. He warns the Captain that he cannot think about or question the instructions if he wishes to win Edmund's favor. The Captain agrees and departs.

Albany, Goneril, and Regan arrive, and Albany praises Edmund's actions on the battlefield before asking Edmund to hand over Lear and Cordelia. Edmund gently refuses, saying that he has placed them under guard in order to prevent the British soldiers, who may still have sympathy for Lear and Cordelia, from turning against Edmund and Albany. Tomorrow, or sometime in the future, Edmund says, he will hand over Lear and Cordelia to Albany for trial.

Albany is angered by Edmund's answer, which seems to imply that Edmund regards himself not as Albany's subject but as his equal. Regan, however, intervenes: she intends to marry Edmund, thus making him Albany's equal; moreover, she says, Edmund's actions on her behalf have raised him to that status already.

Goneril objects that Edmund's actions are enough; he does not need Regan. As the sisters argue, Regan suddenly says that she does not feel well. She tells Edmund to take all of her possessions and her as well; she has taken him for her lord and master. Goneril once again objects, but Albany tells Goneril that granting permission for the marriage is not her right. Edmund replies that giving such permission is not Albany's right, either.

At that, Albany accuses Edmund of treason and Goneril of colluding with Edmund. Albany tells Regan that he cannot allow her to marry Edmund because Edmund is already spoken for: Goneril intends to marry him.

Albany calls for a herald to blow the trumpet. If no one comes forth to back his charge, Albany says, he will prove Edmund's treason through combat. Edmund maintains his innocence and pledges to fight Albany or any other who charges him with treason.

Regan again announces that she is sick, and Goneril indicates to the audience that she may have something to do with her sister's illness. Albany sends Regan to his tent as the herald arrives.

As the trumpet sounds a third time, Edgar arrives, still in disguise. He does not give his name but says that he is as noble as Edmund. Edgar orders Edmund to draw his sword to defend himself against the charges that Edgar now speaks: Edmund is a traitor to the gods, to Edgar, to Gloucester, and to Albany. Edgar dares Edmund to deny the charges, and when he does, the two half brothers fight. Edmund falls to the ground wounded, but Albany orders Edgar to spare Edmund's life. Goneril says that the combat proves nothing, because Edmund did not have to fight an opponent who refused to give his name.

Albany orders Goneril to be quiet and reveals her letter to Edmund. Goneril responds that the letter may be hers, but it does not matter; Albany cannot accuse her of treason, because she, not he, rules the kingdom. Goneril departs, and Albany sends an officer after her, saying that she is "desperate."

Edmund, near death, admits his treason and asks Edgar who he is. Edgar reveals his real name and says that Gloucester has suffered the loss of his eyes through divine justice because of his adultery, which brought Edmund into the world. Edmund now sees in his own downfall that same divine justice.

Edgar tells Albany and Edmund how he guided Gloucester and "saved him from despair." Just before the herald had sounded the trumpet, he had revealed the truth to Gloucester and asked his blessing in the coming

THE KING IS IN HIGH RAGE.

combat with Edmund. Overcome with both joy and grief, Gloucester died. Edgar also reveals that Kent had disguised himself and served Lear as Edgar had served Gloucester.

A Gentleman enters, holding a bloody knife. Goneril has killed herself after confessing to poisoning Regan, who has also died. Edmund says that he will join in death the two sisters to whom he had pledged marriage.

As Albany orders the bodies of Goneril and Regan to be brought out, Kent arrives, looking for Lear. Albany now remembers that he had come to demand that Edmund hand over Lear and Cordelia. Dying, Edmund tries to redeem himself by admitting that he had ordered the deaths of both Lear and Cordelia. Taking Edmund's sword as proof that his half brother has rescinded the order, Edgar runs to the castle to try to stop the Captain. Before Edmund is carried away, he tells Albany that he and Goneril had ordered Cordelia to be hanged so that it would look as if she had committed suicide in despair.

Lear enters, carrying Cordelia and followed by Edgar and the Captain. Lear calls for a mirror in the vain hope that Cordelia's breath will prove that she is still alive, though he knows that she is dead. The sight is so horrifying that Kent asks whether this might be the end of time.

Abandoning hope, Lear announces that he killed the soldier who hanged Cordelia. Lear becomes aware of Kent, who admits that he has been serving Lear in disguise. Kent tells Lear that Goneril and Regan are dead. Albany believes that Lear has descended once again into madness.

THE BLINDED AND REPENTANT
GLOUCESTER RECOGNIZES
LEAR'S VOICE.

A Captain arrives to announce that Edmund is dead. Albany declares that he will return the throne to Lear and will restore Edgar and Kent to their rightful places.

His heart breaking as he mourns Cordelia, Lear dies. Kent urges no one to attempt to revive the king. Albany hands the rule of Britain over to Kent and Edgar, but Kent announces that he will soon join Lear in death.

The play ends with Edgar, now sole ruler of Britain, declaring that those who mourn should "speak what we feel, not what we ought to say." The passing generation—Lear, Gloucester, Kent—lived lives that the younger generation will never live.

ANALYSIS

All of the threads come together in the play's final scene. Edmund, attempting to protect that which he has gained through deception, overreaches in presuming to place himself on the same level as Albany. Albany had intended to save Lear and Cordelia, but Edmund's treachery prevents it. As Albany had suspected, Goneril's disloyalty to Lear foreshadowed her disloyalty to Albany. Goneril's disloyalty extends even to Regan and to herself.

Until his battle with Edgar, Edmund continued to believe that he could make his own fate. Having been mortally wounded by his half brother's hand, Edmund finally realizes that Gloucester was right about the gods all along.

Cordelia's death is the most shocking in the play, because it is the most unexpected. Albany had wished to restore the old order, but when Lear dies and Kent says that he will soon join the king, that order passes away. All that is left is for the young to keep from making the same mistakes as the old by speaking what they know to be true.

LIST OF MAJOR CHARACTERS

Lear: King of Britain; father of Goneril, Regan, and Cordelia; and the protagonist of the play

Goneril: First daughter of Lear and wife of the Duke of Albany

Duke of Albany: Husband of Goneril; loyal to Lear in the end

Regan: Second daughter of Lear and wife of the Duke of Cornwall

Duke of Cornwall: Husband of Regan; puts out the Earl of Gloucester's eyes

Cordelia: Third daughter of Lear and, later, queen of France; remains loyal to Lear despite being disowned by him

Duke of Burgundy: Suitor to Cordelia; loses his interest in Cordelia after Lear disowns her

King of France: Suitor to Cordelia and, later, her husband

Earl of Kent: Adviser to Lear; continues to advise Lear in disguise after the king banishes him from Britain

Earl of Gloucester: Adviser to Lear and father of Edgar and Edmund; loses his eyes for remaining loyal to Lear

Edgar: Legitimate son of Gloucester, half brother of Edmund, and, in the end, ruler of Britain; disguised as Tom o' Bedlam, guides Gloucester after the Duke of Cornwall puts out the earl's eyes

Edmund: Illegitimate son of Gloucester and half brother of Edgar; attempts to usurp both his brother and his father and pledges to marry both Goneril and Regan

The Fool: Lear's fool; remains loyal to Lear during the king's insanity and always tells him the truth, though often in riddle and rhyme

Oswald: Steward to, and close confidant of, Goneril

Doctor: A physician in the company of Cordelia; cures Lear of his insanity

Old Man: one of Gloucester's tenants

A Captain: An officer under Edmund's command; sets Edmund's order to hang Cordelia into motion

A Herald: A messenger in the service of Albany; blows the trumpet that brings Edgar out of hiding to confront Edmund

Various other Captains, Gentlemen, Attendants, and Servants

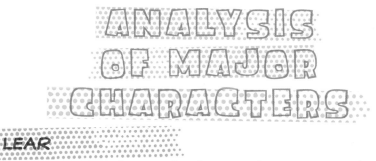

ANALYSIS OF MAJOR CHARACTERS

LEAR

In even more ways than may be obvious at first, King Lear is the central character of the play. Lear's decision to divide his kingdom sets the entire plot into motion. That decision, though, was not properly thought through, as characters as different as Kent, Gloucester, the Fool, Goneril, and Regan can see. Lear wishes to avoid strife in his kingdom after his death, but his action brings strife into his kingdom while he is alive, resulting in the deaths of all three of his daughters and of Lear himself.

Lear's willingness to give up his kingdom reflects his desire to forego his responsibilities. While he is upset when Goneril and Regan demand that he reduce the number of his knights, his daughters are right that the knights have grown riotous, reflecting Lear's own childlike behavior. The very contest that Lear devised to aid in dividing his kingdom—"Which of you shall we say doth love us most" (I.1)—is a child's game. Lear wants the privileges and honors that go with being a king but without the responsibilities.

As the play unfolds, it becomes clear that this is not simply Lear's old age at work. Lear did not realize how members of his court, or even his

UPON THESE EYES OF THINE I'LL SET MY FOOT.

own daughters, thought of him, because he demanded that they "say 'ay' and 'no' to everything that I said!" (IV.6). When Kent showed his loyalty to Lear by opposing his action, and when Cordelia showed hers by remaining silent, Lear banished both.

As the king of Britain, Lear personifies the kingdom. As he descends first into rage and then into madness, nature itself reflects the disorder in Lear's soul. The storm ends only when Lear realizes his errors, rests, and comes to his senses. Along the way, he gains a newfound humility, acquires the wisdom that the Fool told him he should have earned with age, and recovers his royal demeanor.

Peace returns to the kingdom when it returns to Lear's soul, but only at great cost. Lear, though more than eighty years old, shows himself a man worthy of respect when he kills the soldier who hanged Cordelia. But Lear's time has passed, and the younger generation must now apply the lessons of Lear's life to their own.

CORDELIA

Of all of the characters in *King Lear*, only the Fool and Cordelia remain constant in their traits throughout the play. Indeed, there is some speculation that, in the original productions of *King Lear*, the Fool was played by the actor who played Cordelia. The two characters never appear in the same scene. Cordelia is mentioned immediately before the Fool's first appearance, and, at Cordelia's death, Lear refers to Cordelia as his "fool" (V.3)—a term of endearment in Shakespeare's time, but perhaps also another sign that the two characters are really one.

Yet while the Fool says that he always tells the truth to Lear, he admits that he lies to Goneril and Regan. Cordelia, however, never lies. When she refuses to take part in Lear's contest for the division of the kingdom, it is the depth of her love—not the lack of it—that compels her to remain silent. As Cordelia predicts to her sisters when she leaves with the King of France, she will prove through her actions that she loves Lear far more.

Cordelia, however, cannot put that love into words because anything she says would be less than what she feels—in other words, it would be a lie. That is why, when Lear says to her, "So young, and so untender?" Cordelia replies, "So young, my lord, and true" (I.1).

Lear's response is to disown Cordelia, and once the King of France has taken her for his wife, Cordelia could easily have lived the rest of her life with no duty to her father. Yet her love for Lear does not allow her to do so. The King of France has spies in the households of both Goneril and Regan, and their reports of how Lear is being treated prompt Cordelia to come to her father's aid. France is the historical enemy of Britain, yet its forces invade to aid Cordelia's father—and thus to restore order to Britain, not to conquer it.

Goneril and Regan deserve to die because of their actions toward Lear; however, Samuel Johnson, who produced an influential annotated edition of Shakespeare's plays, found Cordelia's death so contrary to justice that for years he could not reread the final scene of *King Lear*. Yet Cordelia's death is a sacrifice of love, and through its senselessness, Shakespeare shows the depth and the constant nature of Cordelia's devotion to her father.

GLOUCESTER

Gloucester is one of the most complex characters in *King Lear*. From the opening lines of the opening scene, we know that he has been unfaithful to his wife at least once, resulting in Edmund's birth. Gloucester's belated acknowledgment of Edmund, however, is a sort of faithfulness, an

LEAR MOURNS THE DEATH OF
CORDELIA, HIS ONLY LOYAL DAUGHTER,
IN A PRODUCTION BY THE UTAH
SHAKESPEARE FESTIVAL.

acceptance of the bonds of flesh and blood that would not have been required either in Lear's or in Shakespeare's time.

While Gloucester speaks of the role that the gods, nature, and fortune play in the lives of men, he does not blame his adultery on them. Edmund regards his father's piety as a cover for irresponsibility, but Gloucester takes responsibility for his actions. For him, as for Kent and Cordelia, loyalty is very important, which makes his previous adultery seem all the more out of character.

Gloucester's loyalty puts him in an awkward position. His lands lie in the part of the kingdom that Lear gave to Regan and Cornwall, so Gloucester is naturally loyal to Cornwall; but his loyalty lies, above all, with Lear. Forced to choose, Gloucester chooses Lear, and that choice costs him his eyes and brings him to the brink of despair.

Gloucester's willingness to accept almost without question Edmund's claims against Edgar is itself a measure of the earl's faithfulness. Having acknowledged Edmund, Gloucester does not doubt him; he assumes that Edmund has inherited his father's honesty.

Gloucester's misplaced loyalty brings him great regret, and his attempted suicide is motivated as much by his recognition that he has mistreated Edgar as by his desire to end his own misery. In his despair, Gloucester forgets his loyalty to the gods. Edgar's ruse does not so much restore his father's faith in the gods as it reminds Gloucester that his fate is not his own to decide.

Gloucester's acceptance of a life of blindness is an acknowledgment of the truth of Edgar's statement: "Thy life's a miracle" (IV.6). As Lear, at the height of his madness, told Gloucester when they were reunited at Dover, "A man may see how this world goes with no eyes" (IV.6). Gloucester himself had told the disguised Edgar, "I stumbled when I saw" (IV.1). Relying now on the gods to determine when his life will end, Gloucester has restored his loyalty to nature, and to himself.

ASK ME
NOT WHAT
I KNOW.

In his annotated edition of Shakespeare's plays, Samuel Johnson mentions that some critics thought that "the intervention of Edmund destroys the simplicity of the story." Johnson, however, believed that any such injury "is abundantly recompensed by the addition of variety, by the art with which he is made to co-operate with the chief design and the opportunity which he gives the poet of combining perfidy with perfidy, and connecting the wicked son with the wicked daughters, to impress this important moral, that villainy is never at a stop, that crimes lead to crimes, and at last terminate in ruin."

If Gloucester is one of the most complex characters in the play, Edmund is the opposite. From the first moment he appears on stage alone, in Act I, Scene 2, Edmund is plotting and scheming against his half brother, Edgar. When he succeeds in usurping him, Edmund switches the object of his plot to Gloucester. With the earl out of the way after having been blinded and banished by Edmund's patron, Cornwall, Edmund sets his sights on both Cornwall's wife, Regan, and her sister Goneril.

The key to understanding Edmund is found in his three soliloquies in Act I, Scene 2. In the first, Edmund complains that others regard him as "base"—that is, ignoble—because of the circumstances of his birth and declares himself by nature better than Edgar.

In the second, Edmund mocks Gloucester's belief in signs and portents, saying that men who bring misfortunes on themselves are quick to blame "the sun, the moon, and the stars; as if we were villains on necessity." Edmund puts no stock in such superstitions, yet he says that "I should have been that I am, had the maidenliest star in the firmament twinkled on my bastardizing." In other words, Edmund has chosen to live an immoral life and thus justifies those who call him "base." (I.2)

For Edmund, the only measure of right is success. Thus Edmund ends his third soliloquy with the line, "All with me's meet that I can fashion fit" (I.2)—that is, everything is right that I can make happen.

Edmund's villainy ends only as he lies dying, but even then his attempt to redeem himself is too little, too late: his actions have directly caused the death of Cordelia and indirectly the death of Lear.

A CLOSER LOOK

- THEMES

- MOTIFS

- SYMBOLS

- LANGUAGE

- INTERPRETING THE PLAY

The 1985 Japanese film *Ran*, ▶
written and directed by Akira
Kurosawa, was partly based on
Shakespeare's *King Lear*.

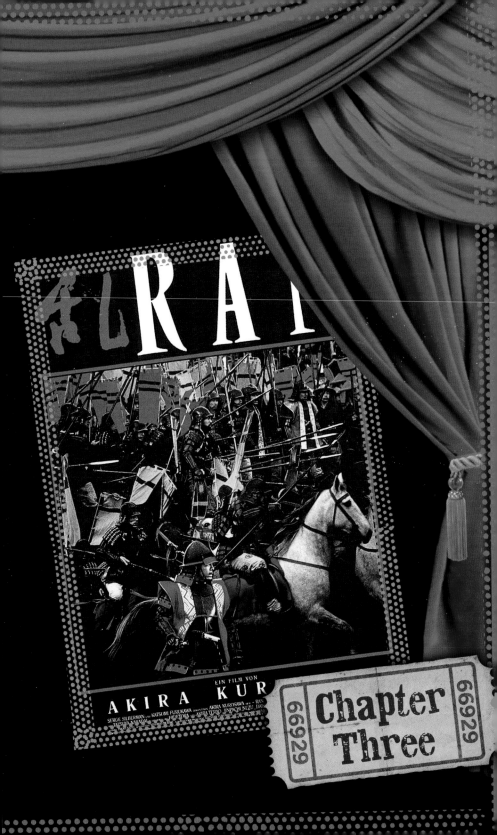

RA

EIN FILM VON

AKIRA KUR

SERGE SILBERMAN and KATSUMI FURUKAWA directed by AKIRA KUROSAWA with RAN
TATSUYA NAKADAI HIDETORA AKIRA TERAO JINPACHI NEZU DA

Chapter
Three

66929

66929

a Closer Look

THEMES

HUMAN NATURE

In *King Lear*, characters often make reference to "nature" when they wish to present something as fixed or constant. The nature in question is not the natural world, but rather human nature or the proper ordering of human affairs, both within one's own life and with respect to others. "Nature" is not simply a way of saying what a person *is* but, even more importantly, of saying what a person *should be.*

Lear in particular speaks of his own nature and of the offenses offered against it by others. In Act I, Scene 1, Lear says that Kent's defense of Cordelia—especially his attempt to get Lear to break his vow to disown her—is one that neither "our nature nor our place can bear." Lear tells Kent that he has "never yet" broken a vow; it would be wrong not just for a man to do so, but even more so for a king. Lear's nature is more than the sum of his actions; it is both the source of his actions and the standard to which his actions must conform.

Because each person's nature is an objective standard, that nature must be respected by others. In other words, the natures of men must stand in their proper place with respect to one another. Lear's first error—his disavowal of Cordelia in Act I, Scene 1—came about, he says, when his most beloved daughter exhibited the "most small fault" of not making a show of her love for him. That action, "like an engine, wrench'd my frame of nature / From the fix'd place; drew from my heart all love / And added to the gall" (I.4).

Lear calls his own action a "folly" (I.4) that came about because he forgot his own nature. Later, when he leaves Goneril and expects to find sympathy from Regan, Regan tells him that "Nature in you stands on the very verge / Of her confine" (II.4). In other words, Lear, in the ravages of age, is finding it harder to act in accordance with his nature.

Lear's decision to divide his kingdom and divest himself of the authority that belonged to him by his nature has led to his mistreatment by others. Goneril and Regan owe Lear respect and loyalty on two accounts: because he is their king, and because he is their father (what Lear refers to in Act II, Scene 4, as "The offices of nature, bond of childhood, / Effects of courtesy, dues of gratitude"). When Lear gives up the exercise of his royal authority, however, he acts contrary to his nature, and Goneril and Regan no longer feel the need to respect his nature in any aspect—even as their father.

Cordelia, on the other hand, remains true to Lear in his true nature, even when he is mad—or, as Lear puts it, when "nature, being oppress'd, commands the mind / To suffer with the body" (II.4). By respecting his nature, both as father and as king, Cordelia is able to bring Lear back to his true nature.

In his final act—avenging Cordelia's murder—Lear, in accordance with his true nature, shows himself again both sovereign ruler and devoted father.

THE DESTRUCTIVE POWER OF RAGE

Closely related to the theme of the need to act according to one's nature is the theme of the destructive power of rage. All of the major characters in *King Lear*, with the notable exceptions of Cordelia, Edgar, and the Fool, fall into misfortune because they let their rage get the better of them. This is true even when the rage is, in some sense, justified, as in Lear's anger toward Regan, Goneril, and their husbands, and Kent's anger toward Oswald.

Lear's rage has drastic consequences. Lear banishes Cordelia from Britain and forces Kent to don a disguise, drives himself insane, and even upsets the order of the natural world, causing a tempest. At the height of his anger against Regan and Goneril—just before he departs from Gloucester's castle—Lear begs the heavens first for the "patience I need" to control his rage, and then for "noble anger." But Lear's rage overwhelms his nature as a father, and he swears "such revenges on you both" that "they shall be / The terrors of the earth!" His rage, he says, will keep him even from weeping for his daughters, which a father should do. Rage has altered his nature, and Lear declares to the Fool, "I shall go mad!" (II.4).

Immediately after Lear exits Gloucester's castle in Act II, Scene 4, a tempest begins, and when Gloucester returns, he confirms the cause: "The King is in high rage." When Kent goes looking for Lear and meets the Gentleman, the Gentleman speaks of the storm itself in a phrase that also describes Lear: "eyeless rage"—that is, blind rage (III.1). The storm will not subside—nor will Lear's sanity return—until Lear can rid himself of his rage through rest.

Cordelia recognizes this when, in Act IV, Scene 4, she sends the soldiers to find Lear as he wanders the countryside near Dover crowned with weeds: "Seek, seek for him, / Lest his ungoverned rage dissolve the life /

DIRECTOR TREVOR NUNN OPTED TO USE SPRINKLERS FOR THE SCENE IN WHICH LEAR (MCKELLEN) IS OUTSIDE DURING A STORM.

That wants the means to lead it." "Ungoverned rage" stands in contrast to the "noble anger" for which Lear prayed, because the latter is placed in the service of wit or intelligence.

In a much less dramatic way, Kent falls prey to his own rage. While he had reason to be angry at Oswald for delivering to Regan a letter from Goneril that undermined Lear's letter to her, Kent ends up in the stocks because, as he tells Lear, "Having more man than wit about me" (II.4), he drew his sword on Oswald. Similarly, Gloucester allows his rage at Edgar's supposed betrayal to blind him to Edmund's actual betrayal.

Against all of these, Cordelia stands in marked contrast. In Act IV, Scene 3, the Messenger tells Kent that when he delivered the earl's letter to Cordelia, "It seemed she was a queen / Over her passion, who, most rebel-like, / Sought to be king over her." To which Kent replies, "O, then it moved her." and the Messenger answers, "Not to a rage." Because she never lets rage overwhelm her nature, Cordelia is able to act properly to restore sanity to Lear and, thus, order to the natural world.

THE DANGERS OF MORAL BLINDNESS

If the characters in *King Lear* often act against their nature and fall prey to rage, the chief reason is their moral blindness, as the stories of Lear and Gloucester show.

At the beginning of the play, Lear is old, but physically he can see well enough; he is incapable, however, of seeing the true nature of those around him. Lear thinks the words of flattery uttered by Goneril and Regan reflect true love, while Cordelia's unwillingness to commit her love to words means she is "untender" (I.1). In contrast, the King of France can see Cordelia's true nature, and he is willing to accept her as his wife despite Lear's unwillingness to provide her with a dowry.

Lear's moral blindness is reflected in his words. When Cordelia prepares to leave with the King of France in Act I, Scene 1, Lear mentions that he will never "see / That face of hers again." When Kent attempts to talk Lear out of his rash action toward Cordelia, Lear orders him, "Out of my sight!" Kent, understanding that the king's blindness is moral, replies, "See better, Lear, and let me still remain / The true blank of thine eye."

Lear's moral blindness toward Goneril and Regan lasts far longer than it should. Even after learning that Regan and Cornwall ordered the disguised Kent to be put in the stocks, Lear believes that Regan still loves him as she should. Faced with the evidence of his daughter's treachery, Lear turns back to Goneril, thinking that her ingratitude no longer looks as bad. When

Lear finally recognizes that Goneril and Regan are morally the same, he loses control of himself and descends into madness.

Gloucester suffers from a similar moral blindness. Edgar has never given his father a reason to doubt him, yet Gloucester, out of affection for his newly acknowledged son, Edmund, falls prey to Edmund's plot.

Gloucester, Edmund says, is credulous—that is, too ready to believe that which he has been told, even if it contradicts his own experience. While Gloucester's loyalty to Lear helps him to come to his senses more quickly than Lear does, at least with respect to Goneril, Regan, and Cornwall, the damage has been done. Gloucester loses his eyes because he was blind to the true natures of Cornwall and Edmund (and Edgar, for that matter). After Regan orders the eyeless Gloucester cast out into the storm, Gloucester tells the Old Man who guides him, "I have no way, and therefore want no eyes; / I stumbled when I saw" (IV.1).

In other words, physical sight is less important than moral judgment. Lear, even in his madness, recognizes as much when he and Gloucester are reunited near Dover. Lear says to Gloucester, "Yet you see how this world goes" and when Gloucester replies that he sees "feelingly" (that is, with his hands, having no eyes), Lear replies: "What, art mad? A man may see how this world goes with no eyes" (IV.6).

The truly blind in *King Lear* are not those who cannot see, but those who cannot properly judge the true nature of others.

MOTIFS

BETRAYAL

Betrayal is one of the first motifs to emerge in *King Lear*, and also one of the most common. Throughout the play, each betrayal leads to another. In the opening lines, Gloucester reveals his betrayal of his wife, a betrayal that produced Edmund. Edmund, in turn, will betray Edgar and then Gloucester, and Edmund's plot leads Gloucester to disavow Edgar—another form of betrayal.

Lear views Cordelia's refusal to speak words of love as a betrayal and Kent's defense of Cordelia as the same. The Duke of Burgundy, when he finds out that Cordelia will not come with a dowry, drops any pretense at loving her—another betrayal.

Goneril and Regan, despite flattering Lear to gain their portions of his kingdom, betray him both as a father, through their insolence and ingratitude, and as their king, through their unwillingness to allow him to keep his knights, a symbol of what remains of his royal authority. Goneril betrays both her husband and Regan by pledging herself to Edmund. Regan betrays Goneril by asking Oswald not to deliver her sister's letter to Edmund, and Oswald, out of his own desire for Goneril, seems willing to betray Goneril by honoring Regan's request.

In the end, Edmund betrays more characters than any other, pledging marriage to both Goneril and Regan and betraying his allegiance to Albany by ordering Cordelia and Lear to be killed. Although he repents as he is dying, Edmund is unable to prevent the results of that betrayal—and thus betrays even himself.

DISGUISE

Disguise is one of the most striking motifs in King Lear, especially since it is hard to understand how characters fail to see through what seem to be obvious disguises. Kent has been one of Lear's most faithful advisers, yet when Lear banishes him, Kent is able to reappear in disguise just a few days later without Lear recognizing him.

Gloucester has known Edgar all of his son's life, and yet Edgar, by stripping to a blanket around his loins, messing up his hair, covering himself in dirt, and disguising his voice, can make himself unrecognizable to his father, even before Cornwall destroys Gloucester's eyes. When

Gloucester is blind, Edgar can assume various disguises just by changing his voice.

Even the Fool is in a type of disguise, speaking truth by pretending he is unable to do otherwise.

These obvious disguises are adopted in the service of loyalty—of Kent and the Fool to Lear, and of Edgar to his father. Those who would betray others adopt more subtle disguises. When Lear reunites with the blind Gloucester near Dover, he makes reference to disguise by calling Gloucester "Goneril with a white beard" (IV.6). The flattery of Lear's advisers, which kept the king from tempering his own desires and gaining wisdom, was a form of disguise.

Likewise, Goneril's and Regan's expressions of love for Lear, and Edmund's for both Edgar and Gloucester, disguised their true feelings. Both betrayal and disguise are more dangerous when they are more subtle.

INSANITY

Insanity is the most obvious motif in *King Lear* because Lear spends all of Act III and most of Act IV in madness. Lear's rage overcomes his nature and physically weakens him, taking a toll on his mind. Having been flattered for decades by members of his court and by his two older daughters—who had disguised their true feelings—Lear is mentally unable to bear betrayal.

Insanity, however, is Lear's path back to reality. By taking leave of his senses, Lear allows his rage to flourish and wears himself out physically. He becomes more aware of the condition of those around him—not only of the fact that he has been lied to by those he most trusted, but also of the torments suffered by his subjects, such as Tom o' Bedlam, the insane beggar portrayed by Edgar.

Edgar's insanity is not real, but it has a similar effect. As Edmund noted in Act I, Scene 2, Edgar was "noble," with a nature that was honest and would not harm others. By pretending to be insane and thus experiencing the effects of insanity emotionally, he is able to guide Gloucester out of his despair and develops the character necessary to confront Edmund in the final scene.

Like Edgar, the Fool may seem to be insane to others, but his insanity is an act, a cover that allows him always to speak the truth to Lear. The Fool sees clearly from the beginning what Lear cannot see until he has lost his sanity and recovered it.

SYMBOLS

CROWN

The symbol of the crown does not appear very often in *King Lear*, but when it does, it is always significant. In Act I, Scene 1, before Lear himself enters for the first time, a coronet, or small crown, is brought into the palace. This crown is the symbol of Lear's royal authority, which he is about to give up. When Lear has divided his kingdom between Goneril and Regan and disavowed Cordelia, he orders Albany and Cornwall to divide the coronet itself between them as confirmation of the transfer of Lear's royal authority and property.

Immediately after Lear has done so, Kent rises to Cordelia's defense, saying that Lear is mad. Thus the crown is a symbol as well of Lear's wit or intelligence; the division of it is the first crack in Lear's sanity.

Kent urges Lear to "check / This hideous rashness" (I.1)—that is, the foolish action symbolized by the division of the crown. While Lear had divided his kingdom to prevent destructive divisions after his death, the destruction of the crown symbolizes the destruction of the kingdom that he has unwittingly begun.

The crown next appears in Act I, Scene 4, when the Fool says to Lear, "Nuncle, give me an egg, and I'll give thee two crowns." The Fool plays on multiple meanings of *crown*. Lear, in dividing his royal authority, threw away the reason why others, including Goneril and Regan, respected him. The Fool talks of dividing the egg and eating the yolk—which represents Lear's wit—leaving Lear with two crowns (the white of the egg) with nothing in them. Driving the point home, the Fool contrasts "thy bald crown"—that is, Lear's head—with "thy golden one," his royal authority.

When Kent finds Lear wandering in the storm, he mentions the crown obliquely: "Alack, bareheaded?" (III.2). The lack of a crown symbolizes how far Lear has fallen and the loss of his wits.

At the height of his madness, Lear fashions a new crown out of weeds, which he is wearing when he encounters Gloucester near Dover. While still insane, Lear begins once again to act like a king, ordering members of the court around. The fake crown symbolizes the real authority, and the real wit, that Lear has by his nature. In wearing the crown of weeds, Lear prepares himself for the recovery of both his sanity and his authority.

CLOTHES

Just as the crown symbolizes more than Lear's royal authority, clothes in *King Lear* reflect deeper truths about the characters. When Lear objects to his daughters' plan to deprive him of his one hundred knights, he compares the knights to a woman's clothes. Clothes symbolize a man's authority and a woman's beauty. As Lear tells Regan, "Allow not nature more than nature needs"—that is, clothing that merely keeps one warm—and "Man's life is cheap as beast's" (II.4).

Edgar, in adopting the disguise of Tom o'Bedlam, removes all of the clothing that marked him as Gloucester's son and wraps his waist only in a blanket. The lack of clothing symbolizes the loss of sanity and intelligence. Seeing Edgar dressed that way, especially in a storm, Kent, Lear, and the Fool immediately think him mad.

Indeed, Lear, recognizing Edgar's madness, tears at his own clothes, symbolizing the loss of his own senses. Clothing, Lear says, separates the man from the beast, and Lear no longer desires to be a man.

When Edgar, still posing as Tom, is reunited with Gloucester in Act IV, Scene 1, the earl refers to Edgar as "the naked fellow"—naked of both clothing and his senses. Gloucester asks the Old Man to bring Edgar some clothes. Once Edgar is dressed, Gloucester notes a change in Edgar's voice and manner of speech. Edgar denies it, saying, "In nothing am I changed / But in my garments." But the clothing reflects the changes that Edgar is going through. He is disguised now not to save himself but to try to bring Gloucester back from his despair.

Still, clothing can obscure reality, as Lear tells Gloucester when they are reunited near Dover: "Through tattered clothes small vices do appear; / Robes and furred gowns hide all" (IV.6). Clothes are a symbol of power; those who would flatter the powerful overlook their vices.

When Lear tore at his garments to become like Edgar, he shouted, "Come, unbutton here" (III.4). In the final scene, as he holds the dead Cordelia in his arms before dying himself, Lear asks for someone to "undo this button" and immediately slips back into madness, thinking that Cordelia is still breathing.

LANGUAGE

Shakespeare's status as a master of the English language is unparalleled. Yet he had an advantage that most other writers have not: he made up the English language as he went along.

Shakespeare was writing at a time of enormous creativity in the English language. In *The Mother Tongue: English and How It Got That Way*, Bill Bryson notes that, from 1500 to 1650, "Between 10,000 and 12,000 words were coined, of which about half still exist." Shakespeare, who lived for about fifty-two years in the middle of that period and whose writing was confined to less than three decades, contributed more than his fair share.

According to Bryson, Shakespeare "used 17,677 words in his writings, of which at least one tenth had never been used before."

In other words, Shakespeare may have coined almost one in every five new words between 1500 and 1650. When we look at individual years, Shakespeare's creativity seems even more astounding. In *A History of English Words*, Geoffrey Hughes examined the *Chronological English Dictionary* and found that "of the 349 new words and meanings recorded for 1605, the combined contributions of *Macbeth* and *King Lear* total 45 items or 12.8 percent."

Not all of those words entered into common usage. "Shakespeare," Bryson writes, "gave us the useful *gloomy*, but failed with *barky* and *brisky* (formed after the same pattern but somehow never catching on) and failed equally with *conflux*, *vastidity*, and *tortive*."

Hughes notes that Shakespeare was responsible for more than six hundred Latinate neologisms—new words formed from Latin roots. Thirty of those new words are found in *King Lear*, and at least five remain in common usage today.

Imagine being in the audience at the first production of *King Lear*. In one scene alone you would have heard Edmund deliver two of those neologisms. Complaining that others view him badly because he was conceived and born outside of wedlock, Edmund cries, "Why bastard? Wherefore base? / When my dimensions are as well compact, / My mind as generous, and my shape as true, / As honest madam's issue?" (I.2). *Generous* was a word unknown to Shakespeare's audience, and yet it is introduced here without any explanation. The same is true later in the scene with *admirable*, when Edmund is mocking Gloucester for believing in fate: "An admirable evasion of whoremaster man, to lay his goatish disposition to the charge of a star!"

Other characters have an opportunity to make their mark on the English language as well. Verbally sparring with Oswald in Act II, Scene 2, Kent swears, "A plague upon your epileptic visage!" In Act IV, Scene 2, Albany, furious at Goneril for her treatment of Lear and fearing that she might be equally disloyal to him, declares, "Were't my fitness / To let these hands obey my blood, / They are apt enough to dislocate and tear / Thy flesh and bones." Thus *epileptic* and *dislocate* enter into the English language.

Not all of Shakespeare's neologisms are uttered by characters in the heat of passion. In Act IV, Scene 7, Cordelia awakens Lear with this fond wish: "O my dear father, restoration hang / Thy medicine on my lips, and let this kiss / Repair those violent harms that my two sisters / Have in thy reverence made!" A few decades after Shakespeare wrote *King Lear*, *restoration* would not only be in common use but would come to be the title of the age, after the monarchy was restored in England in 1660, following a little over a decade of rule by a Puritan Parliament. The restored king, Charles II, also brought about the restoration of public drama (including performances of Shakespeare's plays) after it had been outlawed for nearly two decades (from 1642–1660).

Today, if we do not know the meaning of one of Shakespeare's new words in *King Lear*, we can look it up in a dictionary (if it entered into common use) or check the notes in almost any edition of the play. However, Shakespeare's audience did not have a text (much less an annotated one); in addition, many of those watching *King Lear* would not have been able to read it if they had one. The context in which the word appeared gave the audience the necessary clues to its meaning.

We owe those audience members their own measure of thanks, since Shakespeare's new words survived because they began to use them. The most marvelous aspect of Shakespeare's influence on the English language may be that it began, not in the pages of books or in a college classroom, but in a rowdy theater.

VERSE AND PROSE IN KING LEAR

Everyone agrees that Shakespeare's use of verse and prose in his plays is significant, but there is much disagreement over the reasons this is true. No single theory can fully predict when Shakespeare will have his characters speak in verse and when he will have them speak in prose. There is always at least one significant exception to any rule we can devise.

One of the most common assumptions is that those characters who are of the nobility speak in verse, while those who are more common speak in prose. However, the opening lines of *King Lear* show otherwise: Kent and Gloucester, both earls, are shown speaking in prose. Yet Kent speaks in verse later in the scene when he attempts to convince Lear to change his mind about his decision to disavow Cordelia.

That suggests another common interpretation: that characters speak in verse when showing respect to others (particularly to their superiors), while speaking in prose shows disrespect. However, when Kent first approaches Lear in disguise in Act I, Scene 4, he clearly wishes to show his respect for the king, yet he speaks in prose. Kent also speaks in prose when he is attacking Oswald in Act II, Scene 2, yet no one would suggest that Kent views Lear in the same way as he does Oswald.

Lear himself switches between verse and prose, and at least two explanations are commonly offered. Lear has a few lines of prose in Act I, Scene 1, but they are all single lines and thus not significant. Lear's first prose lines of any length occur in Act I, Scene 4 after he has divided his kingdom and now lives at the mercy of Goneril and Regan. Thus it is common to see this as a sign of Lear's loss of authority.

If it were that simple, however, we would expect Lear to speak in prose not only throughout that scene, but until he is rescued by Cordelia and restored to his rightful place. Instead, both during the time when he comes to recognize the treachery of Goneril and Regan, and throughout the period of his madness, Lear switches back and forth between verse and prose.

There are patterns in Lear's choice of verse and prose, though they are not perfect. When Goneril appears in Act I, Scene 4, Lear returns to verse to demand the respect that he is owed as king and father: "How now, daughter? What makes that frontlet on? / Methinks you are too much of late in the frown." When, in the following scene, he begins to suspect his sanity, he drops into prose: "I will forget my nature. So kind a father!" Yet Lear appeals in verse to the gods to preserve his sanity: "O, let me not be mad, not mad, sweet heaven! / Keep me in temper; I would not be mad!"

This switch between verse and prose is commonly explained as illustrating Lear's loss of sanity: his speeches in verse are saner; those in prose less so. When Lear first encounters Edgar disguised as the insane beggar Tom in Act III, Scene 4, the king has one of his longest passages in prose, ending with him tearing at his clothes—a sign that he has lost his senses.

Yet some of Lear's lengthiest speeches during his madness appear in verse. In many cases they represent the king recalling his former authority. So, for instance, when Lear is reunited with Gloucester near Dover in Act IV, Scene 6, he first speaks to Gloucester in another long prose passage, though one that suggests that Lear has learned something in his madness: that the members of his court flattered him rather than offering him good advice. But when the blind Gloucester replies in verse, "The trick of that voice I do well remember. / Is't not the King?" Lear finishes the line in verse ("Ay, every inch a king!") and then delivers a lengthy speech in verse before alternating again between verse and prose.

In the end, the simplest explanation may be the best: Shakespeare switches between verse and prose when he wishes to draw the audience's attention to a particular speech. Thus Goneril and Regan, who speak in verse throughout Act I, Scene 1, when they are flattering Lear, change to prose at the end of the scene, as they resolve to rob him of the last bits of his authority.

Still, the various theories concerning Shakespeare's use of verse and prose can provide important insights into his plays—as long as we take them all with a grain of salt.

INTERPRETING THE PLAY

THE CHRISTLIKE CORDELIA

King Lear is full of religious imagery—both pagan and Christian—and one of the most powerful Christian images is that of Cordelia as a Christlike figure. Through her actions and words, Cordelia exemplifies a self-sacrifice that Shakespeare's audience would have identified with Christ and that critics down through the centuries have noted.

MANY CRITICS SEE THE CHARACTER OF CORDELIA AS PART OF THE RELIGIOUS UNDERTONES IN *KING LEAR*.

In addition, there are symbolic parallels to the biblical account of Christ's life. When Cordelia, who loves Lear more than her sisters do, is accused by her father of loving him less, she accepts her fate as Christ did when falsely accused before Pontius Pilate. Christ, who told Pilate that his kingdom was not of this world, remained silent before his accusers, and Cordelia, when asked what she would say to win "A third [of the kingdom] more opulent than your sisters," simply replies, "Nothing, my lord" (I.1).

Saint John writes that Christ "came unto His own, and His own received Him not" (John 1:11), and Cordelia's exile from the kingdom of Britain represents Lear's rejection of the only thing that can (and, indeed, will) save him. Throughout the play, Cordelia, while emotionally moved at times, maintains perfect composure. She is the only character in *King Lear* to speak always in verse (except in some short lines where verse is not possible). Both of these represent a perfection that none of the other characters matches.

When Lear and Cordelia are reunited in Act IV, Scene 7, Lear has "slept long," and "in the heaviness of sleep / We put fresh garments on him." The imagery of this scene would remind Shakespeare's audience of Lazarus, dead in the tomb, wrapped in burial cloths. Just as Christ called Lazarus from the tomb, Cordelia wakes Lear through words of love.

Cordelia's death is not by crucifixion but by another type of hanging, but the scene of Lear cradling her dead body would recall for Shakespeare's audience one of the most moving Christian images—the pietà—in which Christ's mother, Mary, holds her dead son in her arms.

IS *KING LEAR* ONE PLAY OR TWO?

Many of Shakespeare's plays exist in multiple versions, but the differences among the versions of *King Lear* have led some scholars to suggest that the two main versions should be treated as separate plays. Depending on which version of the text one consults, different themes are emphasized.

SO YOUNG, AND SO UNTENDER?

King Lear was first published in the First Quarto of 1608; a different version appears in the First Folio of 1623. The First Quarto contains about 285 lines not found in the First Folio, while the First Folio has between 100 and 130 lines (depending on how one counts a line) not contained in the First Quarto. That has led most recent scholars to conclude that the text of the First Quarto is drawn from Shakespeare's working papers, while the version in the First Folio represents the play as it was performed sometime before 1623. It is possible, though, that the version in the First Folio was edited before publication.

Complicating the matter is the fact that later editors created a hybrid version of the two texts, containing all the lines of both. That version is the one with which modern audiences are most familiar (and it is the one that is examined in this book).

Both the idea that Lear is dividing his kingdom to avoid future strife and that he is giving up all his royal authority are stressed more in the folio version, as are Gloucester's remarks about the destruction of order in the kingdom. These lines reflect contemporary concerns about the divine right of kings and the indivisibility of royal authority. The final lines of the play are uttered in the quarto by Albany, who represents the older, pagan world, but in the folio by Edgar, Lear's godson (a Christian reference) and the new ruler of Britain.

With recent scholarly editions of *King Lear* printing the quarto and folio versions alongside the hybrid form of the play, interpretations of Shakespeare's greatest tragedy are likely to become more varied rather than less so.

Chronology

1564 — William Shakespeare is born on April 23 in Stratford-upon-Avon, England

1578–1582 — Span of Shakespeare's "Lost Years," covering the time between leaving school and marrying Anne Hathaway of Stratford

1582 — At age eighteen Shakespeare marries Anne Hathaway, age twenty-six, on November 28

1583 — Susanna Shakespeare, William and Anne's first child, is born in May, six months after the wedding

1584 — Birth of twins Hamnet and Judith Shakespeare

1585–1592 — Shakespeare leaves his family in Stratford to become an actor and playwright in a London theater company

1587 — Public beheading of Mary, Queen of Scots

1593–1594 — The Bubonic (Black) Plague closes theaters in London

1594–1596 — As a leading playwright, Shakespeare creates some of his most popular work, including *A Midsummer Night's Dream* and *Romeo and Juliet*

1596 — Hamnet Shakespeare dies in August at age eleven, possibly of plague

1596–1597	*The Merchant of Venice* and *Henry IV, Part One*, most likely are written
1599	The Globe Theater opens
1600	*Julius Caesar* is first performed at the Globe
1600–1601	*Hamlet* is believed to have been written
1601–1602	*Twelfth Night* is probably composed
1603	Queen Elizabeth dies; Scottish king James VI succeeds her and becomes England's James I
1604	Shakespeare pens *Othello*
1605	*Macbeth* is composed
1608–1610	London's theaters are forced to close when the plague returns and kills an estimated 33,000 people
1611	*The Tempest* is written
1613	The Globe Theater is destroyed by fire
1614	Reopening of the Globe
1616	Shakespeare dies on April 23
1623	Anne Hathaway, Shakespeare's widow, dies; a collection of Shakespeare's plays, known as the First Folio, is published

Source Notes

p. 41, par. 3, Maynard Mack, *King Lear in our Time*, rev. ed. (reprinted New York: Routledge, 2005), 45–46.

p. 49, par. 5, *Bedlam*, a shortening of *Bethlehem*, refers to an infamous insane asylum—St. Mary of Bethlehem—in London.

p. 92, par. 1, William Harness, ed., *The Complete Works of William Shakspeare: With Dr. Johnson's Preface: A Glossary, and an Account of Each Play* (London: Scott, Webster, and Geary, 1843), 797.

p. 107, par. 1, Bill Bryson, *The Mother Tongue: English and How It Got That Way* (New York: William Morrow and Company, Inc., 1990), 76.

p. 107, par. 2, Geoffrey Hughes, *A History of English Words* (Malden, MA: Blackwell Publishing, 2000), 180.

p. 107, par. 3, Bill Bryson, *The Mother Tongue: English and How It Got That Way* (New York: William Morrow and Company, Inc., 1990), 77.

p. 107, par. 4, Geoffrey Hughes, *A History of English Words* (Malden, MA: Blackwell Publishing, 2000), 181.

A Shakespeare Glossary

The student should not try to memorize these, but only refer to them as needed. We can never stress enough that the best way to learn Shakespeare's language is simply to *hear* it—to hear it spoken well by good actors. After all, small children master every language on Earth through their ears, without studying dictionaries, and we should master Shakespeare, as much as possible, the same way.

addition — a name or title (knight, duke, duchess, king, etc.)
admire — to marvel
affect — to like or love; to be attracted to
an — if ("An I tell you that, I'll be hanged.")
approve — to prove or confirm
attend — to pay attention
belike — probably
beseech — to beg or request
betimes — soon; early
bondman — a slave
bootless — futile; useless; in vain
broil — a battle
charge — expense, responsibility; to command or accuse
clepe, clept — to name; named
common — of the common people; below the nobility
conceit — imagination
condition — social rank; quality
countenance — face; appearance; favor
cousin — a relative
cry you mercy — beg your pardon
curious — careful; attentive to detail
dear — expensive
discourse — to converse; conversation
discover — to reveal or uncover
dispatch — to speed or hurry; to send; to kill
doubt — to suspect

entreat — to beg or appeal

envy — to hate or resent; hatred; resentment

ere — before

ever, e'er — always

eyne — eyes

fain — gladly

fare — to eat; to prosper

favor — face, privilege

fellow — a peer or equal

filial — of a child toward his or her parent

fine — an end; "in fine" = in sum

fond — foolish

fool — a darling

genius — a good or evil spirit

gentle — well-bred; not common

gentleman — one whose labor was done by servants (Note: to call someone a *gentleman* was not a mere compliment on his manners; it meant that he was above the common people.)

gentles — people of quality

get — to beget (a child)

go to — "go on"; "come off it"

go we — let us go

haply — perhaps

happily — by chance; fortunately

hard by — nearby

heavy — sad or serious

husbandry — thrift; economy

instant — immediate

kind — one's nature; species

knave — a villain; a poor man

lady — a woman of high social rank (Note: *lady* was not a synonym for *woman* or *polite woman*; it was not a compliment, but, like *gentleman*, simply a word referring to one's actual legal status in society.)

leave — permission; "take my leave" = depart (with permission)

lief, lieve — "I had as lief" = I would just as soon; I would rather

like — to please; "it likes me not" = it is disagreeable to me

livery — the uniform of a nobleman's servants; emblem

mark — notice; pay attention

morrow — morning

needs — necessarily

nice — too fussy or fastidious

owe — to own

passing — very

peculiar — individual; exclusive

privy — private; secret

proper — handsome; one's very own ("his proper son")

protest — to insist or declare

quite — completely

require — request

several — different; various

severally — separately

sirrah — a term used to address social inferiors

sooth — truth

state — condition; social rank

still — always; persistently

success — result(s)

surfeit — fullness

touching — concerning; about; as for

translate — to transform

unfold — to disclose

villain — a low or evil person; originally, a peasant

voice — a vote; consent; approval

vouchsafe — to confide or grant

vulgar — common

want — to lack

weeds — clothing

what ho — "hello, there!"

wherefore — why

wit — intelligence; sanity

withal — moreover; nevertheless

without — outside

would — wish

Suggested Essay Topics

1. Compare Lear's relationship with his three daughters to Gloucester's relationship with his two sons.

2 Some scholars suggest that the Fool is really Cordelia in disguise. What evidence is there for this idea? What evidence is there against it?

3. What does Lear mean when he says, "I am a man / More sinned against than sinning"? Is he correct? Why or why not?

4. Once Edgar is no longer concerned about saving his own life, is his disguise really necessary? Why does he not reveal his true identity to Gloucester until the final scene of the play?

5. In the end, does fate or free will win out in the universe of *King Lear*? Support your answer with examples from the play.

Testing Your Memory

1. Why have Gloucester and Edmund been distant from each other in the past? a.) Edmund has been traveling abroad. b.) Edmund lived with his mother rather than with Gloucester. c.) Edmund was conceived out of wedlock. d.) Edmund has been away at school.

2. Why does Burgundy not marry Cordelia? a.) Because Burgundy suddenly realizes that he does not love Cordelia. b.) Because Lear will not give Cordelia a third of his kingdom. c.) Because the King of France proposes to Cordelia first. d.) Because Lear gives Cordelia the worst third of his kingdom.

3. In Act I, Scene 2, why does Edmund pretend he does not want to show the letter to Gloucester? a.) Edmund is trying to protect Edgar. b.) Edmund does not want to upset Gloucester. c.) Edmund is not sure whether Edgar wrote the letter. d.) Edmund wants to make Gloucester more interested in the letter.

4. In Act I, Scene 4, why does Lear ask Goneril if she is his daughter? a.) Because Lear thinks that Goneril may have had a different father. b.) Because Lear has already begun to lose his sanity. c.) Because Goneril does not treat Lear with the respect that a father deserves. d.) Because Goneril is in disguise.

5. In Act II, Scene 1, why did Cornwall and Regan go to Gloucester's castle? a.) To seek Gloucester's advice concerning the dispute between Lear and Goneril. b.) To hide from Lear and his knights. c.) To help Gloucester in his search for Edgar. d.) To seek shelter from the coming storm.

6. Why does Kent beat Oswald with the flat of his sword? a.) Because Oswald tells Kent to put his horse in the swamp. b.) Because Oswald refuses to draw his sword and fight Kent. c.) Because Kent wants Oswald to leave before delivering Goneril's letter to Regan. d.) Because Kent suspects Oswald of being in love with Goneril.

7. Why does Lear insist that he be allowed to keep one hundred knights? a.) Lear needs the knights to help him on his hunts. b.) The knights are a symbol of his former royal authority. c.) Lear wants them for protection

in case his daughters turn against him. d.) Lear wants to reward the knights for their loyalty to him when he was king.

8. Why does the King of France decide to invade Britain? a.) Because his spies have told him of divisions between Albany and Cornwall. b.) Because he is upset that Lear did not grant Cordelia a third of the kingdom. c.) Because Kent has asked him to invade. d.) Because Cordelia has tired of her husband and wants to return home.

9. Why does Lear attempt to tear off his own clothes? a.) Because they have been damaged by the storm. b.) Because Lear wants to become a natural man, like Tom o' Bedlam. c.) Because Lear no longer wants any mark of his royalty. d.) Because Lear wants to disguise himself for safety.

10. Why does Cornwall name Edmund the earl of Gloucester? a.) Because Gloucester has disappeared. b.) Because Cornwall needs Edmund's support against Albany. c.) Because Edmund reveals that Gloucester concealed a letter about the French invasion. d.) Because Edmund bribes Cornwall to do so.

11. Why does Kent try to get Lear to sleep? a.) Kent is tired of listening to Lear's insane rantings. b.) Kent knows that they cannot travel in the storm. c.) Kent plans to betray Lear while he sleeps. d.) Kent thinks that rest will help Lear recover his sanity.

12. Who first suggests that Gloucester's eyes should be plucked out? a.) Edmund b.) Cornwall c.) Regan d.) Goneril

13. How does Cornwall die? a.) Regan stabs Cornwall after he puts out one of Gloucester's eyes. b.) Edmund kills Cornwall for destroying Gloucester's eyes. c.) Gloucester stabs Cornwall after he puts out one of Gloucester's eyes. d.) One of Cornwall's servants mortally wounds him while defending Gloucester.

Answer Key

10. c; 11. d; 12. d; 13. d

1. c; 2. b; 3. d; 4. c; 5. a; 6. b; 7. b; 8. a; 9. b;

Further Information

Books

King Lear. Folger Shakespeare Library. Edited by Barbara A. Mowat and Paul Werstine. New York: Simon & Schuster, 2005.

King Lear. The New Cambridge Shakespeare. Edited by Jay L. Halio. New York: Cambridge University Press, 2005.

King Lear. The Oxford Shakespeare. Edited by Stanley Wells. New York: Oxford University Press, 2008.

Websites

http://absoluteshakespeare.com

Absolute Shakespeare is a resource for the Bard's plays, sonnets, and poems and includes summaries, quotes, films, trivia, and more.

http://larryavisbrown.homestead.com/files/Lear/lear_home.htm

The Complete Text of Shakespeare's *King Lear* with Quarto and Folio Variations, Annotations, and Commentary. Compiled by Dr. Larry A. Brown, professor of theater at Lipscomb University in Nashville, Tennessee, this site offers an easy way to compare the various versions of the text of *King Lear.*

www.online-literature.com/shakespeare/kinglear/

The Literature Network offers a straightforward presentation of the text of *King Lear,* with a very active forum discussing questions and issues raised by the play.

www.playshakespeare.com

Play Shakespeare features all the play texts with an online glossary, reviews, a discussion forum, and links to festivals worldwide.

www.william-shakespeare.info/site-map.htm

Extensive information on the life and world of Shakespeare, as well as texts of all the published works of Shakespeare, including *King Lear.*

Bibliography

William Shakespeare

Bryson, Bill. *Shakespeare: The World as Stage*. New York: HarperCollins, 2007.

Pearce, Joseph. *The Quest for Shakespeare: The Bard of Avon and the Church of Rome*. San Francisco: Ignatius Press, 2008.

King Lear

Bloom, Harold. *King Lear*. New York: Riverhead Trade, 2005.

Bloom, Harold, and Neil Heims, eds. *King Lear*. New York: Checkmark Books, 2008.

Bradley, A. C. *Shakespearean Tragedy: Lectures on Hamlet, Othello, King Lear and Macbeth*. New York: Palgrave Macmillan, 2007.

Elton, William R. *King Lear and the Gods*. Lexington: University of Kentucky Press, 1988.

Kahan, Jeffrey. *King Lear: New Critical Essays*. New York: Routledge, 2008.

Kahn, Paul W. *Law and Love: The Trials of* King Lear. New Haven, CT: Yale University Press, 2000.

Mack, Maynard. *King Lear in Our Time*. New York: Routledge (reprint edition), 2005.

Milward, Peter, S. J. *Shakespeare's Meta-Drama: Othello and King Lear*. Tokyo, Japan: Renaissance Institute/Sophia University, 2003.

Rosenberg, Marvin. *The Masks of King Lear*. Newark: University of Delaware Press, 1992.

Woodford, Donna. *Understanding King Lear: A Student Casebook to Issues, Sources, and Historical Documents*. Santa Barbara, CA: Greenwood Press, 2004.

Index

Page numbers in **boldface** are illustrations.

About the Author

Scott P. Richert is the executive editor of *Chronicles: A Magazine of American Culture* and the Catholicism Guide for About.com. His monthly column in *Chronicles*, "The Rockford Files," examines political, economic, social, and cultural trends in America from the vantage point of a middle-sized town in the Midwest. A graduate of Michigan State University, he holds an MA in political theory from the Catholic University of America. He lives in Rockford, Illinois, with his wife, Amy, and their seven children. Scott has also written *Bill Bryson*, in the series Today's Writers and Their Works, for Marshall Cavendish Benchmark.